RUTHLESS
Princess
A MAFIA ROYALS ROMANCE

by
RACHEL VAN DYKEN

Ruthless Princess
A Mafia Royals Romance
by Rachel Van Dyken

RUTHLESS PRINCESS
Copyright © 2020 RACHEL VAN DYKEN
ISBN: 978-1-946061-55-3

Cover Design by Jena Brignola
Editing by Oxford Comma Editing, Theresa Kohler
and Kay Springsteen
Formatting & Editing by Jill Sava, Love Affair With Fiction

DEDICATION

TO ALL THE READERS WHO STARTED
WITH ME BACK IN 2010 AND TOOK A
CHANCE ON MAFIA ROMANCE AND
TO ALL THE NEW READERS WHO
PICKED UP THIS BOOK.

Welcome to the fold.
Blood in, no out.
Hugs, RVD

AUTHOR *Note*

This is a standalone and a brand new series; I know you probably already know that since you picked up this book, but hey, let's just repeat it again! ;) If you recognize some of the names in this book, it's because back in 2010, I wrote a series called Eagle Elite, and the parents in this series are the OG's of Eagle Elite. That series got extremely long (as you can imagine), so I decided we needed fresh blood back at Eagle Elite University, and that starts with Ruthless Princess!

If you are an EE fan then this is the part where you may nerd out and want a family tree, I have that on the very next page, NEVER FEAR! If you're new, just scroll on by, it won't matter to you, haha, and you'll be like yeah, I don't care. And you don't NEED to know any backstory, because again this is a new series (do you like how I keep repeating that), oh by the way it's a new series.

Okay, I'm done, haha, grab a glass of wine (you'll seriously need it), and might I suggest some vodka? It's gonna be a rough ride, but it's going to be soooo worth it.

This is actually the first book I've written in over a decade where I threw caution to the wind and went meh, no more censoring my characters, let them be them, so yes this book has sexy times (a lot), and yes this book does have cursing, but one thing remains true. This book is my soul, and I hope that when you read the very last page, you can't stop thinking about these characters.

Blood in, no out. Let's get Ruthless...

WHO'S WHO IN THE
Cosa Nostra

*N*ixon and Trace Abandonato. Nixon is the boss of the Abandonato Family he's a bit psycho, has a lip ring, and in his mid-forties, looks like a freaking badass. Think if Jason Momoa and Channing Tatum had a baby. SURPRISE, Nixon! Trace is the love of his life. Nixon's daughter, Serena, is his pride and joy, she's the heir to his throne. His adopted son Dom is ten years older than Serena. At thirty, he's ready to step in if he needs to, but he really doesn't want to, not that he's thinking about a family of his own. Nixon's youngest, Bella, was a most welcome surprise.

Phoenix and Bee Nicolasi (formerly De Lange) have one son, Junior, and he's everything. The same age as Serena, he only ever has one thing on his mind. Her. But pursuing her is like signing his own death sentence. The one rule that the bosses gave all the cousins, all the kids, no dating each other, it complicates things. They all took a blood oath. But he's willing to risk it all, for just one taste.

Which brings us to Chase and Luciana Abandonato, their love story is one for the ages. He had Violet first, gorgeous, Violet Emiliana Abandonato. And then he had twins, God help him. Asher (Marco) and Izzy. All are attending Eagle Elite University. Violet is more into books than people. And the twins, well they are polar opposites. While Izzy is quiet and reserved, taking after her uncle Sergio in the tech support part of the mafia, Asher was an assassin at age twelve. He takes care of everyone even though he's younger than Serena and Junior. He feels it's his job to make sure everyone is safe, including his girlfriend, Claire. She's his soul mate, and he'll do anything for her. And don't forget the baby of the family, Ariel, who everyone dotes on.

Tex and Mo Campisi. He's the godfather of this joint, gorgeous, he's a gentle giant unless he's pissed and his wife, Mo, is just as violent as he is. They have two sons, Breaker and King. Breaker is in his sophomore year at Eagle Elite and he can't wait to release his own flirtations onto the campus. He's a force to be reckoned with, just walks around with chicks and shrugs. King on the other hand is vying for top whore at his own high school, I mean they say high school is supposed to be memorable right? He just can't remember any of the girls' names, so he calls them all Sarah. It's a thing.

Sergio and Valentina are also Abandonatos. While Val is quiet and reserved, Sergio is the resident doctor of the Families. He's also really into tech and loves spying on people. They have two gorgeous daughters. Kartini has her daddy wrapped around her little finger. He just hopes he survives her last year of high school without shooting one of her boyfriends. With

Lydia, he knows she can take care of herself. She already beat up the class bully, making Sergio quite proud.

Dante and El don't have things easier, they're one of the younger mafia families, he's the head of the Alfero Family. And he has two twin girls at age ten who are making him pull his hair out. Raven and Tempest are adorable, but they're feisty like their mom. He lets them have more screen time than he should, but they say he's their favorite in the world, sooooo… he lets it pass.

Andrei and Alice have been through a lot. Their name single-handedly brought the Russian Mafia into the Italian fold. Andrei is both Petrov and Sinacore, meaning that the oldest Italian mafia family is now part of the Cosa Nostra. Forever. Their son's name is Maksim, and weirdly enough he's a total flirt, he takes nothing seriously, but can flip a switch in a minute if someone he loves is threatened. Anya is his little sister, and he would do anything for her, she seems fragile but studies Krav Maga, so nobody messes with her.

These are the Families of the Cosa Nostra.

Welcome to the Family.

Blood in. No out.

MAFIA
Royals

Mafia Royals Romances

A little kingdom I possess, where thoughts and feelings dwell;
And very hard the task I find of governing it well.
—Louisa May Alcott

PROLOGUE

Serena

"Shhhh," Junior clapped a hand over my mouth as voices sounded around the corner.

Our dads.

Both of them.

I grinned against his palm while he rolled his eyes and leaned in, pressing me against the wall, we were blanketed in darkness, just us. His scent wrapped around me in a way that felt like a fantasy. He tasted like cinnamon; the heat between our bodies would sear a normal person alive.

But we weren't normal.

We were best friends.

Who just happened to be sleeping together.

At sixteen.

And he was a few months older—the dads would flip if they knew—all of them.

They wouldn't approve. It was one of their many rules.

And only they knew the real reason they didn't want any of us together.

But telling me I couldn't have what I want was basically like begging me to do it, I snuck into Junior's bedroom when I was fifteen.

And the rest was history.

We'd been inseparable ever since.

"Mmmm…" Junior ran his hands down my sides, his fingers grazing skin as he tilted his head at a different angle. The hushed voices coming from the living room only made the moment hotter, more urgent. They'd kill us for being together.

I wasn't even exaggerating.

That was the price we paid for being born into mafia royalty.

And yet, I didn't care, maybe I would if I had a gun pointed at me, but right now? All I wanted was him.

With every kiss, I lied and said it was worth a life, life is fleeting anyway, why not spend it in someone's arms? Better yet, why not spend it in his bed?

"We're going to get caught." Junior pulled away and sighed, then pressed his forehead against mine, his eyes were an ocean blue almost teal, I always had trouble focusing when he watched me like he wanted me to know he saw everything and what he saw, he wanted—desperately.

"Not today, we won't." I wrapped my arms around his neck. "Besides, we know how to fight."

He gave me a dubious look. "You do realize that the body count of both of our dads' rivals that of the Capo…"

I ignored the mention of the glorified Godfather of the Five Families and pressed against his rock-hard body and winked. "Worth it."

"Fuck." He kissed me, again and again, pressing me so hard against the wall that I could feel every inch of him burning into me, dying for me.

My hands tangled in his hair as I tried to hold on to him, wrapping my legs around him, holding him prisoner.

The voices got louder.

We broke apart at the exact minute my cousin Ash rounded the corner and stared at us in frustration. "You're going to get caught, and I'm not gonna go down with the ship."

I grinned. "Awww, you're just pissed because you aren't getting any." I loved teasing Ash. It was too easy to get him to react, just like his dad Chase, like a bomb ready to go off.

"You shouldn't be getting any at all!" He clenched his teeth. "Uncle Nixon's gonna flip his shit if he finds out about you two."

"Dad will be fine." I sounded more confident than I felt. My dad was a killer and the boss of the Abandonato Family. I loved him more than life itself. He would understand this; he would side with me; he always did.

Right?

I mean, I was his princess, heir to the throne, and we were best friends, me and my dad, not that he didn't love Bella. My little sister was spoiled rotten, but she was ten years younger than me, which meant all the responsibility of the Family would fall onto my very capable shoulders.

"It's not just that..." Ash looked between us. "If it was anyone else..."

"What the fuck is that supposed to mean?" Junior shoved Ash's chest, causing Ash to stumble backward. He looked more annoyed than anything; I expected knives to get pulled any minute.

It's how we solved everything.

Violence.

"Phoenix Nicolasi, former De Lange—"

We both gaped while Junior shoved him again. "The hell, man! You can't say that name... not here."

Ash made the motion of the cross over his chest like it would somehow prevent the past from haunting our future and sighed. "Look, all I'm saying is, if it were anyone else, they'd probably look the other way, but precious Serena shacking up with dipshit—" he grinned at Junior "—that's you, by the way."

"Fuck. You." Junior pulled out his dagger.

It still had blood on the blade.

Awesome.

"You guys don't know the history between them. Sure the bosses all look happy now, but Phoenix did some serious shit back in the day. Let's just say there's no way that this is gonna slide. One or both of you are going to end up dead, and then who would braid Izzy's hair?"

"Low blow," Junior grumbled while I laughed. He loved Izzy, Ash's twin sister, more than anything, even resorting to helping braid her super thick hair when she broke her arm a few weeks ago.

"Look, this has been fun." I slapped Ash on the shoulder. "But I have a guy to screw, so if you could just be anywhere but here... that would be great."

Junior snickered then shoved Ash again and winked. "Maybe you should be our new lookout."

"Fresh out of earplugs."

"You'll survive." Junior grinned, then jerked me into his bedroom and shut the door.

We were a mixture of laughter, soft sighs, moans, hands, and all the touching in the world.

"He's wrong, you know," Junior said in between kisses. "You're mine, and you will always be mine."

"Yours." I lifted my shirt over my head while he tugged my jeans down. "Always yours."

"Damn right, you are." His kiss was punishing.

And I took it. Again and again, never believing there would be a day where our love would start a war.

And our friendship would shatter into a million pieces.

Then again, the worst thing you could do in the mafia is hang on to hope that your life would be normal.

The second worst thing?

Fall in love with your best friend.

Enemy.

And heir to the Nicolasi throne.

"Shhhh..." Junior smiled against my mouth before he grabbed his black tank and pulled it over his body. Even at sixteen, he was gorgeous, muscular—we had our parents to thank for that.

We were a dynasty in the making.

We'd had no choice but to learn how to fight.

I raked my nails down his chest, already he had tattoos lining his right arm, the only reason Phoenix let it slide was because most of the bosses knew that the pain in getting a tattoo helped develop a tolerance for pain from a gunshot wound or blade.

Sick but true.

I yawned behind my hand, earning a quick smirk from Junior. "Really? You're just going to lay there naked?"

I turned to my side. "See something else you like?"

He cursed. "I'm going to hell, aren't I?"

"Probably." I laughed, and then we heard more voices down the hall, mainly Asher yelling like a banshee.

"Quick!" Junior tossed me my jeans, I hurried and put them on, shoved my underwear under his bed then pulled over my sports bra and tank just as the voices grew louder.

It was my dad.

And Phoenix.

Chase.

It was all of them.

All of the bosses! I could hear each distinct voice and then an accented one meaning that Andrei the Sinacore-Petrov boss was also here.

"Why are they here?" I mouthed to Junior.

He just shrugged. "Family dinner?"

I burst out laughing just as the door opened. We looked as casual as ever, me on the bed texting, Junior at his desk working on a nonexistent paper.

See? We knew how to not get caught.

Chase stepped into the room. His eyes narrowed in on me and then Junior. "You guys studying?"

"Failing, he's failing." I pointed to Junior and earned a middle finger and grunt in response.

"You look fancy today, Uncle Chase." I grinned wide. "Good day saving the world?"

"He's a U.S. senator, not the president," Junior mumbled under his breath. "This is why you go to school, Serena, to learn shit."

"And so eloquently spoken," I said sarcastically.

Chase watched our exchange too closely. And then he sniffed the air like some freaking tracker!

My pulse picked up.

I could see Junior's slow swallow as he kept typing. His body was completely rigid. Okay, so maybe we weren't the best liars, but we were teenagers! What did they expect?

"Something wrong?" I stood and crossed my arms.

Chase's icy stare returned to me, his eyes laser-focused, his hair was longer now, swept to the side, I could see tattoos swirling out from underneath his black button-down shirt. "I would cut the shit before your dad finds out, Serena."

I scoffed. "Finds out that I let Junior do my homework?"

"The hell you do," Junior yelled.

"It smells like sex," Chase said through clenched teeth. "We'll talk about it later, but for now, you've been summoned."

I gulped. "Just me and Junior?"

Chase's expression hardened. "All of you, everyone over the age of thirteen."

I mentally did the math.

So that meant Junior and me, as well as Asher, Breaker, Violet, Izzy, Maksim, and—I wanted to vomit— my younger cousin King, but he was only thirteen. A sickness washed over me as I nodded once to my uncle and waited for Junior to walk with me.

I needed his strength.

Because I knew what a summoning meant.

It meant we had to choose.

But that word was even a lie, wasn't it?

To live meant to bleed for the Family.

To die, meant to turn your back on blood.

Bile rose in my throat as we followed Uncle Chase down the hallway, I knew I would remember each step, the way my heart thumped against my chest as we reached the main living room and looked around.

Everyone was there.

And I do mean everyone.

Aunts, uncles, cousins, and more importantly—the five bosses, Abandonato, Nicolasi, Alfero, Sinacore-Petrov, and our Capo dei Capi, Tex Campisi.

This was no family dinner.

My dad eyed me; my mom wiped a tear from her cheek. I almost asked who died, and then my dad, the strongest man I have ever known—pulled out a gun.

My dad never scared me. Because it was in my blood too, the need to destroy so I could make sure I was still alive. Blood of my blood. Soul of my soul. We were one and the same. Why would I ever be afraid of him? It would be like looking in the mirror and screaming out of terror for myself.

But in that moment, I was afraid.

"Serena," he rasped. "Come forward."

My legs took me to his six-foot-two frame. He was wearing a black on black suit; his lip ring flickered under the lights. His blue eyes searched mine. And then he pointed the gun to my forehead and whispered. "Make your choice."

I almost hurled all over his Armani suit. I could see my mom out of the corner of my eye, silently weeping—hoping I would choose the Family, choose blood, and a life of war. "If you stay, you earn your patron saint when you make your first kill—if you aren't with us, you are against us, you will turn and walk seven steps, counting each one out loud until there are no more steps to take, and your heart will beat no more."

Shaking, I stared my dad down and whispered. "Blood in,

no out." Then I very slowly kneeled in front of him and waited as the blood of my father dripped slowly over my head.

Crowning me Queen.

I was his firstborn, after all.

His legacy.

And I would rather chop off my own arm than disappoint him.

He held out his bloodied hand.

I took it and stood.

He flipped my hand over and sliced across my palm. It stung like hell, and he immediately pressed his bloodied palm to mine and said in such a sad voice that I wanted to burst into tears. "I have taken over thirty-seven souls from this earth. You will do that and more for the Family—your soul is no longer yours—it's ours. Welcome to the Family." He bent down and kissed each cheek, and then in a shaky voice, whispered, "Next."

One by one, the cousins went.

Ash was next.

Chase was ruthless, but Chase was notorious for having no moral compass. He didn't even give Ash the option. Then again, Ash had been doing a lot of killing lately. He was already a made man, so all he had to do was swear fealty to the Family—or at least, so I thought, and then I saw a knife get jabbed somewhere between rib one and two.

"Remember the pain." Chase gritted his teeth. "Let it burn down to your very soul, and remember that you are in the business of giving death—not life." He pulled the knife out Ash swayed a bit then nodded.

"Next," Chase said in a bold voice.

Junior walked up to his dad, Phoenix. If there were ever a

person to be petrified of, it would be Phoenix. He didn't even know the meaning of the word good. He dealt in death and secrets. He kept the Five Families safe.

And had a history nobody would tell any of the kids about.

But I saw the times my dad flinched when Phoenix talked to my mom. Even when they were laughing, there was an underlying tension.

Phoenix went through the pledge, Junior knelt in front of his father, and when he stood, it wasn't just his dad that slit his palm and pressed it to his, but mine stepped forward.

Tension swirled around the room.

What the hell?

I gulped as my dad gripped his still bloody dagger and then grabbed Junior's forearm, digging the tip of the knife into his skin and very slowly creating a bloodied circle.

Junior clenched his teeth in pain as my dad leaned in and pressed his bloodied palm to the fresh wound and with venom in his words spat. "The sins of the father are passed down— break my trust, and I'll remove this scar from your body and make you wear one around your face."

I gaped.

"Yes, sir." Junior didn't look at me.

He didn't give us away.

But I knew… the stakes were higher now.

The rest of the ceremony was a blur as Breaker stood in front of his father. Maksim was next, and our bloody oaths continued as the younger kids watched with wide eyes.

Their own mothers not even telling them to turn away.

Because why would they do them such a great disservice of not preparing them for their future?

When it was all over with, everyone cheered, wine was

poured, and I went into the bathroom. Asher didn't even knock, just walked right in, followed by Junior, Maksim, Violet, Izzy, King, and finally Breaker.

We sat on whatever surface we could find.

"One tear," Junior whispered. "You get one tear, and then we walk back out there and celebrate."

I nodded, and sure enough, one tear fell. Asher wiped it away from my cheek since he was closest, and then we all stood and stared at one another.

"We won't fail," Junior said, voice hoarse. "Because everyone's lives depend on us now."

"Us," Asher repeated.

My heart broke for Breaker as his eyes searched mine. I gave him a reaffirming nod.

And then his small voice piped up. "Blood in."

"No out," we said in unison.

CHAPTER One

Serena

Five Years Later

Being Nixon Abandonato's oldest daughter had its perks, I mean I should at least get something being the daughter of one of the Cosa Nostra's most powerful mob bosses. At sixteen, he let me pick out whatever car I wanted, and when I say whatever car, I mean—in the world.

And because I knew that it would piss Junior off and I lived for his constant scowls in my direction... I asked for the new Maserati Gran Tourismo MC, the exact same car he got the year before only better because mine was newer.

Swear every time I drove it, he wanted to purposefully get me into an accident.

This day was no different.

Day one of hell.

Day one of my senior year at Eagle Elite.

Just like it was Junior's.

It wasn't supposed to be like this. In fact, we had been told repeatedly when we grew up that we could go to college wherever we wanted. Could have whatever life we wanted—as long as we swore our loyalty to the Five Families of the Cosa Nostra, we'd be good.

And then *it* happened.

They refused to tell us what it actually was, but I'll never forget the look on my dad's face that day as he placed a small white toy horse in the middle of the kitchen table and whispered. "We have to talk."

A white horse apparently had been sent to every single boss, and with that, a cryptic note that said: *You should have killed them all.* It was signed MP. Nobody knew who it was from, but the symbolism wasn't lost on any of us. After all, a white horse never meant surrender to the mafia—it meant war.

And this time, we had no idea who the snitch was, or who wanted us dead, which meant I had to say goodbye to Stanford. I'd only been there a year, and for the first time in my life, I hated the mafia for taking that away from me.

We all transferred to Eagle Elite, the University the Five Families of Chicago owned—the one place we would be safe.

We had no choice.

The dads, the bosses, whatever you wanted to call them, decided they'd been too easy on us anyway, that we wouldn't survive in this world if we didn't know how to rule it.

Part of me wondered if they used that as an excuse, so they didn't terrify us of what was coming.

Either way, it had been a hard lesson.

I shuddered, recalling that first day.

It was a lesson I never wanted to remember but was forced to relive every single time I saw Junior kiss another girl, every time he watched me flirt with other guys and invite them to drive my car.

I ignored the goosebumps that erupted all over my body when I thought about that day, the day it all went to hell.

The day I was forced to ignore my heart, ignore the blood that pumped through my veins, and recognize that it had never been mine in the first place.

His. My dad's. The Boss of the Abandonato Family.

I gripped the steering wheel with my red leather gloves and hit the accelerator, wondering what it would feel like to just run right into that tree; my dad would be so pissed, we weren't allowed to go out that way, it was blood in, no out for the rest of our lives.

The mafia refused to let you die until it said you could.

And I was no different.

I could feel Junior's car on my ass; I hit my brakes as dirt puffed up around my back tires, he swerved and pulled out to the right so that both our cars were side by side.

I rolled down my window. "Junior, you know texting and driving is a crime punishable by ticket, right?"

He stared me down and then very slowly lifted his hand and showed me a middle finger. "Says the princess who tries to put on lipstick with one hand while stuffing her bra with the other."

Heat rushed to my face. I would kill him one day.

Unfortunately, today was not that day.

"Cute, Junior, it's almost like you don't remember how much you fumbled with these." I weighed my breasts in my hands. "Then again, if I were you, I would try to forget all those awkward moments too. What was it that one time? Five seconds? What a record!" I slow clapped.

His smile was cruel but so beautiful I ached. Straight white teeth, a small dimple on the right corner, jet black hair and teal eyes. "You're forgettable. That's not my fault, is it?"

Maybe I would murder him today. It wasn't like anyone would blink an eye at me. Then again, he was the heir to the Nicolasi crime Family. Ugh, why did he have to be important? And why the hell had I ever allowed him to see me naked on numerous occasions?

"See you in class, princess." He sped past me.

I followed, slower this time, maybe because I thought this year would be different. This year things would be... normal.

I almost laughed out loud. Right, when has my life ever been normal? I was basically born with blood on my hands. I would die the same way.

At least I had a nice car and unlimited cash. There were worse things in life than being forced to work with your ex-boyfriend and cousins at Eagle Elite.

Oh, it looked like we were just average college students, but everyone, including the faculty, knew the truth, knew who our parents were.

Who ran the world?

The Five Families.

The Chicago mafia.

Crime syndicate.

Whatever you wanted to call it.

We were it.

It... owned us.

Talk about it... and you might just get killed.

Brag about it, you're already dead.

A freshman last year was found hanging outside his dorm room with the word "rat" spray-painted across his chest.

The faculty said it was a suicide and told his parents he was depressed—but we all knew the truth.

It's not like I pushed him anyway.

Ash always did the dirty work, not me.

Junior spray painted it across the kid's chest.

Breaker pushed.

And I took a picture for my social media.

Because that kid could have gotten our family killed, or worse, in trouble, and blood protects blood. And he was bragging about having intel on our families. It didn't matter that he had nothing—what mattered was that we still had enemies, and I would do everything to protect my blood.

We had to warn people that this wasn't some sort of social experiment. This wasn't a reality show. And this wasn't a TikTok you could just go viral with.

This was our lives. And the fact that we let anyone live by our sides meant that they had to follow the rules... and follow us.

The idea was this: make sure that the world around the University understood how dangerous you were—as individuals and as a group—and then make sure that they followed our rules, which created fear. And that fear seeped into the students' friends, families, to the most influential people in the known world, because—newsflash—those were the only people allowed in the University. This fear then trickled quite joyfully down the line until everyone in power understood that the Five Families of Chicago were here to stay, and there wasn't jack shit anyone could do about it.

I used to hate that it would eventually put me in the spotlight, eventually force me to put on a mask that said fuck the world—I ran it, but now... now it just felt like putting on a fresh coat of lipstick and fluffing my hair.

All in a day's work.

Who ran the world?

Us.

I pulled into a parking spot next to Junior and waited while Ash's Tesla pulled up behind me at least four minutes later.

He got out of the car and wrapped an arm around his girlfriend Claire and my cousin Izzy, his twin. Sometimes she rode with me, but she'd told me that her dad put her on spy duty so she was the bad cold they couldn't get rid of.

It's not like Izzy would stop them from having all the sex, Claire and Ash went at it like they would die without touching each other. And honestly, I had to bite back the jealousy that at least one of us was happy.

I made a face at the happy couple while Izzy managed to walk toward me, cell in hand, texting one of her many boy toys. She never did anything but flirt, which almost made it worse, especially since all of us knew Maksim held a bit of a candle for her, which she promptly ignored since she didn't want to die.

"Put that away," Ash barked at her. "We got shit to do."

Izzy held up a finger.

Ash looked ready to break it.

Typical Monday.

"Cool nails." I winked and grabbed a thumb. "I like the red, nice touch."

She laughed, put her phone away, then glared at her brother, who was already kissing Claire like his life depended on it. I mean, would it kill them to come up for air and stop groping?

"Gross." She made a face. "Could you guys not do that in public?"

He ignored her like always.

Claimed he was in love.

We were all taking bets on when he got bored because Ash was too good looking and charismatic to just stick to one girl—we knew it, he denied it, it was a thing.

I sniffed the fresh Chicago air. This would be my year, the year I wouldn't let Junior get under my skin, the year I'd have fun at least half the time while getting groomed by my father the other half.

Most students my age were looking at job prospects, while mine was already embedded in my skin—quite literally.

Blood in, no out.

I was the heir to my father's throne, and I was going to reign supreme over all my silly little subjects, this school included.

Most days it felt like we lived on a different planet, maybe even in a different realm, where mere mortals walked among us and did mundane things like accounting and math—we learned how to cook the books, make murder look like an accident, and spied like we were part of the CIA—like they would even want to catch us, since we had friends in high places, very, very, high places.

"Ash, you're late and drive like Grandpa Frank." I finally brought my thoughts back down to earth and checked my gold Rolex. Already my black Gucci glasses were so tight that I felt a headache forming at my temples.

"He's always late." Junior hopped out of his car and gave Ash a high five and hug while Claire gave Izzy and me a sweet smile.

I didn't do sweet.

I was more… salty. There, that sounded better.

And Claire, well, she had mafia blood, but she seemed too pure for this sort of life. Then again, she helped Ash do some serious shit, so she'd at least earned my respect that way and earned her way into our group.

I cracked my neck. "You guys ready?"

"Always." Ash wrapped an arm around Claire again and let me walk ahead of him. Izzy hung back with them, and Junior flanked to my right. Never had there been such hatred between a king and queen.

I knew Maksim and Breaker were already around; they had earlier classes than us, and frankly, since we were the eldest, we stuck together more, while the younger cousins got more freedom. Someone had to rule the free world, and it wasn't going to be smart-as-shit Maksim who skipped ahead a year and entered into EE with Breaker only to break so many hearts I wondered if he was going to actually contract a sexual disease of some sort.

We let them play.

Because we had work to do.

Fear to build.

Enemies to make.

My stiletto heel hit the cement in perfect cadence to the increased heartbeats around us. The fear, you could almost smell it—I lived for it—it was all I had now that love was gone, now that my heart was obliterated.

I gave my head a shake and kept walking. Along our path, students parted, they stopped talking, they gave us a wide berth, and when we finally made it to the simple white building in the middle of the campus, I felt my hand shake a bit.

Behind us, Ash cursed. He hated this part; we all did.

But it was necessary.

We all turned and glanced at the student body, watching them watch us.

A person would come forward. Someone always did.

Finally, one of the football players stepped forward. I could have predicted that. It was usually an athlete, mainly because they were the only ones who could typically take it.

"Z!" Ash gave the guy a once over. "Damn man, you put on at least twenty pounds over the summer."

He gave Ash a tentative smile then rocked back on his heels. "I knew it was probably time." His eyes flickered from Ash to the rest of us. "Maybe with the added muscle, it'll hurt less."

"Yeah." Was it me, or did Ash sound sad? "Maybe."

Zac took a deep breath, clutching his fists at his sides. "I'm ready."

"Swell." I sashayed toward him, then did a small circle around him, he was at least two hundred pounds of pure American beef. He had a nice smile, sandy brown hair, and I was one hundred percent convinced he'd grow up to be an accountant.

And not the cool ones that burn the books for you and help you hide money but the really shitty ones who looked forward to pot roast on a Tuesday the way I looked forward to a manicure.

"All right, Zac, you know the rules," I said in a low voice. "Not a sound."

I held out my hand, and Junior handed me the wooden bat. More and more students filed around us, along with a few faculty members drinking their coffee; one yawned.

Eagle Elite, ladies and gentlemen, it would be comical if it didn't steal our souls, wouldn't it?

But that's what the parents wanted. Make us hurt, make us suffer, make us understand, so that if the time ever came where we had to choose between ourselves and our family—we chose family every time.

Bred into our bones, the idea that blood trumps self.

I raised the bat and slammed it across his right arm, he winced but didn't say anything. I threw it in the air, caught it with my other hand, and hit him right in the left kneecap.

Zac squeezed his eyes closed; his lips were trembling.

"Who are we?" I asked in a sweet voice that sounded fake even to my own ears. I was a lot of things—sweet was not one of them.

"The Elect." His pain-filled voice was like nails on a chalkboard.

I tossed the bat to Ash, who wasted no time in slamming it into Zac's back, causing him to stumble forward. "Do not touch The Elect." He gave Zac a shove then held out the bat to Izzy.

She took it and hit Zac in the right shin. "Do not look at The Elect."

Junior was last. I ignored the way his swagger made my stomach flop. Damn Zac wasn't the only one who'd lived in a gym this summer... he'd put on at least fifteen pounds of muscle. His tatted fingers gripped the bat. With an evil grin, one I felt all the way to my toes, the bat went soaring right into Zac's stomach, he doubled over and spat out blood, and Junior leaned over him and said in a lethal voice. "Do not speak to The Elect."

Claire watched, her expression stoic.

Junior dropped the bat and crossed his arms. "Any questions?"

No student said anything.

"Good." Junior smiled. "Let's get out there and have a really safe and fun year!"

The sarcasm alone made me want to burst out laughing even though I wanted to drown him half the time.

Ash looked away.

"You heard the man," Ash barked. "Go!"

And off they went, with their rich parents and perfect lives. They'd graduate to the most powerful positions in the world— and they'd remember this moment in their nightmares.

Zac wobbled and then stood. "Thank you."

Yes, he was thanking us, because if someone volunteered at the beginning of the year, that person and any friends weren't just given a free pass to talk with us—they were allowed to hang with The Elect, party with us. That person just had to go through the pain in order to get there. I was glad it was Zac since we actually tolerated him and his friends.

"Welcome." I blew him a kiss and then tilted my head. "No girlfriend this year?"

His eyes heated. "Not yet." He licked his lips. "New skirt?"

"Go." Junior shoved him. "You have class."

"I do?" Zac looked confused.

"Yeah, you do." Junior rolled his eyes, then pulled out his knife.

"All right, all right!" Zac held up his hands. "Hell, you guys are crazy."

I lunged for him.

"Shit, man, don't call her crazy," Junior mumbled under his breath while Ash held me back.

"Didn't you almost lose a testicle last time?" Izzy asked Junior.

Zac must have gotten the picture because he turned and ran.

"You're welcome!" Ash called and then released me.

I stumbled forward, nearly colliding with Junior. He steadied me.

Our eyes locked.

Damn that man's eyes.

Teal... who had teal eyes?

I hated that the only times he touched me now were to push me away when it used to be to pull me close.

I hated what we'd been forced to become.

Hated it.

"You've got mascara—right here," He flicked my chin.

I licked my middle finger and wiped off the makeup earning a grin from him before he sobered and looked away.

Ash and Claire were a few feet from us talking with Izzy.

It was rare for me and Junior to be standing next to one another without shouting, pulling weapons... Was this new school year going to be a cease-fire?

"One day... I'm going to kill you." He said it like a promise.

And I answered in truth. "You can't kill what's already dead."

For a brief moment, I felt his fingertips graze mine.

And then he pulled back.

I exhaled and reminded myself that the sting of tears meant I was still alive, still breathing, still making my family proud, mainly my dad.

I looked around the fancy brick buildings and sighed. "Welcome to Hell."

CHAPTER *Two*

Junior

I would take it to my grave.

The wrongs done against her mom.

The things my father said he did in the name of blood—De Lange blood. The name wasn't spoken out loud—*ever*. And the last time that it was, the person was found not long after with a slit throat.

The thing about the Cosa Nostra… we always have enemies; I just never thought the very Family that used to be a part of the five would be the ones to try to destroy us.

The De Langes tried to do it from within, but according to my dad, they failed, and hits were put out for every last one of them. He and a few of the guys went out, and the rest is history.

The only problem with history?

It quite often repeated itself.

And it was only a matter of time before that happened.

Because they were here.

At this school.

In our city.

The kids that were left alive.

When the mafia does a cleansing of a line, they're supposed to kill every last soul, but instead, our fathers—the bosses—offered mercy.

And now, the kids had to pay for the fathers' sins.

They had gone soft; they refused to kill innocent children, which would have been great, respectable even, but where did that leave us?

Here.

Our lives completely derailed because of them—and now I was paying for it along with my cousins.

I clenched my fists at my side.

It was never supposed to go down like this. We were never supposed to step into the picture until after college graduation.

Until after we got the partying and freedom out of our systems.

After swearing fealty at such a young age, we thought hey at least we have some freedom for a while—but the arrival of that white horse meant calling all of the kids back home. And no matter how many times I asked my dad why the second arrival of the cryptic message was enough for him to call us home, he simply shook his head and said because.

Right, as if that didn't burn like hell.

Because?

We were teenagers.

Teenagers with plans.

Girlfriends.

Feelings.

And now all I felt was pain.

And most of it was because of her.

We walked side by side toward class. I looked down at my schedule and cursed. Why the hell was I in a junior-level history class?

Students gave us a wide berth as the five of us made our way down the narrow hall.

Me in front with Serena.

Ash in the middle with Claire.

And Izzy in the back.

I stopped in front of the classroom and barely kept my groan in when Serena did the same.

Not. Happening.

I could feel her hatred dripping off her like an expensive perfume. Her head snapped in my direction. "Must you stalk me?"

I sneered down at her. "Must you want me so much?"

Hurt flashed across her face before she recovered. She had never been good at hiding anything from me, least of all, her emotions, and in the end, her heart.

Mine. It had all been mine.

Until we were both forced to choose.

And choosing her—would have killed us all.

She had to know that.

She had to know what her dad would do to me, to us.

She had to know that my dad would have no choice.

That I would take those seven steps, and this time, it wouldn't be an option.

I shoved past her and found a seat in the back, and by the time class started, she had recovered back to her bored resting bitch face and was furiously texting someone—probably Izzy— to tell her what a horrible human being I was.

Get in line, princess. Get in fucking line.

"Welcome to day one!" Professor Dick Face's eyes roamed around the room, purposefully scanning over us even though I had a middle finger raised in greeting right along with Serena. Well, at least we could agree on something, pissing off the professors enough to scare them shitless. "If you'll all log onto your blackboard app, we can go over this year's syllabus."

"Overjoyed," I said under my breath.

"Do you mind?" Serena hissed. "I'm learning here."

She literally had Snapchat open.

"Uh-huh." I elbowed her side only to feel the steel of a knife against my dick.

I kept my smirk in and lost when we both locked eyes.

Shit, I knew that look.

And I knew what typically followed.

The best sex of my life.

"No," I whispered hoarsely, even though I let my eyes freely roam over her tight leather skirt down to gorgeous legs that I wanted to lick my way up. "Hell no."

I jerked in my seat and nearly impaled myself on her knife when her hand slid across the front of my jeans.

I gritted my teeth to keep from reacting, braced my hands on the table in front of me, and shook my head slowly as she kept touching, and I kept just responding. Because it was Serena, and eons ago before she fucking broke my heart—she was mine.

"Choose me," I'd said in my head. *"Choose me in front of them all!"*

She didn't.

She never would.

Our love was impossible.

And I knew more than her—how easy love could start a war.

She still wasn't pulling her hand away, so I took matters into my own hands, and scooted my chair back, then slid my fingers up her thigh, digging into her skin the entire way up until I felt the string of her thong.

With a jerk, I tugged it until it broke, bunched her underwear in my hands, and then very somberly shoved them into my pocket all without looking away from my handy app.

"Give those back," she said through clenched teeth.

"Better not draw attention to us," I said in a bored tone. "Wouldn't want you to get detention on the first day—again."

"That was voluntary, and you know it!" she hissed.

I chuckled under my breath. "Whatever you say."

"Junior, I mean it! I can't walk around like this!"

"You can." I shrugged. "You will."

"Junior—"

"Just admit defeat. You tried to win, and instead, you just lost—embarrassingly. It's going to take more than your hand to get me off, or do you forget?" Then I did turn toward her. "I'd rather drink poison than have you touch me ever again."

Something sharp jabbed into my thigh. I winced and squeezed my eyes shut, then opened them and looked down.

And there was her knife, stuck in my thigh through my jeans, embedded at least a half-inch.

Perfect.

I nodded slowly. "Is that the Abandonato crest?"

"Beautiful, right?" She beamed then flipped her dyed golden hair in the air giving me a whiff of her cherry shampoo.

I jerked out the knife and handed it back to her. "Don't be creepy and lick the blood off—that's weird, even for you."

She just rolled her eyes. "More like use it in a spell to make your favorite appendage fall off."

"Your favorite appendage," I grumbled. "Remember? Oh God Junior, right there, so good, it's so—"

She clapped a hand over my mouth while a few students in front of us chuckled. "I get it, just. Stop. Talking."

I nipped her hand with my teeth and grinned.

She smiled and looked away, down at her phone. "It shouldn't be like this."

"I'll hate you for as long as we both shall live," I uttered the mantra we'd been repeating to each other for years.

"Hate you," she repeated in a soft voice. "For as long as we both shall live."

And so, the hurt continued.

The pain followed swiftly, and I was suddenly grateful she'd stabbed me in the leg so I wouldn't feel the daggers in my heart.

Thank God for small favors.

CHAPTER
Three

Serena

I remember the first time I saw my dad cry. We were driving away from Uncle Chase's house, I was small, like really small, and I remember him saying a bad word under his breath—it was the first time he'd cursed around me. I knew the word was bad because my mom made all the bosses, my uncles, put money in a swear jar every time it was said.

Dad drove for another twenty minutes, then pulled off to the side of the road. Without looking, he reached back and squeezed my foot, and then he put the SUV in park and turned. "You're never dating."

I giggled, what was dating anyway?

He shook his head; his handsome face pale, as a tear fell from his cheek down his chin. "Serena, sweetheart, I can't let you go, I don't think I would survive it."

Ten years later, on my thirteenth birthday, he caught me kissing a boy from school behind the house, and the first thing he did was hold a gun to poor Dylan's head and say, "You use tongue?"

Dylan didn't pee his pants, but he looked ready to as he shook his head vehemently and then whimpered.

My dad lowered his weapon and growled, straight up growled, Dylan shrieked and ran off while I glared daggers at my father. "What was that for?"

"You're not dating." He clenched his teeth. "And you sure as hell shouldn't be luring victims behind the house and kissing them!"

"Boys aren't victims!" I yelled, stomping my foot.

He took one look at me, wiped a hand down his face and muttered, "When it comes to you? They may as well be." He shook his head. "Hell, you're only thirteen, and they notice you, they all notice you."

"I like being noticed."

The gun pointed in my direction. I scowled. "The point of this life, of this Family, sweetheart, is to become noticed only after you've won."

"And how do I know if I've won?"

"The other person will no longer be breathing." He shrugged. "Don't tell your mom about Dylan; she'll grab her gun."

I sighed. "Mom's not as terrifying as you."

He snorted out a laugh. "Yeah okay, don't ever let her hear you say that, she's turned into a bloodthirsty woman."

"Wonder whose fault that is." I giggled as he pulled me in for a hug and kissed the top of my head.

My dad was my protector.

He was my best friend.

He was my hero.

And I knew that every time I kissed Junior, I was betraying him, every time I touched Junior, wanted him—I was making small cuts with a knife into my dad's heart.

But I couldn't stop.

Not until I was forced to.

Not until Junior chose this life over me, over us, not until he stared at me while touching another girl and smiled.

I hated him beyond all reason.

"Class dismissed," our professor suddenly said.

I'd been daydreaming that entire time.

Fantastic.

Junior shoved back his chair and gave me an annoyed look. "You gonna stare into space all day?"

"You gonna annoy me all day?" I snapped in a sing-song voice.

"Probably." His full lips drew up into a smirk that had every single memory of his mouth on my body coming back full force. "Feeling a bit of… air princess?"

I ignored the way my bare skin felt against the tight leather skirt I was wearing and the way his eyes seemed to heat every single time they lingered on mine like he was waiting for me to snap and was willing to be on the receiving end of whatever that meant as long as he could torture me some more. That was Junior for you; he could make a person believe they were getting nothing but pleasure when he was doing nothing but offering pain. I squeezed my eyes shut. "Let's go."

"Whatever you say, princess," he muttered, following behind me—because it was his job to protect me.

Protect me at all costs.

But nobody ever warned me that the very man who

destroyed me was the one man who was supposed to protect me.

And sometimes I was afraid I wouldn't ever be able to fix what he broke.

Not with him so close.

And yet so far away.

I kept my head held high as I walked down the hall toward the doors. And without even asking, two football players winked in my direction and opened them wide for me to step through.

"Such gentlemen." I winked.

"Always." Xavier was deliciously gorgeous, with firm muscles in all the right places, perfect mocha skin, and a jawline to die for.

I was about to say something, maybe suggest we should hang out this weekend, when Junior cleared his throat behind me.

"Care to be annoying elsewhere?" I seethed without turning around.

"No. Not really," he said with a careless air. "Hey, Xavier, how's the leg healing up?"

Xavier shrugged. "Pretty good, coach says I should still start this weekend."

"It would be a shame then, wouldn't it?" Junior moved past me and started circling Xavier while his friend Penn held up his hands like he wanted nothing to do with us.

Great, another guy bites the dust.

"Junior," I warned him, finally turning to face him.

"What would be a shame?" Xavier puffed his chest out. Bad idea. Bad idea! Couldn't he tell Junior smelled blood and actually liked harming people? Got off on it in a way that was

34

so horribly necessary in our world that nobody had ever held him back? Only encouraged it?

"If you lost it." Junior's grin was fierce.

"Lost it?" Xavier looked genuinely confused. "How would I lose my leg? I'm not really following, Bro."

I almost groaned out loud.

"I'm so fucking glad you asked, man." Junior wrapped a bulky arm around Xavier, and it was shocking how incredibly built Junior was even standing next to a collegiate athlete. "First, I'd give you a head start. What do you think, Serena? Maybe like thirty seconds?"

There was no point in stopping him, Junior had sniffed the blood, and now he would attack, and I had to keep up pretenses even when all I wanted to do was tell Xavier to run. I lifted one shoulder and let it fall like I didn't care. "At least thirty."

"Perfect," Junior rasped, enjoying the game more than was natural, or human. "And after that thirty seconds, I'd, of course, come after you with a gun in my right hand, and a knife in the other, and you'd naturally notice some psycho chasing you so you'd run faster, but the shit deal here is this, I'm really fast, and also I have a gun. Ask Serena if I play fair."

Xavier gulped and locked eyes with me. "Does he play fair?"

"Cheats at everything and on everyone," I said with venom noticing something flicker in Junior's eyes before he turned back to Xavier.

"So…" Junior semi-backed off. "You'd most likely go down after I shoot directly through your Achilles, and well, I'm not a total monster. I mean, I would for sure want to put you out of your misery, so I'd shoot your leg again, and then, I don't know man, sometimes the ambulance, it takes forever to get on campus…" They stood chest to chest. "Feel me?"

Xavier wasn't backing down. "Try me."

"All right then." I grabbed Junior by the arm, ignoring the flex of his bicep. "He gets it, Junior, no flirting."

"Fuck." Xavier shook his head. "This is because I'm talking to your girl? Just tell me next time, man."

"She's not mine," Junior snapped.

And I felt it again, the slow spread of pain that started exactly where my heart was supposed to be, the cold metal of his blade as he twisted and twisted until it hurt to breathe.

She's not mine.

She's not mine.

She's not mine.

"Then you have no claim." Xavier flipped him his middle finger and turned to me at about the same time Junior lunged.

I blocked the first punch with my own body, nearly doubling over from the pain. "Junior, he's right, let's go."

"If you so much as breathe in her direction—"

I shoved Junior out the door.

Thankfully he let me, probably because he knew he was acting like a petulant asshole.

"The fucking nerve of that guy!" Junior turned apparently to go back and tell the guy he was going to shoot him anyway.

"Leave it." I yawned. "I don't want him anyway."

Junior's chest heaved. "Nixon would murder you if you started sleeping around with the football team."

I stopped walking. "I flirt with one guy, and suddenly I'm whoring myself out for the football team? Are you for real right now?"

Junior shrugged. "All I'm saying is—"

I punched him in the jaw before I could get my anger under control and felt at least two fingers crack, followed by the rapid swelling of my hand. I'd have to ice them later. Worth it.

He went down to the grass.

At least a hundred students saw.

Silence descended as I stepped over Junior with my stiletto heels and then called over my shoulder. "Got a little something, right here."

He jumped to his feet and lunged for me—that's the other thing; if you start a fight, you best be ready to continue it.

I kicked off my heels and moved to the grass while he peeled his shirt over his head and tossed his gun and knife to the ground.

I threw my bag to the grass, took out my hoop earrings and dropped them onto my bag, then slid up my leather skirt and grabbed both daggers that were strapped to my thigh and tossed them with his weapons and shrugged. "Gun's in the purse."

"We doing this?" His eyes lit up with amusement.

"Wait." I took two steps toward him. "I need a little slit so I can do my roundhouse kick justice."

"No problem." He gripped my skirt with both hands and looked up at me with those teal eyes, grabbed his knife again and dug it a few inches into the leather, and then ripped all the way up to my thigh, "Ah, memories, memories."

"Pretty sure you never ripped my skirt like that."

"Only your panties." He winked. "Which I feel the need to remind you—I have in my pocket, I'd be careful not to give everyone a free show—at least charge something, Serena…"

And just like that, I wanted to end him.

Sweaty bodies.

His tongue.

I gave my head a shake as he wet his bottom lip and then slowly stood until we were chest to chest. I wasn't short, but he was massive compared to my five-foot-seven frame.

"First blood wins?" He cocked his head to the side, a smirk playing at his full lips.

Without answering, I kneed him in the balls. "Sure, first blood."

He made a face and dropped to his knees. "You slut!"

I bowed. "What? You in too much pain?"

"One day," He moved to his feet, teeth clenched. "I'm going to murder you in your sleep."

"That day, dear Junior…" I did a little curtsy. "Isn't today."

He charged me, throwing me over his shoulder, and slamming me onto the ground.

I rolled out from under him, as he came down with an elbow, then jumped to my feet and kicked him in the stomach, he grabbed my foot and spun me out onto my back then straddled me with his body.

"Surrender." He pinned my wrists to the grass.

I moved under him, and then realized he wasn't packing—a gun at least, but something extremely hard was pressing into me.

I sucked in a sharp breath while he ground his hips into mine, then leaned down and tugged my right ear with his teeth. "Methinks you're just sexually repressed. All you had to do was say something, and I could be of service…"

I jerked my head away from him. "I would rather die."

"And you just might." He chuckled darkly.

My body responded even though I didn't want it to, I

squeezed my eyes shut, remembering all the years of tedious training from my family and relaxed beneath his touch. "Junior?"

"Surrendering?"

My eyes snapped open as I bucked against him then managed to get a foot out from underneath him enough to wrap up.

He flipped me back around, but I was able to get on his back and get an arm underneath his chin, I pulled tight, my legs wrapped while I tried to cut off his oxygen.

"Let me guess, this turns you on too?" I bit his neck and vaguely realized that we were being watched by a ton of people.

I didn't care.

I just wanted to win.

He started pulling at my arms, and then he stilled and flipped me over his front, slamming me back into the ground and knocking the wind out of me.

"I win."

"You said first blood," I pointed out, a bit breathless, and then I smiled, knowing he'd see the blood on my teeth.

"The hell?" He touched his neck where I'd bitten him.

I licked my lips and winked. "I win."

He burst out laughing and held out his hand to me. "Fair's fair."

I jumped to my feet and started grabbing my stuff while he put his shirt back on and continued to shake his head.

"What the hell was that?" Ash and Claire ran over to us with Izzy in tow.

Junior just shrugged and then turned around to the crowd. "Are you not entertained?"

Cheers erupted.

I gave Junior a high five. "Sorry Ash, he was cockblocking me again."

Claire laughed. "So, this is all over what? A guy asking you out on a date?"

I scrunched up my nose. "Didn't get that far because dick for brains over here threatened to shoot off the star quarterback's Achilles tendon!"

"Nice." Ash gave Junior a fist bump.

I sighed. "Can we be done with the first day of classes now and party?"

Claire grabbed her phone. "Ugh, I have one more class, but I'll meet you guys later tonight?"

"Same spot?" Ash was clearly following her to class, more like stalking her.

"Same." I needed to shower first and rub some CBD all over my already achy and bruised body, but other than that, I was ready to let loose.

Izzy's blue eyes searched my body before she looked back at Ash, "I actually have some homework, I'm gonna head back. Maksim said he'd help."

Of course he did, Maksim was a friggin' genius.

"Iz," Ash wrapped an arm around her. "Homework can wait. It's the first party of the entire year; you know they expect us to host."

Izzy sighed. "It's embarrassing."

"Sitting on a fucking throne?" Junior piped up. "No, that's our right."

"The elite of the elite," I added. "It's the expectation, and you know the real reason for all of this. To be so blatantly arrogant that we draw out our enemies and pick them off one by one."

"Well." Izzy sighed. "The fight sure helped things!"

"Hey," Junior sobered. "All that matters is keeping our family safe, and if we get to act like idiots in the process, that's our gain, not our loss."

"I know." Izzy's face fell. "I just… sometimes I worry you guys are getting too distracted, not paying attention, I mean did you even look over the new student registration today?"

"Yes," Junior and I said in unison.

"Why?" Asher and Claire shared a confused look as Breaker, Tex's son, jogged over to us all six-foot-five of him.

Kid was huge and still growing at nineteen. "We've got a problem."

Dread filled my stomach. "What?"

He ran his hands through his long reddish-brown hair, girls compared him to a young Johnny Depp, and he looked it more and more every day only somehow more attractive.

Tex said it just meant his sperm was the best even though we all knew that Breaker was adopted.

Ah, the Capo, couldn't live with him, would die without him.

"So, I was making out with this transfer." He stopped his story to give high fives to both guys.

"Get there faster, Breaker. We get it; you're a manwhore, please continue."

"Is it whoring, though, if they just throw themselves at me?" he wondered out loud with a cocky grin.

I glared.

"Fine." He sighed. "So, things were getting hot and heavy—"

"Naturally," Junior said in a bored tone.

Breaker ignored him. "And then she starts talking about

how she was so excited to transfer to Eagle Elite because last year she saw some of the kids from the fence and wondered if the rumors were true."

"Wait, back up." I held up my hand. "The fence?"

"I'm getting there." He sighed. "So I asked her what fence and who the hell just stares at people?"

"We do. We do that all the time." I pointed out. "But our goal is to scare them shitless, not build shrines to people's hair."

"One time," Breaker said, becoming irritated. "Anyway, so she takes me to the opposite end of campus where sure enough a brand-new fence was put up dividing our property and that old community college that can barely keep its doors open. She said the college got a grant last year and was able to hire better professors, offer scholarships... but the weird part is that the only reason she even knew about what went on here at EE was because the new brochures for the college use our families' names as a selling point."

"Did you get a—"

"Yes." He rolled his eyes and held out a brochure.

I snatched it while the rest of the group huddled around me to read it. And sure enough, on the brochure advertising Chicago Community, was a teaser line that said: "Located next to the notorious Eagle Elite University, funded by the original Five Families. Study side by side with mafia's elite, and maybe you'll even be lucky enough to study with them!"

Below that were several student testimonials of not only hanging out with us but with edited pictures of us.

Including Breaker.

My hands shook. "This is bad."

"They have our pictures," Junior cursed.

"How did this get through our intel?" Breaker asked.

"Paper." Izzy sighed.

I wanted to scream.

"The only trail is paper," she elaborated. "No social footprint, nothing online; this is all word of mouth."

"The question is, are they trying to make money and boost enrollment, or is this something else?" Ash took the paper and examined it. "What do you think, Junior?"

Junior was quiet.

It was unsettling.

"I think…" He shared a look with me that I knew meant he didn't like this, not one bit. "I think we're being targeted. While the De Lange kids can't enroll in Eagle Elite without getting their parts chopped off and sold—they sure as hell can enroll in the community college next door, and all we have is a fucking fence separating us."

My stomach dropped. "We'll have to vet every single student."

"Shit, who has time for that?" Ash groaned into his hands.

"We have no choice." I tapped my fingers against my cold leather skirt and nodded at Junior. "We're going to host our usual back to school party."

"And kill everyone?" Claire asked.

I burst out laughing. "No, we aren't killing everyone. We're moving the first party of the year, and we're inviting our new neighbors."

"Uh, is that really the best idea?" Izzy asked, her blue eyes wide. "I mean if people are intoxicated—"

"No drinking more than one drink." I crossed my arms. "And everyone needs to be armed, even you, Claire."

Ash wrapped an arm around her.

"I guess all that needs to be decided is…" Breaker looked around the group. "Who gets to tell the dads?"

"Not it!" we all yelled in unison.

I groaned. "Fine, we'll just all go together. Family dinner time!"

Breaker cursed. "I nearly lost a pinkie last week."

"Then stop stealing the bread basket!" I all but yelled. "We have one rule! It's communal, and I won't be held responsible for my fork if you try to take more than one roll before it's been shared with the table!"

"Best Friday night ever." Ash burst out laughing.

Breaker narrowed his eyes. "Yes. So fun. Losing limbs."

"Let's go, no more classes, we gotta decide how to angle this, so nobody gets shot over chicken parmesan."

"A year ago, I would have thought you were kidding," Claire said under her breath.

"And now?" I grinned.

"Now I'm alarmed when nobody has a weapon."

"Ain't that the truth," Junior muttered as we all started walking toward the parking lot.

I was lost in my own thoughts until I felt a hand on my ass.

I froze.

Junior squeezed and then whispered. "Forgetting something?"

I turned around and frowned, and then he pulled me against him and very strategically shoved my underwear back into my hand and winked.

"You're a monster." I hissed.

He leaned over and kissed my right cheek, then my left, his teal eyes narrowed in on my mouth. "I'm taking that as a compliment since we both know you prefer monster over man."

CHAPTER
Four

Junior

People warned me from a young age that there was something tainted in my blood. I laughed it off. After all, my dad was one of the most bad-ass bosses on the planet.

Not just powerful, but he was my hero.

He knew everyone's secrets and used them against them like a chess game that only he knew the rules to.

Masterful would be one way to describe Phoenix Nicolasi.

I had no idea that while I was making plans, the rest of the bosses were moving behind our backs, making a list of our strengths, weaknesses, of ways to break us over and over again until all we felt was this craving to win.

This intense need to prove ourselves.

To kill in order to do it.

To crave the blood as much as our next breath.

"Why!" I yelled at my dad, blood dripping from my mouth

as he took another swing at me. I ducked; he narrowly missed my front teeth. "Why!"

I was screaming.

And for the first time in my life, at the age of fifteen, my dad shed a tear; it mixed with blood as it slid down his chiseled hard face.

"Because," he finally rasped. "It's the only way."

"Fighting me is the only way? Making me bleed?" He went from hero to monster that summer.

"No, son." He peeled off his shirt showing too many scars to count; scars that were covered by tattoos and thick bands of muscle that I knew packed a punch that could easily knock me unconscious or hospitalize me. "It's the only way to keep you safe."

The next blow knocked me off my feet, and the hero-worship I'd had for my father was lost to the darkness of that final gut-wrenching hit. That day he reminded us we were pawns.

That day I decided... I would be a king.

I didn't tell anyone, but I cried myself to sleep that night.

And there she was, my angel, Serena.

She slipped into my bedroom when nobody was looking, she took my face between her hands and kissed each bandaged cut and promised that one day everything would be okay.

"One day, Junior, the fighting will be over."

"Promise?" I could barely get the word out. My body hurt in places I didn't even know existed.

She gripped my hand in hers. "I promise."

I tried not to think about her promises just like I tried not to think about her kisses; it pissed me off knowing she lied.

Knowing that when it came down to it, she didn't trust me the way I'd trusted her, didn't understand that we were still on the fucking chessboard playing a game we had to win.

I tried to shove my feelings aside, but that's the really inconvenient thing about emotions, they tend to just pop up out of nowhere when you're constantly around the only person who has the ability to make you feel less shitty.

We had an hour before family dinner, everyone had already gathered at Nixon's, wine was passed around by the bottle, and I was already bemoaning the fact that we had to tell the bosses what was going on.

And there was no way of doing it gently, not with this crew.

It was too noisy to think, and I had too many damning memories of that house, of being with Serena, sneaking off to her room.

My body felt tight.

I needed to fight someone.

Preferably her.

I touched my neck, couldn't believe that psycho had bitten me. Then again, it was Serena, and she didn't like losing.

I almost smiled but kept it reined in. The last thing I needed was for her to see me touching my neck with a dopy lovesick grin on my face.

Not only would I never hear the end of it, but I'm pretty sure she'd pull a knife on me for making her remember all those stolen moments we were never supposed to have had.

"Hey." My dad rounded the corner into the kitchen. His brown eyes had a hard glint to them even though Mom was holding his hand. She leaned up and kissed him on the cheek.

She was the light to his dark.

Which just reminded me that I had nothing tethering me to anything good, maybe there really was something wrong with me, wrong with my blood, wrong with the way my brain worked, with the way my heart wanted what it could never have.

"What's up?" I tried to appear casual as I went in for a hug with Ma, she held me tight as always, barely coming up to my shoulder as she squeezed me and then sighed. "What?"

"Who bit you?" She just had to ask, making all conversation cease in that ginormous kitchen, including the chatter of the younger kids, who seemed to stop playing altogether and gawk in my direction.

"Yeah, Junior," Serena bit into a red apple that matched her lipstick and winked. "What happened to your neck? Get in a fight?"

"I wouldn't really call it a fight since you never play fair." I grinned and flipped her off.

"You?" My dad's expression was priceless. "Bit him?"

"Hey." Serena chewed and hopped off the countertop. "He said first blood, I agreed."

"I meant with a knife, you psychopath." I clenched my teeth, and there we were, yet again, head to head in the middle of the kitchen.

I lost count how many times family dinners started with both of us staring each other down, ready to draw blood until one of us gave in or begged for mercy.

"Up top." Chase walked by both of us and held up his hands for high fives.

Serena hit his hand then scowled in my direction. "Why does shit for brains get a high five if I'm the winner?"

I tapped Chase's hand and shook my head. "Aw princess, your panties in a bunch?"

She flashed red.

And I suddenly wondered if she'd put a new pair on or was still strutting around remembering what it was like during class.

Shit, I needed to really not focus on what she was or wasn't wearing beneath her skirt.

"Because he fought you, a girl. I've never been so proud to be an uncle." Chase winked, and then something sinister flashed across his face. "You know what they say about love and hate—"

"Can we eat yet?" Tex barged into the room. "I'm starving, and Breaker just told me that something went down at school today."

"Not it!" all of us yelled again in unison.

The moms simultaneously took a step back like they wanted no part of this conversation if it was going to end in bloodshed.

I sighed and eyed Ash, who eyed Claire, who gazed over at Serena with a pleading look.

"Yeah, we can do this all day," Ash said under his breath.

"Loser of the fight gets the short straw." Serena beamed at me.

I let out a strangled cough. "Fine."

We all moved around the huge table and took our seats; Violet was next to Asher. Maksim had pulled out a chair beside Izzy; they were probably going to talk about school the entire time, knowing him. It was baffling how good looking the kid was at eighteen and disgusting how he was already a college sophomore. He flipped me off with a wink. I sighed and glanced away. Either he was good at reading minds, or he was good at reading me, probably both knowing him.

Breaker pulled out a seat next to King and watched our exchange with a smirk. Everyone else, meaning the younger ones who weren't in their senior years of high school or college, got to sit at the other table, and I was suddenly thankful that the smaller ears weren't going to hear what we needed to discuss. Though I guess it didn't matter, they were always listening, always asking questions, always saying they couldn't wait to be made.

I could never decide if I was proud or sick when I thought of the violence they would grow into.

Their table was weapon free, littered with plastic forks, and enough juice to feed a small army. Thank God we got the wine.

"Rules," Tex barked.

We all sighed and took out our weapons and placed them on the table so everyone could see—just in case another fight broke out, which almost always happened considering we were hard-headed Italians and discussions were more like yelling matches where we tried to talk over one another until someone finally stood, raised a gun, and pulled the trigger.

"So." Tex leaned back, in his chair like the fucking king of the Cosa Nostra he was and grinned. His reddish-brown hair was messy like he'd run his hands through it more than once, and he was wearing a tight black shirt that did nothing to hide his ridiculously buff body. In a word, he was fucking terrifying. "It must be bad since nobody wants to talk about it."

I grunted, and then I explained everything Breaker had discovered only to get nervous when the room grew quieter and quieter.

"What's your plan?" Chase interrupted, unbuttoning the

front of his suit and taking off his jacket. His expression was hard; his blue eyes flashed with something that I recognized in my own soul—the need for revenge, the need to inflict pain. He was in politics now, though, and he wasn't allowed to get his hands as dirty as he'd like, so he had to live through us vicariously.

"Easy." I grabbed the knife I'd set on the table and thumbed it with a grin. "We lure them into our web by way of partying, gain as much intel as we can, and we keep the Families safe."

Tex looked at each of the bosses, Chase, Nixon, my dad, Dante, Sergio, Andrei. All of them wore similar expressions of trepidation. "What's the ruling?"

Dante, the youngest, spoke first. "Be discreet."

Tex snorted out a laugh. "And by discreet he means, try not to chop anyone's heads off mmmkay? If you need clean up, you know who to call."

"One more thing," Chase spoke with quiet authority. "You remember how to ID them, right?"

"Of course," I said confidently. "They'll be the ones that want in the most."

"Yes." My dad looked up from his plate. "Junior, are you sure you can do this? Maybe it's best if—"

"Are you shitting me right now?" I yelled, jumping to my feet as my chair toppled backward. "Why would you even ask that?"

My dad said nothing.

It was Andrei who spoke. "Because…" His blue eyes flashed. "You could be killing one of your cousins in cold blood." He gripped a knife in his hand, then held it to King's throat before anyone could do anything. "His age, one of them could be his age, and if he attacks, if he tries anything, you'll have to pull this blade across his soft skin—killing an enemy is one thing, killing an enemy that looks like your family, that has the same blood running through their veins... is quite another."

My nostrils flared. "And yet I was ready to kill Serena this afternoon—"

Nixon jumped to his feet.

My dad followed, his right hand moving to his gun like I was the one who needed protection.

I rolled my eyes. "It was an example, chill out, old man. I'm just saying, don't doubt me, and don't doubt us. It's fucking insulting, especially since you created us." I leveled each of them with a glare. "You did this, so I'd really appreciate it if you'd stop looking guilty for forcing us to survive in a world full of people who'd rather see us dead."

"I think—" Tex grinned at me like he appreciated my sociopathic tendencies. "—we have our answer then. It's settled. We eat, and the children... hunt."

I sat back down. My dad didn't grab his gun, but something shifted in Chase's glance as he stared at me then over at Nixon.

I was trying to figure out why they were looking at me funny when I glanced over at Serena and noticed her eyes were glassy.

Shit.

I'd hurt her feelings.

And for some reason, she chose this moment to crack, to show them that it affected her, that I affected her, which meant one thing.

To protect us both.

To honor the love we once had.

I would need to become her greatest enemy.

"Hate you for as long as we both shall live..."

We'd been slipping.

And we couldn't.

Not now.

Not when we had enemies at our door.

"That time of the month, Serena?" I lifted my wineglass to my lips and earned a scowl from her before a knife got thrown in my direction. "Missed."

Ash groaned. "Nope, no, she didn't. Little warning next time?"

He pulled the knife from his arm as blood dripped down his biceps.

Everyone chuckled.

"Maybe if you'd stop trying to feel up your girlfriend under the dinner table," Chase teased, earning a smack in the back of the head by Luc. "Hey, that hurt!"

"He's too young for that!" Her eyes were crazed while Breaker snorted into his cup. "What? Why are you snorting into your cup? Are they sexually active?"

"I love today." I burst out laughing.

And then Ash threw down the gauntlet, his eyes flashing. "He stole a girl's underwear today!"

"Up top," Tex put up his hand.

"How do you even know that?" I wondered out loud.

"Junior!" Ma chucked a roll at my face. I ducked, but it narrowly missed my right eyeball. "That's so rude!"

"He's a guy." My dad winked.

I winked back.

"Stop that! Stop the winking!" Ma shushed him, and somehow it worked. He kissed her on the cheek and was silent.

"Saw them in your coat pocket while you were fighting Serena on the lawn. Actually, I noticed that Serena—"

"Has syphilis, yes, it's very sad." I interrupted.

Serena's face went up in flames. "Are you high?"

"YOU DIDN'T USE PROTECTION?" Nixon roared, face looking slightly possessed as he jumped to his feet and grabbed a knife while Trace did the same.

I burst out laughing while Serena chugged her wine, wiped her mouth with her napkin, and tossed it down onto her plate. "I just lost my appetite, and no, I don't have syphilis, we know who the manwhore is at the table."

Everyone pointed at me.

Including Breaker, who we'd nicknamed breaker of hearts.

"Bullshit! I don't even have a girlfriend!" I roared.

"Family dinners." Ash lifted his wine into the air. "So much fun."

"Cheers." Dante clinked glasses with him.

"Don't encourage them," El, his wife, whispered under her breath. Then she winked at Ash.

They were the youngest, meaning closest to us in age, more like older siblings than anything, and they might have encouraged a lot of bad behavior, not that we minded.

I was still traumatized from when Dante tried to explain sex to me.

And I think my dad laughed for a week straight every single time I saw a girl.

Serena was in the process of storming off while Tempest, Dante's daughter, belted out loudly. "Mama, what's syphilis?"

"Thanks." Dante glared.

"I'm here to educate." I put a hand over my heart and noticed Serena was gone.

It was for the best.

That was what I chanted to myself the entire way back

to campus, in tight jeans, a shirt that showed off every single tattoo I had, and with enough ammo to take out whoever I needed to.

It was for the best, her hate.

Because if I had her love—I wouldn't be able to become the monster my dad needed me to be—the monster she needed me to be—to keep her safe.

CHAPTER
Five

Serena

We always arrived at the on-campus parties together. To an outsider, it looked like we just wanted to make an entrance, but to us? The new Elect on campus? It was survival.

Junior led us with Ash on his right.

Claire and I were in the middle.

And Breaker was behind watching our backs.

Violet stayed back as per usual since she was consumed with her studies. After a ton of arguing—shocker, I know—the bosses decided it would be best that Izzy stayed in the SUV and updated the bosses as we sent her text updates. She didn't have the same stomach for violence that we did, but she loved the behind the scenes gadgetry that Sergio often mentored her with.

We left her with a gun, an earpiece, and enough Coke Zero that she'd be happy just watching the show and hanging out in the background. Plus, if we needed to get out, we needed someone who hadn't had one or two drinks driving us.

After Junior's outburst at the table, I'd decided to dress in leather pants and a crop top that almost showed side boob.

And if I accidentally brushed against him, reminding him of what he was missing? Well, would that be so horrible?

I was still livid he'd said I had an STD.

Granted, I knew he was protecting me—in his own masochistic way—but it still stung.

He was the guy who used to hold me when I cried.

Now he was the reason for my tears.

Talk about messed up.

My heels clicked against the cement as we neared The Spot.

The welcome back party was already raging, thanks to our new friends who literally took one for the team this morning when classes started.

It was their job to make sure we had kegs and to make sure that only those we invited were allowed inside.

Before we were born, the building had been condemned after a few murders took place there, something that Dante and Andrei still argue over.

The minute we were forced back to Eagle Elite, we claimed it as our own. So what if there were bloodstains in the concrete? Or names of people who'd been tortured written in blood on the walls?

Students said it was haunted.

And I always wanted to laugh and say that our families were the ones who haunted it.

Z was at the door. "Guys." His eyes flickered over Ash and Junior, then settled on me, well my chest, and then my legs, until he finally focused in on my mouth. "Looking sexy as always."

I leaned into him. "Thanks, Z."

"No." Junior grabbed my arm. "You can have your fun later, but fair warning, bro, her kiss is poison."

"What a good way to go…" Z said softly, making me actually want to cover up my breasts and lean into Junior, not because he made me feel safe but because Z looked at me like I was a thing.

And as much as I hated Junior, he'd only ever treated me as his equal, a match in every way.

I shivered.

"Maybe if you wore more clothes," Junior hissed in my ear.

"You're still here?" I snapped.

"Guys!" Ash clapped his hands between us. "Focus."

We shuffled inside. Z shut the door behind us. The party was just getting started; maybe thirty students were scattered around the room.

And in the very middle.

Our thrones.

The music suddenly stopped.

Head held high, I waited as Junior and Ash escorted Claire and me to our seats. They were nothing special, just old velvet purple armchairs that had tall Victorian style backs.

Once we were seated, legs crossed, metaphorical crowns adjusted, the guys took their seats next to us while Breaker stood in front, making sure nobody approached without asking.

My phone buzzed in my pocket.

Sergio: Campus-wide email sent out to the school next door, they have five hundred students enrolled total—that's small, even for a community college. Expect more than a dozen at best to sneak over. Be alert.

I quickly texted back.

Me: We've got this, run the facial recognition software.

Sergio: Done, I just sent the ones that were in our database.

I stared down at the two pictures.

A girl and a guy who looked like they had grown up in the perfect suburban home with a doctor for a dad and a stay-at-home mom.

The girl had a friggin' red headband, straight dark hair, and happy green eyes.

And the guy looked about my age, similar build to Breaker, with blue eyes and reddish-brown hair. He had extremely striking features and would be easy to pick out.

"Uh…" Junior looked up from his phone. "Are we sure these are potential targets?"

"A sneeze could blow this girl over," Ash joked.

Claire frowned and looked over Ash's shoulder. "Maybe that's the plan."

I narrowed my eyes in her direction. "You mean, make them as non-threatening as possible?"

Claire shrugged. "Do you really think they're going to come in here armed and ready to start a war?"

"Yes!" we all said in unison.

Claire just laughed. "Maybe ten years ago that's how things went down, but warfare isn't done in the light—it's done in the dark now, through social media, cat phishing, pretending, it's not as easy to see your enemy as you think."

Something about the way she said it made me pause. "Claire—"

"Serena," Ash interrupted me. "We've been over this. Claire's proved herself, drop it."

Claire sucked in her bottom lip, her eyes filled with worry. "I'm sorry I was just trying to help."

"You did well," Ash whispered, standing and walking over to give her an unnecessary kiss on the head like she was his pet.

I gagged and then set my phone back down just as the door opened again, Z let another twenty students in.

One by one, they walked by us, paid their respects by way of a head nod, and then went over to the alcohol.

"I think we need a secret handshake next year," Breaker piped up. "The head nod feels weird."

"Because it is weird." Junior sounded bored. "And what makes us think they're just going to waltz right into here and—"

"Well then…" Ash chuckled as Z let in five more students that were very much not ours.

The guy was tall, not one of the ones in the picture, but he was with the two that we'd just seen on our phones.

"Safety in numbers." I cursed under my breath, and then I stood.

The music stopped.

Students approached us and waited.

"Who wants to party up here with us?" I asked in a sultry voice.

Everyone shouted.

"Aw," I shrugged. "I can only pick five; you guys know the rules."

Hands shot up, compliments followed, shouting.

Junior stood and moved next to me. "What the hell are you doing? We always wait for an hour."

"I'm bored," I lied. "And I want intel, don't you?"

"Shit, you're gonna get us killed."

"Do they look threatening?" I hissed under my breath. "If that girl's not named Karen, I really don't know anything anymore."

Junior smirked and then turned so that his back was to the crowd, his mouth near my ear. "What's your play then?"

"Seduction." He was far too close.

"Mmmm, them or us?"

"Both," I said before I could stop myself. Any excuse to touch him, to make him want, to distract them, and to show them how good it feels—the power.

Junior's eyes flashed as his fingers gripped my wrist. "I'm not... I can't be..." He licked his lips and repeated what he always did when we had to perform, when we had to do our jobs. "I won't be gentle with you."

Our foreheads touched, my chest heaved with exertion like it was hard to breathe when he was so near, but really it was the promise that killed me, a promise that he wouldn't enjoy touching me ever again, that I was more curse than cure, and yet, I knew it was all we would ever get, these fleeting moments where we did our job too well. "Then make it hurt, baby." My voice cracked. "Make it hurt."

His lips parted in a groan as he spun me into his arms and crushed his mouth to mine. It was part pain, part pleasure as he pulled my hair then slid a hand up my shirt like nobody was watching when everyone was.

We broke apart, mouths swollen, my lower lip was bleeding.

A reminder for both of us—this was no cease-fire, this wasn't real, it was all a carefully constructed show.

"Mmmmm…" I smirked. "Looks like Junior's not playing around tonight, ladies."

Screams went up as Junior grabbed my ass and squeezed so hard, I knew I would bruise later. He roughly pulled me against his chest and nipped at my neck.

I told my body it didn't feel good.

I told my heart we were safe.

And I forced myself to believe the lie every single time we touched.

Because to do otherwise—would destroy me.

We broke apart again.

Junior's eyes were wild.

I wanted to capture that look in his depths, keep it all for myself, unleash it on my person with wicked abandon.

But he wasn't mine to keep—he never had been.

"All right," I called out. "Let's see, who needs to get laid the most?"

Chuckles erupted.

And then I pointed at headband girl. "You, you're new."

She lifted her chin a bit. "I'm a nursing student at the campus across the fence."

"Nursing… perfect." My smile was so fake it hurt. "Think you can nurse poor Junior back to health?"

She gulped, looked back at her friends, and nodded her head.

Breaker helped her up the stairs.

And Junior gripped her by the hand. "Like what you see?"

"Y-yes."

"What about…" He pressed her hand to the button of his jeans. "…what you don't see?"

She straight-up paled but still nodded.

"Strip poker it is then," he announced, earning cheers from everyone around us. Tables from the sides of the building were moved toward the middle, and our game of the evening was ready to begin.

"Now for our Queen," Junior announced. "Who's going to get stung tonight?"

I wanted to throttle him.

Instead, I smiled and pointed at the harmless looking guy who'd walked in with headband girl. We didn't have his picture, but he was with her, which meant he knew her.

"Name?" Junior asked.

The guy leered at me like I was half price steak. "Mitchell."

"Well, hope you brought a cup, Mitchell. Let him in, Breaker."

Ash and Claire took our positions and picked the remaining two; each of us played our part brilliantly as they joined us at the main table.

The one with all the alcohol you could possibly want and the company people would kill to be around.

Mafia. Fucking. Royalty.

"Texas Hold 'Em?" I asked the group, already shuffling.

"Brat." Ash huffed. "Are you really still pissed about last year?"

"I had to walk pantless in stilettos back to the car!" I punched my cousin in the arm while he rubbed it as if it actually hurt.

"Dad was so pissed." Ash grinned. "Worth it."

I rolled my eyes. "You're lucky you're my favorite."

"Hey, what about me?" Junior teased.

"Kissing cousins does kind of have a ring to it," Claire said under her breath, making me nearly drop the cards in my lap.

It was a low blow.

One that made me want to launch myself across the table. Instead, I started to deal.

"So…" Mitchell rubbed his hands together. Great, a talker. "Are you guys for real, like in the mafia?"

"Yes," we all said in bored unison.

I could practically feel them deflate around us.

Junior mumbled, "killjoy" under his breath.

I caught it, just like I caught the gaze he gave me before looking back at his cards.

Let the games truly begin.

"Ugh, it's hot." I started fanning myself, Mitchell's eyes immediately shot below my neck then stopped at my mouth. "Y-yeah."

"Drink?" I offered him my cup.

Idiot took it and drank with wild abandon.

Sigh.

If he was De Lange, he got all the stupid.

"And what's your name?" Claire tilted her head and shot a flirty glance at the other guy we'd invited.

"Tank." His voice was low; he was wearing a black beanie and a tight black shirt. He had a full sleeve on his right arm, and his left was bare except for a Rolex.

Money. But the De Langes were fresh out of that unless they found someone else to partner with, which would be impossible since most the adults were dead.

The kids might as well be poor orphans trying to survive in the wild.

But that didn't explain the school next door.

Or the marketing with our pictures.

"Cool name, bro." Junior nodded. "Does it mean anything?"

Another grunt.

"I'm gonna say that was a no, Junior," I teased, earning a smirk from Tank who seemed to examine me with absolutely zero interest.

"And headband girl," I reached for the red monstrosity and gently pulled it off. "That's better. Your name?"

"Annie." She beamed.

"Of course." I smiled back at her. "A perfect name."

The final girl was silent.

With jet black hair that went past her shoulders, a black turtleneck, and jeans that molded to her body.

If anyone was a De Lange, it was that girl right there.

"You're awful quiet," Ash pointed out.

Her eyes shot up and then narrowed like she was trying to figure him out. She looked at him like she was taking inventory, and then she jerked her head to the right and locked eyes with Junior.

He couldn't see it, because he wasn't sitting where I was.

But I did.

I saw the resemblance right down to my core.

She wasn't just De Lange.

She was related.

And everything that Andrei had said at dinner came crashing down into my reality as I reached for my knife and struck.

The silver blade cut into her neck as I held it there, still. "You're familiar, aren't you?"

Her nostrils flared with hatred. "I'm just a student."

"Try again," I said politely.

Everyone around the table had gone silent.

Our new friends looked ready to shit themselves.

"I'm a student." She said it mockingly, with a smile, and then reached for something behind her back.

I didn't think, I just reacted.

Because Junior... she was going to hurt Junior.

And I couldn't bear the thought of him having more scars, more nightmares. It was like his life, his sins flashed before my eyes as I kicked the tip of my boot under the table and hit her in the shin, the hidden needle went into her skin seamlessly. She slumped forward as if she was drunk.

But the Family knew the truth, as they stared at me in shock.

She was dead.

And I, Serena Abandonato, had just had my first kill.

I... had just been made.

CHAPTER
Six

Junior

I tried to keep my expression calm—hell, I was born to keep my expression blank, wasn't I?

But I knew exactly what had just happened even if our new visitors had no clue.

"Wow," I joked. "Must have been one hell of a pre-party before she came over here, huh?"

Serena shrugged a shoulder. "We'll help her home later. You guys know where she lives?"

Tank's eyes narrowed into tiny slits. "Not really, she just saw us head over and said she was coming with us since most the school was invited."

"Right," Ash said carefully, leaning back in his chair. "But only a select few are invited in."

"Why is that?" Annie asked in her innocent voice that was one hundred percent real. The girl's eyes were even this constant wide expression like the world was so big she was having trouble drinking it all in.

I looked over at the dead body.

They had to know... had to have noticed that her chest wasn't moving, right?

Serena had seen her as a threat, but never in my life have I seen Serena act so impulsively without having any of the facts.

And we were going to have hell to pay when we got home and let all the bosses know exactly what went down.

"I need another drink," I stood. "Serena, come with?"

"Whatever." She stood and followed me over to the makeshift bar that was located in the far corner of the stage we were all currently on.

I grabbed a bottle of Gray Goose and tipped it back then handed it to her, my expression calm. "We need to call this in."

"Yeah." Her voice cracked, and then she blinked up at me, her eyes filled with tears. "I just—reacted. She seemed like she was going to hurt you, or us, or—"

"Hey." I tilted her chin toward up with one hand. "Never apologize for protecting Family."

She shuddered under my touch.

We were too close.

I could smell the mixture of vodka and soda on her breath, feel the warmth of her skin beneath my fingertips.

It was all too much.

When wasn't it?

"But there is something you can apologize for..." I said with a teasing grin.

She frowned. "What?"

I slid my hand down the front of her shirt and tugged her body hard against mine, then leaned down until my lips touched her ear. "Apologize for being a fucking tease. Yeah, apologize." I slid my hand beneath her arm and flicked the side of her breast. "For this."

She sighed heavily, her breathing erratic. "Never."

"Mm... thought so." I pulled back and grabbed the Gray Goose from her hand. "It was worth a shot."

She winked. "All's fair in war, Junior, you know this."

"Too damn well," I agreed. "For what it's worth..." I hesitated and then, "I like you better without all of it."

She rolled her eyes. "You would like me better naked."

"Did I say naked?" I tilted my head. "I meant this... without the mask. I like you better when you're just you."

She lifted her chin. "I haven't been me in a very long time, and all you have to do is look in the mirror to know the reason."

"Don't," I hissed. "Don't make this about me when it was always about us."

"You had a choice. You made it. You don't get to live with regrets, Junior. You get to live with pain." Tears flooded her eyes, and she shoved me away. And then she was gone.

And the line was drawn once again in the sand.

Enemies forced to work together.

Die for each other.

That was if we don't kill one another first.

Cheers.

I made my way back to the table. Breaker was already peeling off his shirt.

"Losing already?" I joked.

Serena was staring a hole into the table.

"Nah man, we call this winning, right, Annie." He winked at her, causing her cheeks to go bright red before she averted her gaze to Claire as if she was safer.

"So…" Claire leaned forward. "You guys enjoying this semester?"

Annie's face lit up, and suddenly we were all punished with the knowledge of too many scientific facts about the extinct wolf than I ever cared to repeat. Ever. Even in my worst nightmares.

You know it's bad when Ash starts to fade out, and he could act his way toward an Oscar if you asked him to.

Even Mitchell had left our little table in search for more fun, leaving us with just Tank, Annie, and a dead body.

"Yeah." Serena stood twenty minutes later, saving us from what I was sure was an interesting theory on breeding in the wild. "So, I just got a text from Dad. They need us at the house."

"That's too bad." Tank apparently could use full sentences, good for him. "This was fun."

"Yeah!" Annie grinned. "Let's exchange numbers."

I felt my entire body recoil while the rest of us mentally drew straws. Please, God, don't let me have the short one.

"Why not?" Claire was the first to speak, though I could have sworn Ash muttered a prayer under his breath as his girlfriend got down their info and said we'd hang out later or let them know when the next party was.

"Thanks." Annie grinned. "This was by far the most rebellious thing I've ever done in my entire life."

I frowned. "Then why take the risk?"

"Oh." Her eyes flickered down and then back up, which was when I noticed that they weren't brown, they were blue, a trick of the dark lights and my attention being on the dead body still at our table. "Actually, both my parents died when I was young, I was adopted a few years ago by a really nice family, and they were just really protective of me. I was sick a lot as a kid, and I don't know for whatever reason this just feels like a second chance."

"Wow." I nodded. "And what about you, Tank? Similar story or were you just born bench pressing five hundred?"

He actually laughed. "I have a mom. She's overbearing. And Annie and I met on the first day of orientation, end of story."

He seemed like he was telling the truth.

Hmm, maybe we were wrong.

And just being extremely paranoid.

"So!" Annie clapped her hands together. "Do you guys like go home now and torture people or—"

"Yeah, we're just gonna go." Tank was already steering her away as she tried to fight back and ask more questions.

"I would die," Ash said once they were finally gone. "Actually, die in my seat if I had to sit through class with a girl like that. Even her questions had questions."

Claire laughed. "She was cute."

"A puppy's cute." Ash snorted. "She was more... I don't even know..."

"What's the most annoying animal on the planet?" Breaker asked out loud. "A parrot? Yeah, she's a parrot. Don't worry, I got you, bro."

He and Asher bumped fists while Serena grabbed her cell and dialed her dad, I knew her like the back of my hand. Of course, she'd call him for cleanup.

He would do it without blinking.

Anyone else would ask questions, wouldn't they?

Even my dad.

They'd want to know why.

And Nixon, wouldn't care about the why; he'd just care that we were safe.

"Hey." Her eyes locked on mine while she spoke. "Yeah, we do need cleanup for one. I saw the threat and—" She was quiet. "Yes, it was me—but Daddy—" She squeezed her eyes shut. "I understand. Okay. Yes."

"So?" I asked once she was off the phone.

"We're headed back to my place, Dante's on his way to do cleanup, so get everyone out of here."

"Who wants to do the honors?" Breaker asked the group.

I sighed and then jumped on one of the purple chairs. "Party's over, go home!"

People groaned but slowly shuffled out the door.

The power we held over them was almost ridiculous.

"Let's go." I wrapped an arm around Serena as Ash did the same to Claire and Breaker followed, and out we walked as students parted like the freaking Red Sea.

Kings among mortals and into our waiting Escalade.

The drive was quiet.

But Serena couldn't stop bouncing her knee, so I knew something was up, and when we pulled up to the house and saw the bosses standing outside, I knew exactly what was about to happen.

"Don't let them make you scream," I said under my breath. "And if you need to pass out, give me the signal, and I'll do the honors."

She paled. "What's the signal?"

I smiled and flipped her off. "What do you think?"

"Of course." She shoved at me and then. "I'm the first girl to get made."

"Yeah." I sighed. "Maybe they'll go easy on you."

I helped her out of the car and came face to face with my dad, who was currently holding a machete.

Yeah, or maybe not.

CHAPTER
Seven

Serena

My teeth started to chatter as I eyed the giant knife in Phoenix's hand. The sort of knife meant to cut through hard bamboo. What would it do to a person's skin? What would it do to me?

And why the hell was he still holding it while we all walked out of the car and toward the front door?

It was just Nixon, Phoenix, and Chase.

So, my father, the insane one, and the angry one.

Perfect.

Breaker took one look at them standing there, held up his hands, and then hopped back in the car. "I'm just gonna head back to my place."

"Traitor," Ash mumbled under his breath.

Breaker just rolled down the window and grinned. "I'm the impressionable young one, like the Skywalker to your Kenobi."

"For the last time, it's Obi-Wan Kenobi!" Junior shouted back at him.

Breaker paused and then grinned. "These things, I forget, Master Yoda."

"Son of a bitch." Ash wiped his hands down his face while I just stood there staring at the guys, wondering if Claire was going to bail on us too.

I didn't have to wait long to get my answer.

All Uncle Chase had to do was jerk his chin toward the house, and Claire was sprinting past them at breakneck speed with Izzy hot on her heels.

"The three musketeers." Phoenix shook his head. "The mentors."

I gulped. Probably not the time to say that my cousin Violet was just as much a mentor as we were.

"And now," Chase stepped forward. "A dead body."

My dad's intense blue eyes narrowed in on me. Why did he have to be so terrifying in that moment? I wanted to run into his arms and tell him to take away the sick feeling in the pit of my stomach, the feeling that told me that life would never be the same.

That I had taken a soul from this world, and I'd done it on the assumption that the soul, the body who kept it—was evil.

Junior stepped forward. "It was my fault. I wasn't paying attention."

Phoenix's eyebrows shot up, and then his gaze went from his son's to mine. Well, it was nice knowing them.

"Did you kill her?" Phoenix asked.

"She was as good as dead the minute she posed a threat," Ash casually said, both of them at least had my back.

I tried to even my breathing as Phoenix's cruel smile landed on me. "Serena…"

The way he said my name was cold, calculated, it was the voice of a killer, the voice of someone that had so much blood on his hands the stains would never wash off.

"Yes," I rasped, locking eyes with him.

"What's done is done… it doesn't matter how or why; you were the one responsible, and you put the entire Family at risk because you acted out of emotion rather than information."

Junior opened his mouth to speak but was interrupted by Chase, who held up his hand and slowly walked toward the three of us. My dad followed. Oh man, this was bad, so very bad.

We were their kids.

But that didn't mean we were above the law of the Family.

I was only too painfully aware of the blood oaths we'd made.

Of the promises never to date each other.

Promises to protect the Family at all costs.

And promises to only kill when absolutely necessary— when there was no other option.

At the time, I didn't think there was.

I could have waited.

Hesitated.

But my hesitation could have gotten Junior killed.

And admitting that would do one thing.

It would tell them that I had feelings.

It would tell them that Junior made me weak.

And it worked both ways; it would tell them that I made Junior weak.

So I said nothing.

And knew I would have to take whatever punishment they gave with my head high and with my screams on the inside.

Chase sighed. "Everyone inside."

I started to walk past him, but he grabbed me by the arm and held me in front of him.

My dad looked like he wanted to say something, but Uncle Chase was his second in command, powerful beyond belief. Hell, he had most politicians eating out of the palm of his hand and asking for more. He could give out free poison, and there would be a line a mile long.

I was convinced it was because he was the sort of good looking that made you want to be a victim, and since he was my uncle, I was allowed to say that.

All my life, I'd seen the bosses get open-eyed stares.

Even in their late thirties and early forties, they were like little mafia Jared Leto's running around with too much testosterone and enough weapons to form their own militia.

God help us all.

Once the front door closed, he leaned in and whispered. "Is it truly over?"

I jerked back. "You mean, is she really dead? Yeah, I think—"

"Not that." His nostrils flared as his eyes searched mine. "I mean you and Junior."

I couldn't help the little gasp that escaped my parted lips. "I have no idea what you're talking about."

"You need to learn how to lie better." He cursed and looked away. "Serena, I need the truth, right now. Are you—" He grabbed me by the shoulder and jerked me closer. "—together."

"No," I said honestly. "I think I hate him more than I hate myself right now."

He let out a rough exhale like he'd been holding his breath. "I don't need to remind you what would happen if it was discovered that the daughter of an Abandonato was screwing a son of a De Lange—" It was my turn to gasp. "—and Nicolasi boss."

"That's not fair, Aunt Luciana is half De Lange," I pointed out.

"You hate him," he murmured. "And yet you're so defensive of a family that nearly destroyed your own father. I wonder why…"

"I like to play fair," I said through clenched teeth.

He smirked. "That lie was a lot better, favorite niece."

I scowled. "Say that to Bella's face."

"Hey, a little competition's good for you, right?"

I let myself relax a bit. "Yeah, yeah."

He wrapped an arm around me. "You took a blood oath when you were sixteen, Serena, all of the kids did. The last thing we need is a group of hormonal rage-fueled college students deciding it would be a good idea to sow their oats under the roof of mob bosses who've been known to chop off body parts of men who look at their wives sideways."

I had nothing to say to that, except, "You're joking, right?"

"Why the hell else would we have a machete?" He deadpanned like I was the crazy one.

This guy.

I shook my head. "So, what's my punishment going to be?"

He opened the front door.

The house was quiet.

Too quiet.

I suddenly wanted my mom, but then I didn't want to see the sadness in her eyes for the innocence that I allowed to be taken from me tonight.

Over a guy I supposedly hated.

I risked everything for the hate I had.

If that wasn't a sick and twisted sort of love—what was?

Chase didn't answer me; he just led me around the corner to the stairway that led to the dark basement.

Not a good sign.

My room was upstairs.

I slowly took the stairs in my heels, the same ones that held small little needles in the toes that could kill someone—*had* killed someone—in an instant.

I called them my killer heels for a reason.

A doctor would assume her heart was weak—that it just stopped.

But we knew the truth.

I knew the truth.

I had done that.

I would do it again.

To potentially save the man I hated? I would kill everyone. And I would smile while doing it.

Maybe he wasn't the one with the sickness in his blood.

Maybe, just maybe, it was me.

The lights overhead flickered on as Chase took me to the end of the hall and finally into the sparring room.

We had a nice boxing ring in the middle and enough gear to make you sweat for days.

Junior and Ash were already standing in the middle of the ring.

My dad and Phoenix were standing outside the ropes.

At least the machete wasn't in Phoenix's hands anymore. No, that honor went to Junior.

And when he looked at me, his eyes were empty, like his soul had momentarily taken a vacation from his body—not out of exhaustion but out of necessity for what he had to do.

"Serena." My dad held out his hand. I took it. "When blood is wasted, you need to be punished. It kills me that you were made before your time, before you really had time to experience life, but that's what this is, and as the heir to the Abandonato Family, it's your birthright. As a woman, you're equal to the men standing before you, which means the punishment has to be the same."

I whispered, "I understand, sir."

His blue eyes flickered with emotion before he looked down and ran his hands through his jet-black hair. "Two minutes in the ring with each of them. They won't go easy on you—"

"They've never gone easy on me," I snapped, earning a proud smirk from my dad.

"What happens down here stays down here, when you walk out of this basement, you'll be made just like Ash and Junior. Do you understand what that means?"

It meant my life was no longer mine.

But I'd known that from too young of an age.

I gave him a jerky nod and kicked off my shoes, then went over and grabbed a leftover hoody from one of the benches, so I didn't flash boob at anyone.

With a deep breath, I crossed my arms. "Who wants to get their ass kicked first?"

Ash smirked and held up his fist. "Let's go, little girl."

I hopped into the ring.

And trembled when each of the bosses slowly gave me their back because, at the end of the day, they were parents first, bosses second, and their instincts were always to protect, never to harm.

But this wasn't just their war anymore.

It was ours.

So, I held my head high and blew Ash a kiss. "Let's see if you're roundhouse has gotten any better."

A choked laugh came from Junior as he stepped outside of the ring and watched.

The only rules?

Two minutes, no time outs, no killing, and blood must be shed.

Game. Freaking. On.

CHAPTER *Eight*

Junior

I wasn't allowed to show emotion—so every single time Ash landed a blow to her perfect hateful face, I swear I cried on the inside, mourned the loss of her blemish-free lip, wept over the fact that she would never be the same after this. That the last remaining part of her soul that was still clinging to the dream of a life outside of this—would be crushed—and I would help do it.

I always wondered if Nixon would find an excuse, a way to get her out, and now... now we had no choice because she'd killed—for me. She'd done that for me regardless of what she said with her words, her eyes... her actions, they said it all.

Her words said I hate you, while her soul cried I can't lose you.

I didn't know how to digest both realities.

I didn't know how to protect her and hurt her.

And that's what I was going to have to do in another thirty seconds.

I gripped the machete.

Only one of us got a weapon.

So, when my dad handed it to me, I had to look excited that I was chosen when I wanted to run to the bathroom and hurl every last drop of vodka in my stomach.

Serena got a good punch in, causing Ash to stumble backward, but he had thirty pounds of muscle on her—both of us did.

We worked out to stay sane.

Where we were hard muscle and grit, she was soft and sexy.

Fuck.

The sound of bone cracking had my fingers turning white from gripping the machete so hard.

Ash had just broken two of her fingers.

She had to fight me with broken fingers.

The timer went off.

Ash handed her a towel then pulled her in for a hug. Blood mixed between them as he kissed her forehead with a bloody mouth and whispered. "Blood in, no out, welcome to the Family."

"Blood in, no out," she rasped, landing one more sucker punch to his shoulder that had him grinning, despite the fact that his mouth was bleeding.

At least she had gotten a few good hits in.

Ash left the mat, and it was my turn.

She was allowed to grab a weapon to fight me with, and I wasn't surprised when she shimmied out of her leather pants far enough to grab a knife that was strapped to her thigh.

She wouldn't be Serena if she weren't carrying a knife.

I almost smiled as she struggled to pull her pants back on with her swollen hand,

And then I realized I had to fight her.

For two minutes.

She excelled in hand-to-hand combat.

But against me?

It was a joke.

"Ready spoiled princess?" My voice cracked.

"Yeah, jackass, come at me," she taunted.

From his spot at the side of the ring, Ash chuckled.

She lunged first. I dodged the knife with ease and got a bit of her flesh as the machete went straight through her hoody. Blood dripped from her side down to the mat.

It was a deep cut.

A machete didn't make shallow cuts.

I could chop off body parts.

She held her broken fingers to her side and lunged again. This time she caught me on the arm—and I let her.

Then she was kicking my feet out from under me, slamming me into the mat as she leaned over and hissed, "What the hell are you doing?"

"Fighting." I gritted my teeth.

"No, you're losing." She shoved her knife into my right shoulder; it went in at least three inches. "I don't go easy on you, don't go easy on me."

"So, you want to die?" I whispered.

"A problem?" Chase called.

I shoved her off of me. "No."

"One minute left," Ash shouted out.

"You want to bleed?" I clenched my jaw. "I'll make it burn."

"Bring it!" she yelled.

I went at her with the machete, hitting the back side of her arm before shoving her away, only to come at her again and make a slice down the front of her right thigh, the cut opened wide enough to show muscle.

I'd never hated myself more.

"Again!" she screamed.

And then I realized that it was the scream of a girl who was terrified, the scream of a girl who needed to feel, a scream of a girl who was still numb after taking her first life.

So, I gave her what she needed.

I gave her the pain.

I slapped the knife out of her hand, then kicked her in the stomach sending her toppling backward hard enough for me to straddle her on the mat and drive the edge of my machete directly into her left arm, pinning her there, all the way through her skin to the mat, narrowly missing bone.

Her chest heaved as our eyes locked, and then she whispered, "Thank you."

"Hate you for as long as we both shall live." I pressed a kiss to her forehead.

"Hate you for as long as we both shall live," she replied and then, "Blood in, no out."

"Blood in, no out." I nodded. "Welcome to the Family."

The bosses turned around in time to see me jerk the machete from her still body.

Nixon was pale as he watched me pick her up in my arms and hand her to Ash.

And together, the three of us walked away from the bosses, bloody and beaten.

Made.

Serena moaned against Ash's chest as blood dripped from

her mouth. The deepest wound was the one I had made in her arm. It was going to hurt like a bitch, but thankfully we had good doctors at the house, and I had known if this was gonna go down tonight, that Sergio would be waiting somewhere upstairs to stitch her back up.

We found him in the kitchen with his med kit; already, he was getting a needle and thread ready.

"Hold her down, please," he said without even looking up.

Ash placed her on the kitchen table while I pressed down on her arms.

Sergio grabbed alcohol and poured it over her wounds while she screamed, and I felt my heart crack in my chest as he quickly inserted an IV in the back of her hand and started a morphine drip.

She was out in seconds.

I let her go and watched Sergio stitch her up.

I wasn't sure how much time had passed, but after a bit, Ash said he had to take off, leaving me with the wounded princess.

"How did it go?" Sergio was stitching up the last wound, the most superficial on her side.

I tried to ignore her marred skin, and the fact that it was my fault it looked that way.

"Great," I said through clenched teeth. "We had tea and swapped boy stories. How the hell do you think it went?"

Sergio snorted out a laugh. "Sometimes, I forget you're Phoenix's kid, not Chase's."

"I can't figure out if that's a compliment or an insult," I said.

"Depends on the mood I'm in." Sergio grinned down at

his handiwork and tied the last stitch. "You know there's a method to our madness, right?"

"Yes." *No.* I mean, I did, but some of the rules made no sense.

"I can feel your temper rising, Little Phoenix." Sergio pulled her IV and started cleaning her up.

"Riddle me this," I started, helping him gather all the bloody gauze. "Why the hell was it okay for all of you guys to be hopping into bed with each other—but we have to take blood oaths at sixteen not to kiss behind the damn tree in my back yard?"

"So many good memories at that tree." Sergio peeled off his latex gloves and looked up. His eyes were a staggering blue that reminded me he was more than another made man. He was powerful, and he was Serena's other uncle.

I was surrounded by Abandonato men who would rip my dick through my mouth if they knew it had been anywhere near their favorite princess.

Literally.

"Love triangles may look fun on TV or in books, but they start wars in the mafia, and history has a way of repeating itself. You know the whole Nixon, Chase, Tracey drama." He rolled his eyes. "Nearly snuffed out the Alferos. It was like our own rendition of Romeo and Juliet, and then you have the whole De Lange Family line who not only betrayed all of us but betrayed Chase. Imagine marrying someone close and finding out that the power between you felt uneven. That was how Chase's first wife felt. We thought marrying from within would keep the families strong. Instead, it nearly destroyed us. So, when you think about it that way, it makes sense."

I sighed. "So, what you're saying is, love causes wars, hate ends them?"

"No, I'm saying when emotions run high, and you have a gun, well, not the best combination, you know?" He shrugged. "We learned an important lesson from our pasts. Sometimes when you're too close the way all of the kids are, it causes jealousy, it causes fights, and we need you guys to be strong, not distracted by all the sex you wish you were having."

I burst out laughing. "Oh, I wouldn't worry about the sex we're not having, I mean have you seen how many scrunchies Breaker wears on his wrist?"

Sergio narrowed his eyes. "I thought that was just to piss Tex off."

"Nah." I laughed. "Go check out his Snapchat, man. So many girls, so many I've lost count. If he hasn't slept through half of Eagle Elite by the time he graduates, it'll be because it's a choice."

"Could have lived my whole life without the mental picture of nineteen-year-old Breaker naked and earning scrunchies instead of notches in his bedpost."

"Oh, don't worry man, he has those too." I patted him on the shoulder.

"If Tex ever asks, this conversation never happened. He would shit a brick if that kid got someone pregnant."

"He's a fan of Trojan so I wouldn't really worry about—"

"Yeah, I stopped listening at Trojan."

"Smart man." I nodded.

"The smartest," he agreed with a slow grin. "You need help getting her to her room?"

"I got it; I might crash in one of the guest rooms, though. It's late, and Trace makes better eggs than my mom."

Sergio made a face. "It's like she's trying to poison people."

"Thank you!" I threw my hands up. "She just tries so hard."

"The food can tell. It revolts on purpose," he teased, just as Dante walked into the kitchen like he'd just taken a pleasant stroll down the road.

He had recently showered, no blood, huge grin.

Man, the guy loved taking care of dead bodies, sick bastard.

"Things good?" Sergio asked.

"I enjoy the cement." He cracked his knuckles. "Just had to update you guys on a few things. Everyone still in the basement?"

"Tex is home, but everyone else is here."

"Good." His eyes flashed for a minute, and then he glanced down at Serena. "Shit, that's a lot of stitches."

I winced. "It was necessary."

"Doesn't make it feel any better when you wake up screaming in pain." He pointed out. "Serg, you ready?"

"Yeah." They started talking in hushed tones, leaving me the task of carrying Serena to her bedroom upstairs.

I gently picked her up in my arms and walked up the steps, taking them one at a time, one foot in front of the other, until I finally made it into her large bedroom at the end of the hall.

I flicked the lights on and laid her on her bed and looked around for a T-shirt I could toss in her general direction.

"You look lost," she mumbled, not opening her eyes. "I guess it has been a while."

"Ah, the morphine's talking. Great." I finally settled on a plain white T-shirt and held it out to her. "Think you can move enough to put this on?"

She groaned and then opened an already swollen right eye to look at me. "I can barely see, what do you think?"

"I forgot how much fun you are when you're high."

Her smile was dopey as she lifted her arms for me to dress her.

Grumbling, I pulled what remained of the sweatshirt and her tank off her body, leaving her completely topless.

"Wait." She slumped forward. "Shower, I have blood everywhere; I need to shower."

I sighed in irritation. "Serena, you can barely keep your eyes open, you'd most likely drown standing up."

"That's why you're here, friend."

"Yeah, not your friend, and even if I were in that territory, I wouldn't risk getting shot in your home just because the blood makes you woozy."

"You're helping me. She held up two fingers that Sergio had taped together, the swollen broken ones. "Two." Had she even said one? "I really, really want to forget tonight, not just the blood, I just—please?"

I gritted my teeth. "It's weird when you're polite."

"Don't get used to it."

"Wouldn't dream of it." Decision made, I went over to her door, closed it, and then held out my hands. "All right, lets hurry and get you naked and washed."

"So romantic." She slumped forward and then winced when I tried to take off the remnants of her leather pants.

She was half-naked when I got them off her feet, and then I had the trying task of pulling off her lacy red underwear.

I cleared my throat and quickly tossed them aside, then lifted a girl I refused to stare at, into my arms again, and walked into the bathroom.

I placed her on her feet and then turned on the rain shower.

She steadied herself against the wall while I made sure it was hot.

And then she stumbled into me, nearly sending me into the water with my clothes on.

With a curse, I shook my head. "You can't do this alone at all, can you?"

"Not sure I can even hold soap right now." Her lower lip trembled.

Shit. She rarely cried.

It was probably the drugs, the dead body, the circumstances... hell, take your pick.

"Don't cry." I hugged her tight.

"I still hate you." She sniffed against my chest.

"Yeah, well, I'm not your biggest fan either, princess."

"Let's hurry before my dad shoots you."

"Gotta love a story with a happy ending." I peeled off my shirt and then kicked off my jeans while she leaned against the counter, shoes gone, socks gone. I was completely naked and trying like hell to think about anything that wasn't her pink skin.

"Ouch." She hissed once we were under the hot spray. "It stings."

"The stitches have been cleaned already, so let's just get the rest of you clean, okay?"

"Are you gonna wash my hair now then braid it later?" She slumped forward, forcing me to catch her slippery body against mine.

I ground my teeth. "You know I'm shit at braiding anyone's hair but Izzy."

"True." She laughed, and then the laugh somehow turned

into a sob as I held her tight. "Everything's so messed up. I messed up!"

"You didn't mess up." I cupped her cheeks. "We were all there. You acted on instinct, and nobody can fault you for that—least of all me since I looked like the lucky target. Besides, we can't trust anyone."

"Not even each other." Her eyes searched mine.

I gulped. "Not true. We can trust each other. Trust has nothing to do with liking someone and everything to do with knowing that at the end of the day, that person's going to have your back."

"Is that your roundabout way of saying you trust me despite your hate?" She at least wasn't crying anymore.

I said the only thing I could, the only thing that would keep her safe, and me alive. "My love doesn't matter, not when you have my trust. You're like the keeper of souls, Serena, you keep mine safe, just like I keep yours safe. What use is love when we have that?"

She nodded. "You're right."

"Damn right, I am." I grabbed the body wash and started rubbing it down her shoulders. "Now, try not to pass out."

We didn't speak the rest of the time, and while I tried like hell not to get aroused, it was impossible.

I just hoped she was too high on morphine to remember that my cock very much wanted to show her comfort in about a billion different positions and ways.

No matter how many times my brain and heart told my body to rein it in, my body just ignored it and kept wanting, straining, begging her to pay attention.

We were rinsing off when her hand brushed up against me.

I froze.

She acted like it was an accident, and maybe it was.

But then her other hand did it.

And before I knew what was happening, I was pinning her against the shower wall. "Don't."

"Don't what?" Her sleepy gaze found mine. "Touch?"

"Serena."

"You grabbed boob tonight."

She had me there. "I was taunting you."

Her healthy hand reached down and squeezed my cock so tight I nearly spent myself against her fingers. "Consider yourself taunted."

"We even now, Serena?" My voice cracked.

"I think we'll always battle for that position, don't you?"

"War's boring when both sides are always on equal footing."

"Mmm." Her hand slowly pulled away.

Our foreheads touched as water dripped between our faces. Mouths were inches apart, her chest heaved.

I squeezed my eyes shut and gave my head a shake, hoping reality would set in.

She wasn't mine.

I wasn't hers.

She looked away like she didn't want me to see the truth of the pain in her eyes.

And I let her do it because I couldn't trust myself not to pull her against me and make it better.

Make *us* better.

I turned off the shower, grabbed a towel, and wrapped it around her as gently as I could.

No words were spoken as we got her ready for bed, and when I went to open the door, it was to see Trace standing on the other side of it, her expression one of concern, not accusation. "How is she?"

"Sleeping it off, she wanted a shower, I tried—"

Trace cut me off with a hug. "Thank you. Can you stay with her, do you think? The guys are still downstairs meeting, and your mom stopped by to talk about a few things."

I wanted to ask what things, but instead, I nodded and said, "I'll keep the door open."

"Don't." She smiled. "I trust you."

She walked away, and when I clicked the door shut, I whispered into the air. "You shouldn't."

CHAPTER Nine

Serena

I didn't want to wake up.

Not because I wanted to die.

But because Junior was sleeping next to me, and even though he was hilariously on top of the bed rather than inside the sheets, he was there.

And he hadn't been there, by my side.

For so long.

I swallowed the lump in my throat and put the metaphorical mask of hate back on because it was all I had.

And I would take him in whatever capacity I could.

If that wasn't his love, then so be it.

"Is the cease-fire gone?" His voice was raspy, deep, full of that sort of sleep that makes a girl shiver in all the right places. Hating him was a full-time job, especially with a voice like that, the body of a god, and the stupid teal eyes that always seemed to see past even my bullshit.

For the first time in forever, I admitted the truth, I admitted my weakness and whispered. "Just two more minutes." And then my hand inched across the comforter and gripped his.

I could feel his pulse beneath my skin.

The memories came full force.

"This," Junior gripped me by the thighs and then grabbed my hand and pressed it against his naked chest. "Will always be yours."

"Even though it's not supposed to be?" I asked.

"Sometimes, hearts can't help but beat for the wrong person, and who am I to deny what my heart craves even if it ends up killing me?"

"Don't joke like that."

"I would die for your love," he whispered. "And the last words I would utter would be worth it, fucking worth it."

Tears filled my eyes. "I love you so much."

"As long as we both shall live," he murmured against my lips.

"As long as we both shall live," I said right back, clinging to him like he was my life, my very soul.

Two days later, he had taken the heart I'd so freely given him and thrown it in my face.

I wasn't counting.

Maybe Junior was because seconds later, he slowly pried his hand away from mine. I felt the loss in my chest, the pain was so severe—so much worse than the wounds from the night before, because there was no morphine for this sort of pain.

After all, there were no stitches strong enough, brave enough, for a broken heart like mine.

Best it stayed broken, so it never had to feel that first slice.

The pain is never in the days after you lose your heart to someone.

The pain is in the moment you realize that your forever is no longer your future, but your past.

Junior slowly rose from the bed and put on his bloodied-up shirt from the night before.

I watched him move around the room and gather his things, and then I watched him walk to the door, hesitate, like he wanted to look back—and instead, square his shoulders, yank open the door, and keep walking.

He didn't see the tear that rolled down my cheek.

To the outside world, I was in physical pain.

But my soul knew—it was all the things on the inside that Sergio would never be able to fix.

Ten minutes later, I was dressed in sweats and slowly walking downstairs toward the kitchen.

I blinked in surprise.

Everyone was there?

I mean, we did family dinners, not family breakfasts.

The little ones were in the living room, and by the sounds of it, Frozen Two was on again for the millionth time.

Breaker and King were sitting with them along with Violet, Claire, and Izzy.

Did that mean we weren't invited to breakfast?

Loud laughter had me shuffling farther into the kitchen. Ash was sitting on Junior's lap in a vain attempt to block him from stealing all the bacon.

Tex was holding a plate of eggs hostage while Chase yelled about getting his man hair on it.

The wives were making mimosa's like they were ready to go on vacay, and I was genuinely confused.

"What's going on?" I yawned.

"Sweetheart?" My dad turned, his expression worried, and then I was in his arms, resting my head against his chest. He always smelled so good, always felt so strong, like he could save me from the world, and I never doubted he could.

Not once.

"How are you feeling?" He kissed the top of my head.

"Like I had a spa weekend," I teased and then stood on tiptoes and kissed him on the cheek. "I'm sorry I messed up last night—"

"No." He cupped my chin. "I'm sorry that you had to go through that. But I can't be sorry that you're going to lead this family one day, kinda makes an old man wanna cry."

Uncle Chase burst out laughing. "Like you did while watching Frozen Two?"

I couldn't see it, but I imagined my dad was giving him a middle finger behind my back.

Typical.

Mom came over and hugged both of us. "Other than the eye, you don't look horrible."

"Man, all these compliments are gonna go to my head." I squeezed her back.

Uncle Tex lifted his mimosa into the air and tapped it with his fork. "We have news."

My Aunt Mo grabbed a bottle of champagne and lifted it with him.

"You're pregnant again!" I guessed.

Mo gave me a horrified look. "Do I look like I'm pregnant?"

"No, just say no," Tex said quickly, earning a swat in the back of his head from Mo. "What'd I do?"

She just took a swig from the bottle.

"All right, so Dante brought something to our attention last night after disposing of another body, which by the way I hear congratulations are in order not only was she armed with a knife and two guns, but she was a De Lange. Well done Serena—"

"Hear! Hear!" Ash lifted his mimosa.

Chase shook his head at him. Ash lowered his hand and winked.

I sighed.

"Anyway..." Tex cleared his throat. "Even though things are a bit tense, we've been through way worse—"

Andrei chose that moment to stroll in with his wife. "Who ate all the bacon?"

"Do you mind?" Tex growled. "I'm trying to make an announcement."

"Here you go, man." Ash handed him the plate.

Andrei winked and then scowled at the mimosas and pulled what we all knew was a vodka flask out of his jacket and dumped some in a cup with orange juice, took a sip and handed it to Alice like he was testing her drinks now or something. Then again, a lot of people wanted them dead, so maybe not the worst plan of action.

"As I was saying..." Tex stood now. "Dante brought it to our attention that Phoenix and Bee just had their twentieth anniversary and have yet to take a trip in the last fifteen years. As crazy as things have been lately, they've been worse, so we voted and decided each of the couples will take a trip. And since they just celebrated, they go first, two weeks anywhere in the world. We're big enough to hold down the fort. The only issue is dipshit over there." Tex pointed to Junior.

Junior tore into a piece of bacon. "That's me, right?"

"Yeah, that's you," I said sweetly, earning a middle finger and a wink that I felt in all the wrong places.

"We voted last night and wanted to tell the kids today. We're going to all take shifts, and well, it just feels like it's time, especially now that our kids are growing up and able to take on some of the load."

I realized he meant us.

And part of me wondered if the fact that the three of us were all made had been part of the decision making process.

Meaning, I was the last one, ergo, now they felt safe knowing that the Family had a potential boss in place in case the worst happened.

Just thinking about it made me sick to my stomach.

Phoenix grabbed Bee's hand and kissed it. "We're headed to Fiji."

Her expression was completely stunned, and then she mauled him with her mouth, then her hands, and then it was time to look away.

"Ma, aw man!" Junior threw a piece of bacon. "Not in front of the eggs!"

"Save it for the private plane." Tex laughed. "And I'm happy for you guys, so who takes dipshit?"

"Could we stop with the name-calling?" Junior glared and then smirked with a hand placed on his chest. "I'm sensitive."

"My ass," Ash muttered under his breath.

They started fighting like best friends did, and then my dad sealed a fate he could have never known was ever in the stars by saying, "He can stay here."

I kept my expression calm but didn't miss the panicked look from Ash or the warning look from Uncle Chase.

Nobody said anything.

Because our secret wasn't theirs to share.

But I had a sinking feeling I was going to have to work a lot harder at my hate, so I didn't accidentally lose it to my past love.

And damn us all.

Because our love wouldn't just be a problem.

It would destroy the Families.

Rip them apart.

I knew it in my soul.

I knew deep down, Junior had been right, even though it was so wrong.

I knew that unloving him was the only way we could co-exist.

And now, he was going to be in the guest room connected next door because I knew my dad would want him closest to the living room as well as the gun safe on the west side of the house. Everything was strategic when it came to sleeping arrangements.

God help us all.

Because my dad would kill him if he knew he'd touched me.

And Phoenix would never forgive his own son for doing the one thing he made him swear he would never do—touch an Abandonato heir, want her, be with her, the way he'd been with mom.

Had they dated then? It was unspoken, but I knew there was some sort of bad blood which is why I knew how to press the button, though every time I tried to use it, I knew it was wrong, I never knew how wrong, though, or how horrible, maybe if I did I would have never pushed, but I didn't, my ignorance was a death sentence.

I gulped and shared a worried look with Ash, only to see Junior already getting up and leaving the room in his usual pissed off manner.

And I was thankful that at least one of us was sane enough to do the right thing.

Walk. Away.

That at least his hate would stay intact, making mine solid.

We just needed to stay that way.

And we'd be just fine.

So why was my heart hammering out of my chest? Why were my eyes looking for hiding places? And why did I suddenly feel the need to confess everything?

Uncle Chase looked at me again, his expression curious, and then a slow shake of his head told me all I needed to know. His blue eyes crinkled at the sides with a sad smile as he crossed his arms.

Our secret.

It would be fine.

It was only two weeks.

We'd been enemies for over a year; no way two weeks was gonna shift a year's worth of hurt.

It was impossible.

And yet, my stupid heart beat, *"Maybe it isn't."*

CHAPTER
Ten

Junior

"You excited for your parents to leave town?" Ash asked a few days later when we were on campus sitting outside and chugging our coffees before class.

I snorted into my cup. "I have never seen my mom pack so many swimsuits. If I see one more bikini, my eyes are going to start bleeding just like my soul every single time Dad grabs her ass."

Ash burst out laughing. "Yeah, not gonna lie, I can't see brooding Phoenix Nicolasi grabbing your mom's ass without Tex chopping off his hand. I mean, sure they're married, but I swear his eye still twitches when they kiss."

I grinned, and then my smile fell because I was once again reminded that my mom was Tex's sister, and yet she wasn't off-limits to my dad, and even then, he obviously ignored that glaring problem of dating within the Families.

"When do they leave?" Ash asked, jarring me out of my pity party. I'd been feeling off since leaving Serena's bedroom.

All I'd wanted to do was turn around, pull her into my arms, and kiss every inch of her body.

Chances were she would have probably kneed me in the balls since the morphine had all but evaporated from her system, leaving her pissy all morning, but it would have been worth a try, right?

"Bro!" Ash waved a hand in front of my face. "What's with you?"

"Nothing," I snapped. "And they left this morning."

Another reason I was actually going to class instead of skipping—I needed every excuse in the book to stay on campus until I had to go to Serena's.

"Nice." He put on his sunglasses and waved Claire over. She was texting and walking, typical.

When she finally looked up, she grinned and skipped over to us. "Hey guys, you done for the day?"

"One more class, and then I'm done," I announced and prayed to God that Serena wasn't going to show up for it. Ever since I stole her panties and our brawl on the lawn, she'd avoided our shared class. I called it an answer to prayer.

Claire scrunched up her nose, then looked back down at her phone and grinned.

"You cheating on Ash already?" I teased.

She rolled her eyes. "Hilarious."

"Dude." Ash shoved me.

"Hey!" I held up my hands. "Maybe learn how to please her properly, so she doesn't stray."

"Ash, don't take the bait." Claire shoved her phone back in

her purse. "And I'm actually texting Annie. She's really sweet, and I thought it would be cool if we all hung out again."

Ash's jaw clenched even though his eyes gave nothing away. "Do you think that's the best idea? Partying with them is one thing, setting them up and trying to figure out if they're out to get us, is one thing, but braiding each other's hair?"

"Girls don't actually do that, Ash." She patted his head. "Sorry to disappoint you, but we also don't dance around in our underwear and have pillow fights."

"Why are you telling such a sad story?" Breaker interrupted, taking a seat at the same picnic table and tossing his bag on top.

Claire sighed. "Breaker, you have two hickeys—that are visible, at least. I think you'll make it."

"That are visible," he repeated with a smirk.

She rolled her eyes. "And Ash, think about it, how else are we supposed to get close and get them to trust us? So far Sergio hasn't found anything on any student except the one that—"

I jerked my head in a no motion.

Claire pressed her lips together in a line like she was irritated and then kept talking. "All I'm saying is it's not the worst idea to go hang out or something. Maybe we can all go get pizza? Drinks? Something, anything."

Ash's face dropped to a frown. "What's wrong with all of us hanging out without them? Are you like, unhappy, or something?"

Breaker and I shared an uncomfortable look while Claire gulped and looked down. "No, I love hanging out with you guys, it's just... sometimes a girl wants... normal."

Ash flinched like he'd just been slapped.

"And that's my cue." I stood and prepared to take my leave.

"See you guys later. Let me know what the plan is, and for the record, I'm good with normal or crazy, all right?"

I left before they started fighting.

I hated that Claire had a point.

Almost as much as I hated that it looked like Ash's feelings were hurt. She didn't understand that he was trying to protect her as much as he could.

We weren't like other college students.

Normal would be nice, but that wasn't us. It would never be us.

And if she wanted normal, she needed to get out now before it was impossible for her to leave.

Then again, it was probably already too late.

Ash knew it.

I knew it.

I wondered if Claire did, or if she just fell for Ash's damn charm so hard that she had no idea there would be consequences for wanting a six-pack, dimples, and multiple orgasms all in one package.

I swung my bag over my shoulder, went into the History building, and found my seat at the back of the class.

I smelled her first.

That smell haunted me night and day.

Sometimes it was vanilla; other times, it was sweet like pineapple, but with a spice that made me clench my fists together, made my blood heat to ridiculous temperatures as I remembered all the times she was mine.

And all the reasons why she no longer was.

Shit. I was going to have no time outs for the next two weeks.

No escape.

Just her and her scent and her hate-filled eyes when people were looking, only to look so damn sad when they weren't that I didn't know what to believe anymore.

"Surprised you're not skipping," I said, not glancing up from my phone.

Her chair turned toward me.

I lifted my gaze.

Her face was still a bit bruised, but her expert makeup covered up the worst of it. Faint purple smudges were present beneath her eye, but she was still gorgeous. A queen among men.

Her ribs were probably still sore, and I knew the reason she was wearing her Eagle Elite jacket when she hated wearing it with her uniform because, according to her, it hid her best assets.

Her ass and boobs.

I could attest to them being impressive.

Okay, fine, more than impressive. Out of this world. Nixon and Trace bred a fucking supermodel for a child.

"Yeah, well, one more missed class..." She winced like talking hurt. "...and I fail; I told Dad to get me out of it since I have to suffer next to you, but he said no."

I sneered. "Poor pretty little princess, you mean Daddy said no? To you? I'm absolutely shocked."

Her blue eyes narrowed into tiny slits. "Says the guy who got a new car because, and I quote, 'the tech was just all wrong.'"

"I was sixteen," I said defensively. "And for that expensive of a car, it was all wrong."

"Whatever. I'm just saying I'm not the only spoiled one. What are you going to do without your mom to make you your lunches, pat you on the head when you get a scratch, and tuck you in bed at night? Oh, and before I forget, we're all out of mac and cheese."

Ignoring her, I leaned forward, whispering in a low voice, "You offering to do all of the above, Serena? Because I think I'd like to see you on your knees—kissing every place that hurts."

She smiled wide, shocking me a bit, and then she leaned in and murmured, "I would rather drive this pen through my skull." The sound of the pen clicking might as well be the gauntlet falling.

I gripped her hand and tugged, and her chair rolled into mine. "Funny, because I don't remember a time you ever preferred death over my dick."

Her eyes flashed. "Things change. Plus, I was young, had nothing to compare it to, and now..." She shrugged. "Let's just say I'm not impressed."

"Bullshit," I hissed.

"Oh, please." She rolled her eyes and jerked her hand away. "We threaten to kill each other, but this, this is what gets you pissed?"

The professor was talking about some worthless shit.

And Serena was staring at me like I had two heads.

My body felt numb and hot, all at the same time. Another guy. There had been another guy? How many guys? She'd slept with someone else?

I couldn't breathe.

I'd never had a panic attack before, but if this was what it felt like, I think I'd rather run headfirst into a wall. My chest felt tight, my heart hammered way too hard against my chest, and I had trouble swallowing.

I gripped the edge of the table and tried to slow my breathing to no avail.

"Junior?" she asked in a soft voice, reaching out to me in concern.

I stood, grabbed my shit, and left.

I had just made it outside the building when she charged after me and, in typical Serena fashion, threw her bag at my back. "Junior! What the hell is your problem?"

I stumbled forward a bit from the impact but kept walking.

"Are you serious right now?" she shrieked, chasing after me as fast as she could with all her wounds. "Fine," she yelled louder. "Your dick is huge, best of my life, Junior Nicolasi has a dick of gold—"

"Shut up." I turned on my heel and gripped her by the good shoulder, my fingers digging in. "Keep talking, and I'm switching arms, and Sergio's gonna have to stitch you back up again."

"You're insane." She gritted her teeth. "I can't believe you'd storm out of class over something so stupid—"

"It's not stupid! And I'm not mad about my dick!" I roared, earning odd stares from people hurrying by us.

"Um, were we having two totally different arguments?" Her eyes widened. "You left because—"

"I left because you said you'd compared me," I yelled. "Which means you've been sleeping around. How many, Serena? Huh? How many guys did you suck off while—"

Her good hand came flying at my face, slapping me so hard I stumbled sideways. "Don't." She gritted her teeth. "Don't you dare disrespect me like that."

I rubbed my cheek. "How many?"

"This is stupid." She shoved at my chest. "Do you really

want to play that game? Huh? Where we compare sexual partners? Numbers? How in the hell is that going to help either of us right now?"

I sobered completely on the outside, but the breathing, the pain in my chest slicing up and down over and over again kept increasing. She hadn't waited. She wasn't mine. "Go ahead, ask me."

She rolled her eyes. "I already know you get around, Junior, so I'm gonna put you in the more than two hands category, which is more than double my number."

"Wrong," I whispered as a choking fog descended over me.

"Wow!" She laughed. "So more than?"

I shook my head, too hurt to speak, too angry to form words. "I'm done with this conversation."

"You can't just start this and not end it. Don't make me beat you up again, Junior." Her tone was more teasing. She had no idea that my heart felt like it was getting ripped from my chest.

She didn't know that I felt alone.

Lost.

Forgotten.

So unimportant that it was some colossal joke to her—my feelings.

"One," I finally said. "My number is one."

She paled, her lips parted, but nothing came out. And then she reached for me.

I jerked away and shook my head. "But apparently I need to go out there and get some side by side comparisons too…" I started walking away.

"Junior, wait!" She grabbed my arm again. "Where are you going?"

"To find a few willing girls, obviously." I sneered. "Maybe I'll get lucky and have a threesome."

"You don't mean that." Her voice cracked, and her eyes filled with unshed tears.

"But I do, Serena." I glared. "I really do. Because how the fuck am I ever going to forget this conversation? It's out there now. In my head. Your confession may as well have been a shot to the head, executioner style, or at least to the heart." I took a deep breath. "Fuck. You."

"Junior. Don't!" She yelled. "You can't just—"

"I can. I will. Sorry, Serena, I'm off to find my new queen. God knows I've waited long enough to find a replacement."

"You'll never replace me." Her eyes filled with tears. "Never."

"Watch me." And just like that, we were back to the beginning, back to where things broke.

And it was painfully clear that while I played my part, I never forgot my vow to love her forever.

And Serena?

She obviously hadn't meant it in the first place.

"I'll love you as long as we both shall live."
"I'll love you as long as we both shall live."
"No matter what?" She asked, "Even if this goes bad?"
"A promise in blood is a promise in my soul." I took our hands and pressed the bloodied palms together. "No matter what I say, what you think, what I do—you own me, Serena Abandonato, and one day, I'm going to be yours, just like you're already mine."

I slammed my car door shut.

And screamed.

CHAPTER
Eleven

Serena

I should have known that the cease-fire between Junior and me wasn't going anywhere, if anything, after our fight, where we aired out our dirty laundry on the campus lawn for everyone to see—again—things seemed to feel so tense that I wanted to land a punch to his face just so I could feel better about the way he'd treated me.

He'd made it so believable, the lies he told, the harem of girls he made out with, and felt up, sometimes right in front of me with a smirk on his face.

"Dinner!" Mom called down the hall.

He was already at the house; I heard his voice, felt the tension rolling off of him right along with all that misplaced anger.

Maybe he shouldn't have made it look like he was whoring himself out if he was going to get so pissed about me doing the same.

Not that I'd done it.

I mean I'd done it as in, had sex, but it wasn't with multiple people, it was a week after he'd broken my heart into a million pieces.

And I thought it would make me feel better.

It didn't; if anything, it just pissed me off more.

When I saw the guy on campus I still felt dirty about that night, it was so rushed and so opposite of what I'd experienced with Junior that I wondered if I was defective, if something was wrong with me or if my body just refused to feel good with anyone but him, which just pissed me off more. Because how dare he make it so that I compared every kiss to his, every touch, every moan.

I gave my head a shake and slowly walked out of my room and down the hall toward the massive gourmet style kitchen.

The long wood table was piled high with enough food to feed a small country. Then again, we were Italian; we weren't really fans of portion control.

Broken heart? Have some bread!

Broken finger? Try the wine; it's a Malbec!

Near death? The pasta should help!

My eyes darted around the table. Dad was already seated at the head, staring down at his phone while Mom moved around him and kissed him on the head.

He grabbed her by the waist and spun her around until she was on his lap. "Missed you today," he said in a rough whisper before kissing her.

She sighed into his embrace. "Missed you too."

"Get a room, guys, get a room," I said with a laugh.

"Look who wants another sibling!" Dad teased while Bella sat at the opposite end of the table, giving them a huge grin.

She was in the whole I want a baby sister so I can mother her phase.

I made a gagging motion much to their amusement and pulled out one of the black wingback chairs and winked at Bella.

The front door slammed, and then Junior was sauntering in, with a girl draped all over him.

The first thing I noticed was I could see at least two blond extensions, the next was that her fingernails looked like they could seriously harm someone if they got too close, and third?

She was giggling.

The fun part?

Nobody had said a damn word.

So, she was just filling the air with her annoying giggle for absolutely no reason.

And Junior? He seemed to like the sound of it even though my ears were bleeding.

If a goat could laugh.

It would sound like extension girl.

I gripped my knife in my right hand before realizing what I was doing, then slowly set it back down and counted to three.

The giggle picked up.

Bella made a face in my direction.

Same girl, same.

"Sorry I'm late, guys," Junior announced. "Coco and I just got a little…" He grinned at her. "…sidetracked."

She honest to God touched her neck where a hickey was already forming and let out another ear-splitting giggle.

"Coco." I nodded. "Cool name." Was she a stripper? I mean, really…

She was wearing a black tube top dress, bright red lipstick, and heels.

Fuck my life.

"Thanks." Her heavily shadowed lids lowered into slits. "Are you Junior's sister?"

Deep breaths, Serena, deep breaths. "Kind of, I'm more of a sister-wife."

Her eyes widened. "Whoa, I had no idea he was into—"

"She's kidding."

Coco frowned. "Oh, so you guys aren't."

"Nope!" I answered a bit louder than I should have. "And this actually isn't Junior's house; those aren't his parents; he's staying here as a guest for a few weeks while his parents go on a mission trip to South America where they're going to rescue endangered teacup pigs."

Her jaw hung open as she swung her head back to Junior. "You must be so proud!"

"Yeah, I'm something." Junior shot me a glare while my mom snorted a laugh into her wine.

"Serena." Dad's voice held a warning edge, but I could see his mouth twitch.

"Cool lip ring." Coco eyed my dad like he was on the menu right alongside Junior. I fought not to throw up a bit in my mouth; she'd probably have a stroke if she came over for family dinner.

Dad gave her a chilly expression that made me want to duck under the table. "My wife thinks so too."

Message sent.

Unfortunately, goat-giggler did not receive.

She laughed again and reached for her empty wine glass then held it out to Junior like he was her servant.

I rolled my eyes as he poured her a glass and then started putting food on her plate.

"Gonna cut up her pasta too?" I mumbled under my breath.

"What was that?" Coco asked, twirling a piece of hair that looked minutes away from detaching from her head.

Sigh.

"Nothing," I said it quickly. "So where did you two meet?"

"Oh, it's the funniest story!" Coco took three gulps of wine. "My car broke down on the side of the road, he pulled over to help, and the rest is history, right baby?" She reached for his hand.

He took hers and kissed it while I was still waiting for the punchline in her "it's so funny" story.

"Wow." He was an idiot. "When was that?"

I took a sip of wine as she spit out, "Two hours ago."

I choked down what was left in my mouth. "Wow, you guys move fast. When's the wedding?"

"Serena." Mom shook her head at me like I was the crazy one. "Let's not tease our new guest."

Coco waved Mom off. "Oh, it's fine, I can handle the teasing. Actually, can someone let me know where the bathroom is?"

"Down the hall," I answered before anyone could. "Just turn around, walk, first door on the right."

"Thanks!" She jumped to her feet and practically bounced on those stilettos down the hall.

I used that as an opportunity to throw my spoon at Junior's head. "Are you kidding me right now? Two hours? I hope you get crabs!"

"Serena!" Mom hushed me. "I think it's… um… nice that you're dating."

I barked out a laugh. "This isn't dating!"

"Sure it is," Junior argued, leaning back in his chair, face serious. "Plus, she's really interesting, smart—"

"I'm gonna cut you off right there. I'd be stunned if she could spell cat or tie her shoes without Googling it!"

"Says the single girl with no boyfriend. Actually—" Junior snapped his fingers. "That's funny I've never even seen you date anyone, but then again, you don't have to date to fu—"

"Finish that sentence, Junior, and I'm going to have to punch you in the face," Dad said, all calm like they were talking about the weather.

"Sorry," Junior grumbled and flipped me off anyway.

I sighed and returned with two fingers.

"Well, this is… special," Mom grumbled, reaching for the wine.

Suddenly I remembered my parents' rules. "Daddy?"

Dad shot me a look that said *I know exactly what you're trying to do with that sweet voice of yours.* "Yes, sweetheart?"

"Shouldn't we let Junior know about the rules of your household? I mean, since he's going to be here for two full weeks, it wouldn't be fair that he can have female company when the rules specifically state no boyfriends, girlfriends, or skanks can stay any later than ten at night."

If looks could kill, I would be dead. Junior was glaring holes through my body.

"As much as it pains me to say this out loud…" Dad sighed. "Serena's right. We do have certain house rules. Your, um, friend can stay until after dinner, but then she needs to go home."

"If she can find it," I grumbled, earning another scolding look from my mom.

Coco teetered back down the hall, walking so loud in her heels that I was concerned for the hardwood. She staggered a bit as she approached her chair and then plopped down in it.

I frowned.

Junior leaned in. "Hey, you okay?"

"Mmmm." She swayed toward him and patted him on the cheek but missed, nearly collapsing onto his lap. "Sooo good."

I burst out laughing. "Yeah, she's high as a kite."

"I was nervous." Coco giggled and then stared up at Junior, blinking her eyes so slow that I was afraid she was going to pass out. And then she did, right on his lap.

"Well." I grabbed my wine. "At least you got some action, right, Junior?"

With a grunt, he shoved her away, stood, then threw her over his shoulder. "I'm just gonna go let her sleep it off; then I'll take her home. Sorry guys."

"Real winner, Junior. I mean seriously, good work." I lifted my glass in a cheer.

His eyebrows shot up to his hairline. "Hey Nixon, I almost forgot. Some things came up at school today. I strongly suggest you have the sex talk with Serena. The last thing we need is for her to end up pregnant."

With that, he gave me his back and strutted down the hall with Coco lifeless over his shoulder.

I was choking him in his sleep later.

Slowly, I turned toward my dad's thunderous expression.

Forget choking him; I was going to make him suffer slowly.

Damn it, Junior!

"Dad, he's just being... Junior."

Dad grabbed the bottle of wine and started drinking directly from it; bad sign, very bad sign. "Have you been…" He took a deep breath. "Serena, I've always trusted you, but guys think differently than girls. They—shit." He rubbed his eyes with the back of his hands. "They have thoughts!"

I looked to my mom for help, but she seemed to be enjoying the show as she snorted out a laugh. "Yes, Nixon, boys have thoughts. Care to share the ones you had about me when you were her age?"

"Mom, no!" I nearly shouted. "Some things you can't unhear!"

Dad looked between us and then threw up a hand. "Look, guys are… they're bad."

I waited for more.

But that was it.

Apparently, he was finished talking.

"Wait." I leaned in. "That's it? That's your sex talk?"

"Yup." Dad thrust a finger in my direction. "Oh also, if I find out you're having sex with boys, I'm going to rip out their tongues, chop off their dicks, then let them suffer through life while they beg for death, and that, sweetheart, will be on your conscience."

Eyes wide, I nodded once. "Good talk, Dad, good talk."

He relaxed. "Really? Because I feel like I came on a little strong."

"Nah," I waved him off while Mom laughed and handed him the wine bottle again like he needed comfort. "I particularly liked the rip out their tongues and chop off their dicks… classic mob boss."

"I like chopping things." He shrugged. "But also, I'm

serious. No boys. Focus on school; our life's hard enough without having to bring someone into the fold."

I wanted to say he was already in.

The one who I'd had.

Who I'd wanted.

Who was currently sitting with a drug-using, passed out Coco.

I suppressed a snarl as I reached for my fork and grabbed more pasta. If Junior was trying to flaunt his female fans to make me homicidal—it was working.

CHAPTER Twelve

Junior

By the time I got back to the house, it was already past midnight. Thank God I didn't have class the next day because I was exhausted having to drive someone a good forty minutes back to her apartment.

When we finally got there, Coco had trouble finding her keys, and then she plastered herself against me, kissed my nose because, and I quote, "It's just so damn perfect." Only to follow that up with asking me if I wore contacts and if I was packing.

I think she meant that sexually.

But I truly was packing—heat that was.

Those hours with Coco, I would never get back, but to see the anger on Serena's face?

One hundred percent worth it.

It was the only plan of attack I had.

Hurt her the way she'd hurt me—no, the way she was still hurting me.

I quietly let myself in the house and tossed my keys on the counter; it felt like a second home to me since we had all been close. And all those nights I'd snuck into her room, well let's just say I knew how to get into the fortress that was Nixon Abandonato's house—blindfolded.

I went over to the fridge to grab a water, then nearly shit myself when a too-sugary voice said, "Get lucky?"

"Did Satan at least give you a deal when he took your soul, or did you just freely hand it over so you could lurk in dark corners and curse people?" I picked up the water and closed the fridge. "I'm genuinely curious."

She made a face.

The lights were off except for the glow from the motion sensors outside that I'd activated.

And then, absolute darkness.

"I gave him my soul, and in return, he said when I die, I can haunt you, so I figured it was a pretty legit deal, you know?" she said sweetly.

I rolled my eyes. "Yeah, okay and to answer your question, no I didn't get lucky because I'm not into screwing passed out girls—"

Serena took a step toward me and whispered, "Huh, that's strange, considering what bloodline you come from."

I shoved her so hard she stumbled backward.

And then she was on me, legs wrapped around my waist, hands grappling for a solid chokehold around my neck.

I threw her down onto her back while she tried to get an arm bar, too bad her fingers were still broken or she may have had me.

"Son of a bitch," I groaned as my arm strained inside hers, I got out of position then knocked my head against hers.

She cursed and loosened enough for me to wiggle out and pin her arms to the ground.

Both our chests were heaving; I tried to ignore the fact that her white tank top was nearly see-through, and she was wearing tiny shorts that did nothing to hide her lean legs.

Her hair was pulled back from her face, and she had never looked so angry—or so damn beautiful.

"What the hell is wrong with you?" I hissed. "That was low, even for you."

Her eyes darted away. "I know."

And then it was like our bodies realized what perfect position we were in, her legs wrapped tight around my waist.

My hands holding her hostage against the floor.

Her breasts straining.

We were a tangle of erratic breathing, hatred, and millions of angry, broken pieces.

I could feel the heat from her legs as my dick strained against my jeans. An erotic swirl of tension so thick, so sweet, pulsed between us in a way that was catastrophic.

I lowered my head a fraction of an inch so that I could whisper in her ear, my tongue wetting the outside tip. "Admit it; you like fighting me."

She struggled against my grip. "I can feel you… so maybe it's you who likes fighting me?"

I thrust up against her, feeling the throb of her body against mine. "What was that, princess?"

She arched beneath me.

A light flicked on down the hall.

We scrambled to our feet and jumped apart. I did my best to hide my arousal while she crossed her arms and reached for the bottle of water I'd just taken.

The light turned off, blanketing us in darkness again.

I took a step away from her.

And then Serena grabbed me by the arm and shoved me against the fridge, her mouth was on mine before I could beg.

And then I was shoving my hand down her shorts, gripping her naked ass so tight that she would have bruises.

Our tongues tangled in a mess of want.

I would die for a kiss like this.

I would commit murder.

I would burn down the world.

I let out a groan as my other hand dug into her hair, tugging it, holding her prisoner as our mouths greedily fused harder.

The sound of the water bottle dropping broke us apart again.

"Consider it a favor, Junior." She sounded confident, but she looked shaken.

"The kiss?" I rasped, mouth swollen from her.

"Yeah." She shrugged like it wasn't a big deal when we both knew that blood could be shed over us kissing like that. "Just a friend helping out a friend. I couldn't let you go to bed with her taste still on your tongue. Better you fall asleep with the flavor of someone you hate, don't you think?"

"Better for my nightmares maybe, sure," I agreed, and without saying another word, picked up the discarded water bottle and left. I squeezed the plastic so hard it crinkled in my hand, and I knew I would never look at water or plastic again without getting painfully aroused.

I nearly impaled the guest room door when I turned to close it behind me.

And when Serena's footsteps sounded down the hall and

her door shut, I whispered under my breath. "Hate you for as long as we both shall live."

CHAPTER
Thirteen

Serena

Junior was at breakfast, drinking a cup of coffee when Ash and Claire barged in. None of us had classes today, and typically we hung out together, sparred, shopped, cleaned our guns—not even kidding—but today, Ash looked irritated as he jerked a seat out and shoved a piece of bacon in his mouth with a growl.

"Hangry, party of one," I sang out.

"Ash, it's not a big deal," Claire said softly. She reached for him then seemed to think twice about it and pulled back. "I mean, we just hung out for an hour."

"An hour," he repeated. "Without protection. Without me."

She glared. "Look, I get that I need protection, but you've been teaching me, and I'm pretty sure I can take apart ten different sorts of guns and put them back together with a blindfold on."

He snorted in disgust. Ash was calm until he suddenly wasn't. It was like once he'd had it, he was done.

He was a perfect mini-me of Chase, gorgeous thick dark hair that the girls went wild over since it was a little on the long side, tattoos peeking out from beneath his collar, a few on his right hand, and those damn Abandonato blue eyes.

It didn't help that he was arrogant as hell.

But recently he'd been on edge, especially when it came to Claire.

"Guys, don't fight," Junior said without looking up from his phone. "It just makes Ash angry, which makes him more hungry, which means he's going to steal the last piece of bacon and I'm going to have to stab him in the throat, and I promised Nixon no bloodshed this morning, I said it before prayer and everything."

Ash chose that moment to snatch the last piece and shove it into his mouth then flip him off.

I sighed. "Mature, Ash."

"She started it." He pointed at Claire, mouth full. He chewed a few bites. "She thought it would be a good idea to go hang out with Annie and Tank, so she got in their car by herself, disappeared for over an hour without any security, and strolled her ass back to the house while I had a mini-panic attack thinking I was going to find her body in the back of their trunk!"

I made a face. "You do realize that Annie looks like she'd pass out if she saw a gun in real life, right?"

"You don't know..." His face paled. "...what people are truly capable of."

"And you do?" Junior asked, this time finally looking up.

"What's this really about, man? Is it about Claire not being safe, or you not being in control?"

"No." Ash put his head in his hands and gripped his hair. "It's this really horrible feeling that something bad's going to happen. Ever since that night, I can't shake it. I keep having these nightmares about something happening to us. First, it's to Claire, and then it's you, Junior." He locked eyes with him. "Last night it was Serena and Breaker. Violet saw everything. I just—it's not about control. It's about not knowing anything and having to just wake up every day prepared for the worst."

Claire started rubbing his back with her hand. "I'm sorry, I just—think about it from my perspective. This is all really new for me, the way you guys live, and it was nice to go to coffee, talk about movies instead of people plotting our bloody deaths."

"Shocked," Junior said dryly. "That you don't like talking about death. I mean, it's like my number one favorite thing to do."

"What's your second?" Claire frowned.

Junior's eyes flickered across the table, landed on me for a few heated moments that had me clenching my thighs together. "Kissing, I love talking about kissing and watching a girl's face go from ghost white to red with embarrassment, then arousal. I like to see her eyes dilate; her tongue slide out and wet her lip in anticipation. You know, boy things." He winked.

Meanwhile, I was having a near nervous breakdown at the table.

He just had to bring up kissing.

And I just had to be a few feet away from where we'd had our makeout session last night.

I couldn't lose control again.

But he'd felt so right.

So damn sexy that I just wanted to pretend that we didn't have this chasm of rage and mistrust between us.

I didn't expect him to kiss me back.

But boy, *did* he!

I felt that kiss in my soul.

For the first time in years, I was absolutely terrified, because it would be so easy to give him what was left of me.

And I knew he would break it again.

"Why don't you say things like that?" Claire nudged Ash.

Ash shook his head at Junior. "Thanks, man."

"Any time." A grin slid across his face.

I had to look away from that mouth before I launched myself across the table and took his head between my hands and begged.

"Normal," Ash repeated. "You want normal?"

She nodded.

"With normal people?"

"Hey, I'm normal!" I said defensively, not realizing I was holding my knife in my right hand since I liked always having it on me.

Ash and Junior both looked at the knife then at me.

Ash spoke first. "You literally killed someone with a fucking poison dart you keep in your heels, Serena, so…"

"I'm gonna give you a hard no," Junior agreed. "Nice try, killer, but please carry on, I think you missed a spot of blood on the tip."

I made a face at both of them.

"Yes." Claire bounced in her seat.

"Fine." Ash jerked his head toward me. "Think we can have some people over?"

"Ah, inviting them into the lair, nice." I grinned. "Yeah, we know where all the weapons are just in case, and it's not a secret where we live. Mom and Dad went out for the day, but we have around fifteen suits walking around bored out of their minds."

"Right." Ash let out a rough exhale and cupped Claire's face between his hands. "We have them over, watch some movies, drink some wine, talk about whatever the hell normal people talk about and then, we go home, and you stop going off on your own because you think you're strong enough to kill someone in cold blood when we both know you aren't."

She wrapped her arms around him as Ash pulled her into his lap so she straddled him, and then he started kissing her.

"Yeah, that's our cue." I grabbed my knife and stood.

Claire laughed and pulled back. "Should I text them to come over in an hour?"

"Sounds good." I yawned and then left them to go grab clothes from my bedroom.

I pushed my bathroom door open and dropped my clothes to the floor. "Get out!"

Junior gave me a blank stare as he continued brushing his teeth. "No." His mouth was full of foam.

"This house has five bathrooms, pick one!"

He spat out his toothpaste. "Your father specifically said to use this one because as of today, your mom's decided that she's gutting the other three, thus the reason for part of their outing; I think Home Depot is in the plan. Besides, why would I bring all my shit to a new bathroom only to have to move it back? Use your head, Serena."

I clenched my teeth. "You're going to force me to make us a schedule, aren't you?"

His grin was sexy, devouring me as he leaned against the counter. "Depends. Are we talking more of like a sticker chart schedule? Because I could really go for some positive…" His eyes freely roamed up and down my body like the teal monstrosities had a right to. "…reinforcement."

I grinned and took two steps toward him, then smacked him on the back of his head. "Consider yourself positively reinforced."

When I pulled my hand away, he struck, snatching my wrist and gripping it firmly, his expression amused. "Come on, Serena, be an adult about this, you can shower all you want while I'm in here getting ready. I won't look."

I gaped. "You're such a liar!" I shoved at his chest. "The shower's glass! You can see right through!"

"Right, and as shocking as it may sound, I do possess self-control."

I crossed my arms. "It's not about self-control; it's about reward versus punishment. Why should I reward you with a free show when you deserve to be punished?"

He leaned forward and tucked a piece of my hair behind my ear. I tried not to focus on his aqua eyes and stellar jawline. Everything about him screamed dangerous perfection. "Trust me, sweetheart, you naked, mere feet away from me when I know you're off-limits isn't a reward; it's pure hell."

With that, he walked out of the bathroom.

I was too confused and stunned to do anything but slowly strip out of my clothes and get into the shower and try to forget about how close his lips had been to mine.

The water was hot as steam billowed around me.

I let out a groan as I put my head under the hot water,

letting it slide over my face. This was what I needed, to relax, to think about anything but Junior taunting me. Again.

I was so calm and relaxed, I didn't notice that he was back.

The glass door opened.

And a very muscled eight-pack greeted me like a bomb detonating.

"Hey." He didn't so much as blink as he held out his hand. "Can you toss me the body wash?"

With a curse, I grabbed the plastic bottle and chucked it at his perfect body, obviously on purpose. May it slip and hit his balls, rendering him unable to sleep around like I'd assumed he was doing all along.

I hid my hurt well because I hid it behind the shield of so much anger that I could have sworn I was hooked up to an IV of rage.

He caught the body wash with one hand and smirked. "Shoulda played baseball, princess."

"I'm not the best with balls, you know that, I see something small and I want to squeeze." I lowered my gaze and shrugged like he wasn't completely hung.

He burst out laughing. "Funny, since I remember you grabbing a lot of balls back in the day, even licking them…"

I refused to shiver. "Go be gross elsewhere, dude." I waved him off and grabbed my shampoo, and tried to ignore the way my body pulsed with awareness. He was so close, under the other showerhead, pretending like we didn't hate each other, like we didn't have some serious issues.

It was almost like he was pretending we were friends.

And It confused me more than his hate ever would.

Because I didn't know what to do with it, and it made me

hope, and deep down, I was a romantic. I grew up watching relationships around me borderline on obsessive.

I wanted an obsessive sort of love, the kind that refuses to let go, even if it was unhealthy—it was what I wanted, what I was exposed to.

So, when Junior teased me, it gave me the wrong idea.

"Do me a favor?" I whispered while I massaged shampoo into my hair.

"What's up?"

"Don't—" I took a breath. "Don't pretend we're friends just because we're shower buddies, don't pretend our relationship isn't fucked up when it is, because it's not fair to me, and it's not fair to you, especially when you go back home in less than two weeks, and we still have to work together without killing one another. I may actually murder you if you go from my friend Junior to my enemy in the span of thirteen days, got it?"

He seemed to think about it, and then he grabbed my shoulder and turned me around, so my back was to him, and then he was pulling me under the water and rinsing my hair.

My lips trembled.

My heart cracked in my chest.

It was so wrong it was right.

I hated him for making me feel vulnerable, for making me crave the closeness that I missed so much.

It was so hard, knowing what it was like to love someone, only to have them disrespect and betray you in front of your face and act like it didn't matter, like you didn't matter.

He was sending so many mixed signals I wondered if he was actually going insane.

"What if I'm just your friend now, what if we both put down the weapons and try a different tactic, I'm here for two weeks, and regardless of our friendship we still have to work together until we fucking die—may as well make it enjoyable by not being at each other's throats."

I opened my eyes. "Is the great Junior Nicolasi waving the white flag?"

"I would never wave first." He shrugged. "I'm just saying, this has been going on for over a year, maybe it's time we tried not hating each other."

I swallowed the lump in my throat and said softly, "Junior, my hate is all I have. Please don't take that too."

His face completely fell. "Serena—"

"I'll think about it," I whispered in a hurried rush, and then I was stepping out of the shower and grabbing a towel, but not before a knock sounded on the bathroom door.

"Serena?" My dad's voice filled the bathroom; he was clearly standing on the other side of the door, ready to expose both of us, all of the lies. It couldn't happen. Not now, not ever.

My eyes widened. "Hey, Dad, I'm showering what's up?"

"Oh, I was just looking for Junior. You see him?"

"He's um…" I looked over my shoulder.

Junior gave me an arrogant grin. Ugh, he knew I was the worst liar ever. "He's around somewhere, Dad. I just saw him at breakfast. Knowing Junior, he's probably finding Coco number two, so he can ruin dinner again and get laid."

"Serena, have a little heart. Junior hasn't had it as easy as the rest of you."

I felt Junior go still behind me.

"What do you mean?"

"It's just… Never mind, just know that the mafia doesn't forget. We don't talk about it, but that doesn't mean we don't know, so yes, things have been harder on him because he has to prove he isn't his bloodline, and I wouldn't wish that on anyone."

"But— I held my towel tighter. "Phoenix is amazing; he's your best friend."

Dad was quiet and then. "Honey, we should talk about this later."

"Okay."

"Love you," he said.

And then he was gone.

I whipped around. "Junior, what's he talking about?"

Junior's eyes looked haunted. He gritted his teeth; his jaw clenched like he was ready to lose his shit. "Nothing."

"Junior?"

"I said nothing!" He moved past me and snatched the other clean towel. And then he hung his head. "Sorry, I didn't mean to snap. Just know that it's not something I want to talk about—ever, especially with someone who might look at me the way you are right now."

"How am I looking at you?"

He was quiet and then, "Like I'm unpredictable. Like I could snap. Like something's wrong with me."

"That's not what this look is." I shook my head. "This look is one of concern." I took a deep breath and said it. "From one friend to another."

His head jerked up; long, wet, golden-brown hair stuck to his forehead as his teal eyes locked on mine. "You promise?"

I knew in that moment I should have run in the opposite direction. No good would come from us being friends.

In fact, it almost felt like a bad omen, holding out my hand and shaking his, like we'd both just sealed our fate.

Done something we would never come back from. But I still said, "I promise."

"Hate you for as long as we both shall live." He said it with a smile.

I grinned and said. "Back atcha."

I didn't realize how much I was smiling until I was back in my room and saw my reflection.

And all my heart kept screaming at me was. "We are so screwed."

CHAPTER
Fourteen

Junior

Nothing like calming the arousal down like the reminder of your family's past, the reminder of your blood, of where you came from, of choices made.

The minute Serena left the bathroom.

The minute I knew Nixon was gone.

I slammed my hand against the tile, over and over again, until the pain turned numb, until I couldn't feel my fingers.

She knew that there was a past.

She didn't know what my dad had done.

She didn't know the forgiveness her mom had extended or her dad, for that matter.

And she sure as hell didn't know the shame I carried when I thought of the name I was born with.

Not Nicolasi, but De Lange, the cursed and forgotten arm of the Five Families—my dad took the Nicolasi name the minute he inherited Luca Nicolasi's job as boss, making it even harder for the De Lange name, a name attached to traitors, murderers, and rapists, to survive.

But there's something about a name.

Something that people don't talk about. It doesn't matter that I was a Nicolasi under my father's rule, because I knew, in my heart, in my head, the blood that pumped through my body knew, that I was still a De Lange, that I was part of the original Family that the Cosa Nostra despised.

It didn't matter that Nicolasi covered a multitude of sins.

My blood was still evil.

Serena didn't know the whole story, none of the kids did, but I'll never forget the day my dad sat me down and explained why it was essential to become a Nicolasi and not slide back into what was easy—being what I was born to be: a De Lange.

Fucking evil.

I didn't understand; I mean, I was twelve.

And then he showed me the pictures.

Pictures of strung-out prostitutes, pictures of death, pictures of my grandfather, of business deals made, and finally.

Of him and his friends.

The original Elect.

All four of them standing next to another girl, Nixon's wife, Trace, all of them smiling, all except my father who in the picture was looking directly at the innocent dark-haired girl—his expression dripping with hatred.

A person doesn't forget the first time they see that sort of hate, that sort of brainwashing, which my dad assured me it was, didn't mean that the sins were totally forgiven.

That day I went into my dad's office innocent.

I left with the sins of my father on my hands, and I'd been trying to rectify that ever since. I learned that day that no amount of showers and soap would cleanse me of our sins, of our family's legacy, so I had to be better, do better, and then I'd locked eyes with her.

Serena.

I remember the day things shifted.

The day we went from laughing and climbing our favorite tree, to making out behind her dad's giant ass garage. We went from making out to skinny dipping to our first time when she told me she loved me when I told her I had no idea what I was doing, and when she told me it didn't matter because we were together. J and S.

I squeezed my eyes shut as the memories came like a flood.

I grabbed a towel and quickly wrapped it around my waist and then went into my bedroom to grab some clothes only to find both Ash and Breaker sitting on my bed like they owned the place.

"Um, hi?" I dropped my towel.

"Bro." Breaker burst out laughing. "Cold shower?"

Ash shoved him. "If that's shrinkage, you should only be so thankful. Also, stop staring at his dick, it's weird."

"Almost as weird as a super long shower with Serena?"

I burst out laughing; it was harsh, on purpose, because what choice did I have? God, I was strung as tight as physically possible, wasn't I? "Yeah well, it's fun taunting her. Besides, she knows that the last thing she'll ever get to taste is this." I winked.

"Gross." Breaker shuddered and then made a big motion of covering his eyes like my nakedness offended him.

Ash let out a cough.

"Wow, glad we know where we stand then because I was just stopping by to ask if I could suck your dick, damn it, how embarrassing would that have been?" Serena sauntered into my room, fully clothed.

And there I stood, towel-less and ashamed. "You dressed fast."

"I was motivated." Her eyebrows arched.

Was she talking about me?

The minute I let the thought get out there, Ash tossed her a Snickers.

With lightning reflexes, she lifted her hand, and the candy bar slapped into her palm.

Ah, so candy bar trumps naked Junior, nice.

Ash cleared his throat. "Could you maybe put clothes on so we can talk about tonight?"

"Tonight?" I casually walked over to my dresser, feeling someone's eyes on me. Maybe the Snickers wasn't satisfying? With a smirk, I grabbed a pair of ripped jeans and turned around in time to see Serena eyeing me like I was the candy bar. "Serena, put your tongue back in your mouth, I'm a person, damn it!"

She scowled. "Is that a rash?"

"I hate you," I grumbled as I pulled on my jeans commando and crossed my arms. "So, tonight?"

Ash gritted his teeth. "Look, Claire wants to have everyone over as discussed; I don't know what the hell's going on but—"

"She wasn't born into this like us," Serena said softly. "We kind of gave her a shove into the mafia pit and went 'survive!'"

Ash let out a snort. "I know but, we love each other; it should be... easier."

"Love doesn't make things easier, man." I shook my head. "If anything, it makes things hurt more, it makes things harder, it makes you question everything, and it makes you wish you were dead at least half the time you experience it. Love, if anything, isn't a blessing, it's a curse."

All eyes fell to me.

Shit, I'd said too much.

I didn't know how to recover.

"Been in love before, huh, Junior?" Breaker snickered.

I looked down at the hardwood floor of my room, then to the black area rug next to the guest bed. "Once, but it was doomed before it even started."

"You're Junior Nicolasi. If you're doomed, we're all doomed." He snorted like he didn't believe me.

"Yeah, well." I ran my hands through my hair. "I'm just saying that sometimes it's not. Ash, if she wants normal, we can try to play it that way while we do some research. Sergio hasn't found any trace of chatter on the black market or in the underground, no hits, none of our names mentioned, but make no mistake, there's a reason they're trying to make it look appealing to go to college next to us."

"Bait," Serena muttered. "We're bait, which means they are too. Actually, anyone who hangs out with us is."

"Shit." Ash got up and started pacing. "All right, no need to go to the bosses. We can deal with being bait; we were basically born little worms."

"Does that make us fish now?" Breaker wondered out loud.

Each of us gave him an annoyed look and then ignored him.

"All right, so we have our normal time with Tank and Annie tonight, watch a movie, popcorn." Serena stopped talking as her eyes narrowed. "Wait, do we have to leave our weapons in the room?"

Breaker busted up. "Serena, normal doesn't mean bringing your knife and then throwing it to impress guests."

She pouted.

I had to laugh. "We have enough men outside on the property, and inside, we'll be fine. It's two people, and even if they did get through—well, we have Bone Crushing Breaker."

He did a little bow.

"Angry Ash."

I got flipped off.

"And Sexually Repressed Serena." I winked. "Perfect."

She scowled.

I kind of liked that she didn't deny it.

And then my heart reminded me that it didn't matter, did it?

"Cool." Breaker stood. "So, they'll be here in the next hour. I'm going to grab some candy, order some pizza. And Junior, make sure you put on a shirt. Wouldn't want Annie having a heart attack."

"I wouldn't worry about her watching Junior." Serena laughed. "She only had eyes for Ash." She fluttered her eyelashes while Ash visibly paled.

"You look like you're going to be sick." I laughed.

Ash shook his head. "Bro, if I have to listen to her talk about school, or plants, or insects one more time..."

"She's smart!" Serena argued, winking at me.

"Yeah, man," I agreed. "Smart women like smart men, you should be flattered. You know, since you're an idiot."

"And I'm going." Ash ignored us and followed Breaker out the door, leaving Serena and me in a weird staring war.

If I looked away, did that mean I lost or won?

I swallowed and stared her down.

She bit down on her bottom lip and then blurted, "I want to try it."

"What? Not bringing your knives to movie night?"

She shook her head slowly. "No, this whole... let's be friends thing," Her shoulders slumped. "Honestly Junior, I hate you so much—"

"Is this literally how you're starting our friendship talk?" I burst out laughing.

And then she joined in. "Yeah, pretty much."

"Well, I guess it would be weird if you hugged me."

"So weird." She gulped.

Fuck, suddenly, that's all I wanted. Her arms wrapped tight around me. The memories from our first time filled that room so deep with the past that I had trouble breathing.

"Yeah." My voice was raspy as I took a step toward her. "And you do hate better than anyone I know."

"Was that a compliment?" She tilted her head and smiled.

God, I used to be on the receiving end of so many of those smiles, I almost forgot how good it felt. It was like feeling the sun on your skin the first time, like experiencing life instead of death—love, not war.

"It was." I finally said as she took another step toward me.

And then we were nearly chest to chest as she looked up at me with her bright blue eyes and silky wet hair. "Watch it; you don't want to get soft in these next two weeks." She poked my eight pack.

I grabbed her hand and held it. "I highly doubt being soft has ever been a problem for me, Serena."

Her eyes darted to my mouth then away as she sighed. "Promise me one thing."

"What?"

"I would rather you physically knock me out than let me in," She tapped my chest with a long fingernail. "Agreed? Shields still up?"

I deflated a bit and then nodded. "Shields still up."

"For the Family." Her chin lifted.

I leaned down and whispered in her ear. "For the Family." What we both meant was, for us.

For us.

CHAPTER
Fifteen

Serena

He was getting to me, and even though I talked a big game with my whole Avengers shields up talk, I mean seriously, did I really say shields? I shook my head. It didn't matter; just looking at him was hard.

Being in the same room.

Knowing that all I had to do was make the choice to take a few steps and walk into his arms, knowing that Junior had never denied me his embrace, nearly killed me.

I could do this. I had survived being made; I could sure as hell survive being on friendly terms with the guy who took my virginity, right?

Easy.

I took a soothing breath and walked into the movie room. Annie and Tank had arrived about twenty minutes ago, I heard everyone joking in the kitchen but hadn't felt ready yet, so instead, I sat in my own room and stared at myself in the mirror.

If everyone was trying for normal then I knew I needed to tone it down, so instead of wearing something scandalous or spiky heels, I went back and changed into a pair of gray joggers along with a black crop top Adidas hoody, and as much as it pained me, I grabbed a makeup wipe and removed everything but my mascara.

I looked younger, more innocent, which was almost a joke, I hadn't been innocent in a while, and if I was being completely honest, the girl looking back at me bothered me because the girl without her lipstick looked petrified, she looked easy to wound, she looked soft.

And I couldn't be any of those things anymore.

Especially around Junior.

But this was important to Claire, and regardless of her and Ash's relationship, she was a friend. I never admitted it out loud, but normal, sometimes, did sound like winning the lottery.

The last time I even went to the movies without a security guard was never.

We always had suits watching us, watching everyone else, so pizza and some downtime, where I didn't have knives strapped to my thighs, sounded kind of nice.

God help them if they ate all the pizza though, I smirked as I walked down the long hallway leading into the movie room. I didn't need my knives to make an impression.

Laughter trickled out of the room as Claire and Annie teased Tank, who looked like he'd rather be anywhere but at my dad's house.

He was sitting between them with a piece of pepperoni

pizza held up to his face, his gaze darting between the girls as they talked about something that he obviously didn't find interesting.

"You should probably go save him," Ash said as he walked up. He looked down at me, and then his eyes widened. "Whoa."

"What?" I touched my face. "Is something wrong?"

He gulped and then looked away. "Nope."

"Ash,"

He held up his hands. "Look, I'm not stupid. Doesn't matter that we're cousins; you'd still kill me."

"Truth." I winked.

He just rolled his eyes. "Don't you think you're treading on thin ice already?"

"Huh?"

"Shit," he muttered. I knew what he was thinking; that I looked like I did before the day Junior and I started a war. "Just... I hope you know what you're doing, Serena." He kissed the top of my head and went over to Tank, who looked so thankful to be rescued that he stopped chewing enough to give Ash his attention.

I almost laughed.

From what I'd gathered, Tank didn't really enjoy going to college, at least according to Annie, which made it semi-strange that they were friends, then again, who was I to judge? I was part of the mafia.

I never realized how big Tank was until he was in my house. He was wearing a tight black T-shirt and had enough muscle that if he stood next to Junior, he would at least look like he could hang without dying. His hair was a dark chocolate brown, his eyes green. Maybe I didn't notice that he was attractive because I was broken. Then again, I'd been surrounded by some of the most ridiculously good-looking men on the planet since birth. Most guys couldn't even hold a candle to any of the bosses, let alone the sons.

Tank shifted on his feet and then let out a sigh as he exhaled and tapped his foot while the girls kept talking excitedly with their hands.

Poor Tank. He looked like he'd rather be out on a motorcycle or in a ring, not at a pizza party talking about his latest test.

Who knew normal could be so wonderfully boring?

As if he felt my stare, he glanced over at me; a confident grin spread across his face. A grin that said he knew exactly how to smile at a girl to get her to fall all over herself.

Hmmm, what game was he playing?

I returned his smile with a polite one of my own and glanced around the room.

The big screen had Trolls on, which was so damn innocent I almost laughed; the pizza was stacked in the corner by a few bottles of wine because, duh, Italians. Though I did notice one six-pack of beer that I attributed to the two normals who decided to come to our house for whatever this was.

Junior barked out a laugh from the hallway. When was the last time he'd even laughed with me? I let out a sigh.

My first mistake was getting distracted by the normalcy of what was happening. My second was letting my guard down and actually enjoying the fact that every muscle in my body wasn't tense, ready to attack.

And my third?

Not understanding that an entirely different battle was about to take place.

Between my heart.

And his soul.

"Okay, we have more pizza coming." Junior strolled into the room with Breaker hot on his heels. He took one look at me and stopped, causing Breaker to run right into him.

Junior's eyes locked with mine.

And they said it all. They widened and then narrowed like he hated me more than he loved the way I looked before I was forced to become the Serena Abandonato with her high heels and perfect makeup.

Maybe I'd grown up too fast, but it's not like he wasn't to blame for part of that, right?

"Junior, seriously?" Breaker shoved past him and made a beeline for Tank and Ash while Junior stared me down like he'd never seen me before. Then again, he hadn't seen this version of me for a very long time. I felt naked, exposed beyond what I was comfortable with, and at the same time, I didn't want to look away.

The room felt thick with tension as he slowly made his way over to me and stopped when he was inches away from my body.

I was afraid to blink, afraid this version of Junior would disappear as his eyes drank me in.

"You okay?" I asked in a weak voice.

"No." He shook his head and lifted a hand like he wanted to cup my chin, to feel my skin, to lean forward and press a kiss to my naked lips.

"Movie time!" Ash all but yelled, and Junior jerked his hand away.

I shot daggers at Ash. "It's already started?"

"That was just for background noise." He pointed to the screen. "The movie of choice tonight, as voted on by everyone but you since you take forever to get ready." I flipped him off. "Is going to be Closer!"

I flinched. "Why that movie? It's old." I gulped and turned to Ash, who was already going through our Apple TV to stream it.

"Because—" Ash grinned. "—nobody's seen it, and it's a classic. Besides, Tank's a movie buff and completely convinced us that we needed something dark and twisted with a bit of a love triangle thrown in for good measure."

My breath heaved out of my lungs. "Great."

"Great." Junior hissed next to me.

Did they notice how we stood?

Did they care?

Did they know that every part of my body was pulsing with need, dying a slow death every second Junior didn't touch me?

Shit, I should have never agreed to this cease-fire.

I quickly joined the girls and took a seat.

Not even forty minutes into the movie, and I was already losing my mind. It was sexual. It was hot. It was everything I so did not need to watch with Junior mere feet away from me.

"Gotta pee." I stood.

"Should we pause it?" Tank asked, giving me a look of genuine concern. Poor guy, I would eat him alive. Then again, he might just enjoy it with the way he was staring at me.

"No, go ahead." I gave him a genuine smile that had him smiling back at me like he wanted to get to know me better, which I knew Junior would shut down like he always did.

Sigh.

I marched out of the room while everyone went back to watching and quickly darted toward the kitchen. I poured a glass of cold water and chugged the entire thing then wiped my face with the back of my hand before gripping the countertop.

"This isn't the bathroom." Junior's voice floated toward me like a caress.

I lifted my gaze.

I could see the reflection of him in the kitchen window as he slowly moved behind me, then without saying anything, grabbed my hips and slowly ran his thumbs over the exposed skin above my joggers.

Trembling, I leaned forward so I wouldn't lean back against him, so I wouldn't feel him—my body fought me though because it remembered how his mouth tasted. Since we were friends now, I shouldn't be focused on the way he kissed or the way he tasted, and yet that was what my brain was doing, creating this bonus reel of all the times he bit my lip, all the times he thrust into me, all the times he whispered his love, swore his fealty.

The giant grandfather clock in the living room continued to tell time, and yet the world felt like it had stopped, or maybe we were both moving in slow motion.

"Can we talk?" Junior rasped.

"D-do you think that's a good idea? Us talking?"

He sighed. "Probably not, but I think we should."

"Does this talk include words or is this just your way of getting into my pants?" I tried teasing.

He gripped the band of my sweatpants and gave a little tug. "It would be way too easy, Serena, and you know it."

"Bastard," I hissed.

"You're angry. Good."

"I'm always angry."

"Don't lie."

I lifted my head and stared him down through our reflections. "What do you want to talk about?"

"Tank. He likes you."

I froze. "What?"

"He watches you," he continued. "Like a hawk."

My lips trembled while my heart raced. "So, you wanted to talk to me about Tank?"

He didn't answer just shrugged and continued to touch me like he had a right to. "If he knows anything, he'll crack. I think you should give him more attention and see what happens."

If a heart could break multiple times, mine just had, I swear I felt it crash to the ground, I saw myself fall to my knees in a bloodied frantic mess as I hurried to put the pieces back together before he noticed. But it was Junior. He didn't have to see; he felt it in the way I tensed; he tasted it in the air around us. He knew he'd just hurt me, and I'd shown him yet again that while I was searching for all the vulnerable pieces of my heart—he still owned the ones that mattered.

And I would hate him forever for it.

"So..." I let out a heavy sigh. "You want me to give him more attention, flirt with him, learn his secrets, and what if he's just some normal guy going to college?"

Junior's head rested against the back of mine. "Then, at least we know."

"Right." I was going to murder him in his sleep—Junior, not Tank. "And that's more important than anything, isn't it?"

He stilled his movements. "Keeping the Family safe—keeping you safe is the most important thing right now, Serena, you know that."

"I'll do it." I found my voice.

"Good." I could feel him tensing behind me.

"Great," I added and then tried to walk away only to have Junior grab me by the arm and drag me toward the pantry.

He didn't even flick on the light as he pushed me against the shelves and molded his mouth to mine, invading with his tongue, pillaging more like it. His kiss was full of rage—full of pain as heat exploded between our mouths, he grabbed my hair in his fist and tugged, jerking me forward, his teeth grazing my skin as he placed a bite beneath my ear, only to work his way back up and hold me prisoner beneath his rock hard body. I reached for him, tried to respond, but he pulled back before I could. His eyes were wild as he hissed, "There, now you look primed."

I slapped him across the face then gripped my stinging hand. "I hate you."

"I know." He sighed.

I wiped a stray tear with my hand and got the hell out of the pantry, and I pretended to ignore his softly spoken words, "I hate me too," all the way back to the "normal" movie night.

And when Tank saw me walk in with my eyes wide, mouth swollen, he looked hungry.

For me, not the pizza.

I slowly walked over to him, sat down and put my feet in his lap, and winked. "This okay?"

"Yeah." He nodded slowly, his green eyes flashing with lust. "More than okay."

I smiled; it was fake.

And when Junior finally made it back to the movie room, he sat directly behind us while I flirted with the guy he had thrown in my direction.

Sacrifices, sacrifices.

At least Tank was good looking.

And at least he wouldn't break my heart.
Nobody but Junior Nicolasi held that power.
And by the guilty look in his eyes—he knew it.

CHAPTER *Sixteen*

Junior

All it took was one decision, one night, and we were back to what we considered normal. Back to classes, back to Serena hating me while we were in public, back to her at least talking to me in the privacy of her own home.

Then again, did it really count when all she did was ask me to pass the milk this morning after her mom and dad went out for breakfast, leaving us alone again?

Maybe this was why the bosses forbade us to date each other because when shit needed to get done, jealousy got in the way.

He slept over last night after the movie.

I heard him.

I heard them.

It wasn't yelling or shouting or even moaning—no, they were doing something so much worse—she'd gotten him to talk, to open up. They were bonding, and I hated every single laugh he got from her just like I hated every single time I imagined it was quiet because he was holding her or telling her that he'd fix everything that I'd broken so perfectly with my bare hands.

He didn't stay for breakfast, which was good since I would have slit his throat. I had to keep reminding myself that it had been my idea; he was attracted to her, and she could get information out of him.

Claire and Ash took on the job of Annie, though it was more of Claire just wanting normal. Serena got close to Tank.

And Breaker and I pretended to just be the best friends on the sides, the easy-going non-threatening people that could provide a good time.

Shit, I hated this life sometimes.

Getting people drunk and having a sleepover in order to gain intel was anything but normal.

"You were up late," Ash said once we all got out of our cars and met at our regular spot on campus.

Serena just batted her eyes. "A girl never kisses and tells."

I scowled, even though it was my idea, I didn't have to like it as I clenched my fists at my sides to keep from doing something dangerous like ramming them both into the nearest tree or person.

"Something you wanna say, Junior?" She grinned in my direction while I was greedily searching her neck for any hint of hickey so I could have a reason to end him and end this whole thing. Not that the bosses would listen to me anyway.

Shiiiiit.

"Nope." I smiled. "How was Tank? I heard some talking. You teaching him how to spell the big words now, or are you still sounding words out?"

Breaker choked on his laugh, and Claire punched him in the arm. "Be nice. He's smart, he just doesn't talk much, plus he's cute!"

"A man of few words, some may say more action." Serena shrugged. "Anyway, I didn't get any intel on them per se, but he did say that the college was really nice on the inside and offered to show me around."

I stared in disbelief. Did he even realize what he had all to himself? Why the hell was he even thinking about a public tour when he could just take her to the closest room and worship her like she deserved? Instead, I said, "He wants to give you a tour of the college? Could he be any more lame?"

"It's not really a bad idea," Izzy said, looking up from her computer, a rarity for Izzy, talking and looking away from her work. "I mean, we have a blueprint, but it could be good for Serena to look around, especially while other students are on campus."

"Agreed," Ash said. "Why don't you ask him if we can all come and then we can all go out to dinner afterward or something."

"Good idea." I jumped on the idea. I didn't want them alone. The plan had been for her to get in, get out, get it done, not to actually start dating the guy. "Text him and see if we can meet later this afternoon."

"Eager beaver," Serena muttered under her breath as she pulled out her phone. I looked over her shoulder and nearly died when I saw a heart emoji from him.

Little shit was going to be pissing out of his left eye if he touched her in any way she didn't like.

Then again, what if she did like it?

What if I'd just thrown her toward the one guy that could help her get over everything? Get over us?

My chest got tight.

It didn't matter.

Because we could never be together.

Right?

"Done." Serena looked up from her phone and grinned at us. "Meet back here at five, and he says he's bringing Annie too."

Ash's face fell. "She wears cardigans."

I frowned. "Bro, you're wearing a uniform. How is that different?"

He glared at me, his teeth clenching. "By. Choice."

Breaker and I shared a look of amusement as I put my hand on Ash's shoulder. "Do you need backup? Or are you gonna make it?"

Ash shrugged me away while Claire looked on like she was thinking way too hard. "She's a nerd, there I said it, I'm not sorry." He held up his hands.

Claire wrapped an arm around Ash's waist. "Just because she likes to talk about scientific things doesn't make her a nerd. She just has interests outside of guns. Shocking, I know."

Ash pulled Claire to his chest. "Thank God you actually like talking about guns, huh?"

Claire gulped and then nodded as she flashed him a smile. "I do know how to take them apart and put them back together again, thanks to you."

He winked.

My eyes narrowed as I looked at them both. They seemed perfect, and yet something was off.

Serena jerked her head toward me, and I caught it—she wanted to talk. *Well, here goes nothing.*

"Gotta run to class, guys." I waved them off. "Serena, walk with me?"

"Yeah." We fell into step together.

She waited until we were far enough away from the group to speak. "What the hell was that?"

"I have no clue." I shook my head. "She's been off. Everyone sees it, but it's not just that. It's this sudden need to be normal; it's the fact that she looked excited to talk about science and not guns, which—whatever. It's fine, but Ash doesn't seem to know—"

"He doesn't see it." Serena stopped walking and put her hands on her hips. "He's too in love with her to see it, damn it." She did a small circle. "Call Sergio, have him put a tracker on Claire."

I grabbed Serena's arm. "Why the hell would we ask him to do that?"

"Because…" Serena gulped and met my gaze. "She's scared; there's something wrong. I can tell."

"How do you know it's fear?" I asked.

"Fear recognizes fear," she said softly. "And I see that reflection every damn day in the mirror." She pushed against my chest and said through clenched teeth, "Put a tracker on her now."

"Serena—"

"No." She jabbed a finger at me. "You don't get to be my friend at school, all right? You can ask me about it when we're home, but I probably won't tell you because I refuse to let someone in who only does damage."

I hung my head. "It's in my blood; my blood is damaged."

"No." She swallowed and looked away. "It's not your blood that's damaged."

"If not my blood, then what?" I snorted out a laugh of disbelief; I wanted to tell her then, tell her how bad my line was, tell her I was lucky I didn't get killed for even looking in her direction, let alone taking what wasn't mine to take.

"Your heart," she finally said.

I stared at her for a minute then whispered, "I guess you would know, wouldn't you? Since you still have it."

I walked away before I did do more damage.

And I walked away before I had a chance to pull her into my arms and ruin everything.

Because that's what a De Lange did. They ruined lives. And I felt my internal clock as if I was a bomb ready to go off.

I would destroy her.

And I knew, destroying her, would annihilate what good was left of me.

So I walked away.

Right then and there, I swore a personal oath that it would take an act of God for me to ever reach for her again.

CHAPTER
Seventeen

Serena

I met Junior about fifteen minutes before we were supposed to be meeting up with everyone to go over to the other campus.

We shared a look as a black Escalade pulled up into the large semi-circle lot in front of the Business Building.

It was more private than pulling up in front of Registration or any of the dorms. None of the bosses could escape without somehow ending up on someone's Instagram or Snapchat or God forbid—TMZ.

"How much are we telling them?" I murmured under my breath.

"Enough." Junior crossed his arms and managed to look hot and casual all at once, while my breathing was a bit uneven because for us to ask this wasn't just dangerous, it put a giant target on Claire's back. But I had a feeling, and my dad taught me that there was a reason we had gut instincts, and mine said something was very, very off with her.

Sergio opened the passenger door and slowly stepped out of the SUV. His black aviators and strong jaw made him look like Henry Cavill's brother. His long hair was pulled into a man bun. He unbuttoned his gray suit jacket revealing a chest tattoo that said *Two Twirls* with the letter *A* under a sunset. His story was legendary among all of us, like a fairy tale in the middle of a war. I gulped when I thought of his other tattoos, the tally marks that he kept whenever he took a soul from this earth. We'd stopped counting a few years ago because it was getting a bit ridiculous.

He was a bit too good at what he did.

I sucked in a sharp breath when another boss stepped out of the back of the car. Andrei Petrov-Sinacore. Shit.

"Why's Andrei with him?" I asked through clenched teeth.

"Fuck." Junior's stance didn't budge. "Probably because Sergio doesn't want the other bosses to know, and Andrei's technically related to Claire since she's Nikolai's niece."

Nikolai, as in The Doctor. The Russian mafia used him because he was the best, but he worked both sides just like Andrei, they'd single-handedly taken over the Russian mafia and merged it with the Italians. It was the strangest cease-fire the world had ever seen, and I knew if Andrei was with Sergio, they were taking this very seriously.

Andrei's blue eyes snapped to attention; his neck tattoos seemed to swirl beneath his three-piece suit as his nose ring glinted in the sun. He was in his late thirties and looked like a freaking supermodel. It was stupidly annoying how easy it was for him to break people.

It felt like they were walking in slow motion, but when they finally stopped in front of us, it all happened too fast.

"Here," Sergio held up a small tracking device that looked like one of those batteries they warn kids not to swallow when they're little. It was silver.

Junior took it in his right hand. "I appreciate you keeping this quiet."

"Tell me," Andrei spoke up. "Is there a solid reason you're suspicious, or are we solely basing this off of Serena having a tummy ache?"

I glared. "Hilarious."

"I wasn't being funny," he said, the smooth Russian tilt of his voice thickening ever so slightly. "I'm serious Serena. This is—" He shook his head. "Chase can't know."

Junior snorted out a laugh. "Gee, thanks for the warning, don't tell the scary U.S. senator who likes to have people murdered for sport. Good pep talk!"

Sergio and Andrei both gave us blinding grins.

Sergio angled his head and gave an assessing look. "What do you know that we don't?"

"A lot?" I offered with heavy sarcasm.

"Was I ever this young?" Sergio wondered out loud.

"No." Andrei snorted. "You've always been old as shit."

"Thanks," Sergio snapped.

"You're welcome." Andrei smiled.

"I'll ask again. Is there something we need to know?" Sergio crossed his arms.

I chewed my lower lip and shared a look with Junior.

He gave me a slight nod.

"She seems like she wants out," I said quietly. "But it's not just that. She's distancing herself at a time when we need to be together. Who am I kidding? Isolation is how you get dead."

"Isolation is how our enemies destroy us," Andrei agreed. "Keep the tracker in her purse, you know the drill, put it inside her favorite lip gloss, whatever you need to do. And we'll track her movements."

"You two?" Junior laughed. "You two are working together on this?"

Sergio glared. "Not by choice, but since she's Nikolai's niece..."

"Right, Russian jurisdiction and all that..." Junior nodded.

"You both should go." Andrei jerked his head at us. "Classes are starting to get out, and the last thing we need is for Sergio to get chased again."

I laughed at Sergio's horrified expression. "Admit it, you're more terrified of college girls than you are of dying."

His shudder was all we needed.

Andrei winked at me, and then they were gone. Power in each movement, in each step as they went back to the car and left the same way they came.

I let out a rough exhale. "Damn, he's intimidating."

"Both of them are." Junior elbowed me playfully. "It's their job to be scary, but we know the truth."

"Oh yeah, and what's that?" We started walking toward our meeting spot.

"That Andrei wears Christmas sweaters because he doesn't have the heart to tell his wife he hates them, and Sergio's favorite game to play was Operation when we were little. Oh, and he promised you a pony when you were ten and then actually got you one."

I smirked. "Jealous?"

"No, because for my birthday he got me a stripper."

I stumbled.

He caught my elbow and laughed. "Kidding."

I jerked away. "There was a rock."

"Uh-huh." Junior smirked. "It's okay to be jealous, hey I've got a few ones, do a little private dance for me, and I'll shove them down your skirt."

"And I've got a knife strapped to my thigh. Shove anything close to my ass, and I'm going to use it on your dick."

He shrugged. "Might be worth it to get to spar with you."

I almost stopped walking. "You mean you enjoy getting your ass kicked?"

"I enjoy..." He drew out the word and shoved his hands into his pockets. "...fighting you because at least it means we're doing something productive with our hate; at least when we fight, I can make you sweat in an entirely different way, make you moan with pain instead of pleasure knowing they come hand in hand, make you scream my name in hatred reminding me what it was like when you screamed it in ecstasy. So yeah, I like sparring with you."

My eyes widened as I gave him a hard shove. "You sick pervert, I had no idea fighting was your foreplay."

He stopped walking and jerked his chin up at me. "Liar."

My cheeks heated. "I'm serious!"

"Cut the shit, Serena."

"You think you know me so well?"

"I think if I put my mouth between your thighs, you'd be embarrassed with how ready you are for me."

I gulped as my legs trembled. "Yeah, right."

"Another lie."

"Junior—"

"Because we both know that it's your foreplay too. In fact, I bet you're itching to grab that knife and aim for my heart. Too bad we're out of time." He was looking over my head; everyone was walking in our direction. I looked back at him only to see him an inch away from my face. "Don't worry, when we get home, I'll let you hit me."

I glared and then smiled. "Promise?"

He barked out a laugh. "Damn, even your hatred makes me hard."

I fluttered my eyelashes, then grazed the front of his pants and whispered, "I know."

"Keep doing that, and I'm going to pin you to the nearest tree, and you're supposed to be playing nice with Tank, remember?" His voice lowered. "Just remember that nobody will ever get you the way I do."

"You sure about that?" My voice wobbled.

"You need it as much as I do." His eyes flashed. "You're sick with it."

He wasn't wrong. I hated it when he knew my hot buttons. Already I felt my body burning for his, itching to both punch him, then grab him by the back of the head and force our mouths together while we grind on each other's bodies until we both find release without even taking our clothes off.

"Tonight," I said in a challenge. "I'll spar with you tonight."

His eyes widened in surprise, and then his entire face seemed to go dark. "Don't make promises you can't keep."

"Midnight," I whispered. "Prepare to get your ass kicked."

"I'll be out for blood," Junior promised.

"The only blood you'll be seeing is yours."

"We'll see," he grumbled, and then everyone was

surrounding us, chatting about classes, and pretending to be so normal my head hurt.

"You guys ready?" Claire rocked back on her feet like she was getting ready to sprint to the other college and sing at the top of her lungs. Yeah, something was definitely not right.

"Let's hit it." Junior turned, but not before I saw him palm the front of his pants like he needed to remind himself that walking with an erection could cause physical harm to his body if he tripped.

I suppressed a snicker and earned a sharp elbow in my side, compliments of Junior as we walked across campus and toward the new college, ready to meet our normal friends and the guy I was supposed to crack.

With the sick and twisted relationship of me and Junior hanging between us like an unbreakable thread.

Great.]

CHAPTER
Eighteen

Junior

Watching the girl whom you both loved and hated flirting with someone who could be a sworn enemy while fighting a semi for two hours was sweet hell.

Tank talked how he walked.

Fucking slow.

If we went any slower, we'd be crawling on our hands and knees; he wanted Serena to see everything.

New student center? Check.

New freshman dorms? Check.

Mess hall? Check.

Finally, we ended up at his dorm, which went over like nails on a chalkboard as he swiped his key card over the slot and explained that they had upped their security during the remodel.

"Wonder why," Breaker said under his breath as we all slipped into the main part of the dorm. It was senior housing, which at least let us know how old Tank was since he hadn't exactly told us.

He wrapped an arm around Serena and guided her toward the elevator. She leaned into him and stretched her lips in a smile that I knew wasn't real, but you'd think she just gave him a handjob with how pumped he looked.

I ground my teeth.

"Down boy," Ash said under his breath. "This was your plan, remember?"

"She never listens to me," I grumbled.

"She likes to provoke you. Do you really think she'd say no to a chance to get under your skin? Again?" Ash chuckled and slapped me on the back. "Look, this is good; we get insider information, and we don't have to kill anyone."

"Right, because we already did that, in front of them."

On my right, Breaker winced. "Technically, Serena did that."

"Yes, because blaming someone other than yourself raises that person from the dead," I said dryly as we all got into the elevator.

Claire and Annie were huddled together, staring at Annie's cell phone. When I looked over their shoulders, my eyes narrowed.

They were looking at a pair of Wyn boots.

Seriously? That's what had them as thick as thieves? A pair of boots that any one of us could get for free and just toss at her?

Ash's dad owned Wyn, amongst other things.

I elbowed him and jerked my head down.

He glanced over and smiled wide. "You like the new Wyns?"

Annie paled like he'd just asked if he could lick her boobs. "Um, y-yeah, I mean I could never afford boots like that but—"

"Sure, you could," Claire piped up. "Ash can get you some."

Ash gritted his teeth and then forced a terrifying smile toward Annie that had her taking a step toward me, but the minute we touched, she jumped a foot.

Yeah, if she were a De Lange child, I'd put ketchup on Ash's toe and lick it. The girl was terrified of everything.

"Th-that's okay. I could never pay you back."

Claire made a noise. "You don't need to. His dad owns the company."

"Surprise," Ash said dryly.

Breaker elbowed him again and cleared his throat.

Ash shot Breaker the barest hint of irritated glance then turned his attention back to Annie. "What size are you?"

Annie's eyes went wide as the elevator opened to the top floor. "I'm a seven."

"And you like the black over the knee stripper ones?" He just had to say it like that.

I held my breath while Annie flinched and then hid her phone back in her purse. "Well, yeah I mean my adoptive mom might freak out but—"

"I like it," Ash said in a voice that was a bit gruff around the edges. What the ever-loving hell was going on with those two? "I mean…" He shook his head. "A little rebellion is good. Just promise you won't wear them with a damn cardigan."

Claire looked between them and beamed. "She won't, right, Annie?"

"Right." Annie bit down on her lower lip her big eyes stared through Ash for a few minutes before she whispered. "Thank you for being so nice."

I'm pretty sure Ash just had a stroke at nineteen.

Nobody called him nice.

He was a cold-blooded killer.

And yet she just gave him a meaningful compliment that I know he felt all the way into his icy soul.

"I'm not nice," he said in a clipped voice before he followed Tank out into the hall.

The building was new; everything was new.

All the doors had little whiteboards on them that you could write on; it seemed like a typical college dorm.

But as we walked down the hall, I noticed that doors slowly started to open as if word had gotten around that we were on the floor.

My phone pinged.

And sure enough, I'd been tagged on Twitter.

Serena had been tagged on Instagram.

We were suddenly everywhere from people who had taken pictures of us, so it was a lot like walking in slow motion as people jerked open their doors and blatantly stared.

It seemed oddly familiar, at least the students did.

And that's when I realized.

Every last one of them looked like they could be my cousin.

Serena tensed as Tank stopped in front of his door.

She looked over her shoulder, slowly reaching for the knife in her thigh at the same time I grabbed my gun and held it casually at my side.

Breaker did the same.

Followed by Ash.

They needed to see we were armed even if we were outnumbered five to fifteen.

One of the girls squeaked and closed the door.

It was clearly a co-ed dorm. Great.

A guy who looked about my age stepped out from his room and crossed his arms, hatred dripping in his gaze. He locked eyes with me, and I suddenly felt shame.

The hell?

He shook his head slowly, then mouthed the word. "Traitor."

I gripped my gun so tight I nearly pulled the trigger.

With a curse, I stomped over to him and slammed him against the wall.

People started screaming around us. "What the hell did you say?"

"You know!" he roared, his eyes blazing. "You're a traitor to your own blood!" He spat on the floor between us.

I barked out a laugh. "I have no idea what you're talking about." I slowly let him go. "But I'd tread carefully, I'm the one with the gun, and it wouldn't be wise to fuck with mafia royalty now would it?"

"I'm already dead anyway," he said in a calm voice. "What difference does it make if you kill me now or later?"

I sighed. "I'm not here to kill you."

"Then why the hell are you here?" He gritted his teeth. Damn, he looked like family. It was hard to even glance at him.

Harder than to look at myself in the mirror, even though he'd never know that reality I faced every day.

If I could bleed myself dry, I would.

"We're hanging out," Ash said in a smooth voice behind me as he put a hand on my shoulder. "You'll have to forgive Junior. He doesn't like being taunted."

I released the prick and stepped back.

The guy nodded his head toward Ash. "You're Senator Abandonato's son?"

"I am." Ash crossed his arms. "Why? You wanna pick a fight with me too?"

"No." He gulped. "You've done nothing to offend me."

"Yet." Breaker smirked.

"And you…" He looked at Breaker. "…the Capo's oldest?"

"And brightest." Breaker did a little bow. "Then again, you already knew that."

"Nixon's." He looked at Serena and then at Claire. "But you, I don't know."

"Yeah, I wouldn't look at her if you want to live," I snarled in a harsh voice. "She's under the protection of the Petrov-Sinacore Family."

He paled a bit and backed up.

Of course, the Russian name did it.

"And you?" I just had to ask. "What's your name?"

He said nothing.

"That's what I thought." I slapped him on the shoulder and then turned my back on him.

The minute I was facing away from the guy, he muttered under his breath, "De Lange."

I turned to lunge, but Ash held me back. "Not here, not now, man."

I jerked away from him. "We're leaving. Sorry Tank, another time, let's go, Serena."

Tank's face fell. "Sorry guys, I didn't know it would be a big deal."

My laugh was ugly. "A big deal? You do realize that you just gave that guy a death sentence, right? All because you wanted Serena to see your bed."

The guy was already going back into his room. I shared a look with him and sighed. "Pack your shit."

His eyes narrowed. "What?"

"I said…" I clenched my teeth. "Pack your shit."

"Hell no!" He shook his head. "I'm not packing my shit, so you can shoot me behind the building!"

I frowned and then burst out laughing. "That's hilarious. Ash, when was the last time we just up and shot someone on a campus?"

"That would be, never." Ash grinned. He leveled a gaze on the guy. "But I'd do what he says."

"I'm dead if I do, dead if I don't."

Breaker sighed. "We're not killing you."

"Lies!" he spat.

"Hell, who raised you to be so resentful of the Five Families? You should be on your knees, thanking me for this kindness." I snapped. "Grab your shit and come with us."

"Where are you going to take me?"

I glanced around the scared faces and sighed. "Where you belong."

"In the ground?"

"Eagle Elite University," I said softly.

A hush fell over the crowd.

And a few of them met my gaze like maybe they could trust me, maybe they could trust us to keep our word.

And keep our word we would.

Because as much as the De Langes had a death sentence over their heads, I realized one thing in that moment: it wasn't fair that I was alive just because I got a new name when they were stuck with theirs.

"Any of you want to follow; you have ten minutes." I leaned against the wall as several people ran back into their rooms.

"What the hell are you doing?" Ash hissed.

"What our parents should have done." I sighed. "Keep your enemies closer and all that…"

Serena and I shared a look, she nodded her head once, like she approved of me not killing everyone and for the first time in my twenty-one years, I felt like the made man I was. I felt like I was the new generation of the mafia, and I felt like my dad would be proud of my choice to keep the battle on our own turf.

"If they cross us—" Breaker looked around as people started packing up duffel bags.

"They won't," I said. "Because they know what happens if they do."

"And what? We just waltz back over to Eagle Elite and let them know they have fifteen more students?"

"Of course." I smirked. "Because we run the fucking world, and it's about time everyone knows it, the bosses included."

Within minutes everyone was packed; twelve De Langes came, including the random guy who had tried to pick a stupid ass fight he would have lost.

They were silent, untrusting as we walked them from their campus through the black iron rod gates of Eagle Elite, and you'd think we'd just invited the devil onto campus with the way students stared.

I know what they saw, more mafia.

Except we had no clue if these guys even knew how to fight. For all we knew, they were all adopted, their parents dead.

I was the only connection they had.

Shit.

I stopped in front of the Senior dorm and slid my card against the slot. The dorm mother came running to do my bidding, but she was in her thirties and knew the drill, thank God.

"Got some fresh meat for you. Get them settled, wave all registration fees, and have them fill out their schedules." I turned to the grumpy guy. "Name?"

"Lance." He gulped. His eyes clouded with uncertainty.

"Lance here..." I slapped him on his back. "Is going to be your liaison with the rest of the group. Whatever he says goes unless it's illegal or gets people killed." I was really giving them a lot of power. "And Lance?"

"Yes." He gulped.

"Betray me, and I slit your throat while your friends watch, and then one by one they'll have the same fate, do you understand me?"

"Y-yes."

"Good." I sighed. "I'm placing men outside the building for your protection not to keep you in, but to keep others out, Tank's gonna stay and contact me if you need anything, we'll be in touch."

With that, I left.

It wasn't lost on me that Serena walked by my side like my queen with Ash and a very silent Claire behind us. Breaker was in his spot in the back as always.

When we got to the car, Izzy was on her computer, typing away, while Maksim was in the back on his phone. "Am I seriously finding student ID's for all of them right now?"

"Yes?" I grinned.

She rolled her eyes. "All right, I'll just be up all night,

nothing new. Glad none of you died, now can someone please take me home?"

"I got you." Maksim interrupted with a wink.

She flushed a bit and then whispered, "Okay."

When they were gone, I shared a look with Ash. "Anything going on there?"

"Well, if there is one or both of them will die, so let's hope not because I'm really attached to my sister, and if Maksim touches her wrong or even breathes wrong, I'm cutting his dick off."

"Graphic," Claire muttered next to him.

"What?" Ash shrugged. "She's too young."

"She's your twin dipshit." This from Breaker.

Age talk just reminded me how young Serena and I had been. So I just mumbled, "Yeah," then got into my car.

By the time I got to Serena's house, I was wired, adrenaline pulsing through me, because in a few hours, I was going to get to work off this aggression, and I hoped to God she was ready for me.

Because I sure as hell was ready for her.

CHAPTER
Nineteen

Serena

I put on a pair of black spandex pants and a hot pink sports bra, then threw a loose white tank on and pulled my hair back into a tight braid. The last thing I needed was for him to grab my hair while we were sparring.

My blood buzzed beneath my skin as I made my way down to the gym.

My parents were both sleeping; I checked about a billion times and prayed that my dad wouldn't hear the soft click of the basement door as I headed down to meet Junior.

Darkness wrapped itself around me as I made my way down the stairs and into the main gym where Junior was already wrapping up.

Of course he was early.

And it looked like we weren't using gloves, fantastic. He truly wanted to draw blood.

Funny thing about that, I kind of wanted to kiss him for

what he did today, I wanted to tell him I thought it was ballsy, it could blow up in his face, but the fact that he took that chance for them was huge.

Though I really would not want to be him when all the bosses found out in a few hours.

If he wanted to bleed, all he had to do was wait until Phoenix learned his son not only failed to kill any De Lange survivors, but he'd invited them to live with us.

I almost laughed at that.

He was either very arrogant, stupid or had a soft spot that he refused to let anyone see—anyone but me because I'd known it was there all along. Music pumped from the sound system; I knew my dad wouldn't hear because the dungeon, as we liked to call it, was soundproof—for very obvious reasons.

"You're late." He didn't look up, which gave me adequate time to drink him in. He was wearing low-slung black Nike sweats and no shirt. His golden tanned, muscled skin was in full view. A few tattoos swirled down his right arm, while the larger one, the Nicolasi crest, was drawn in the middle of his chest like the rest of the eldest kids.

I got mine on my back since my dad about had a heart attack when I told him I was going to have to lay topless in order to get it done.

I hadn't meant it, but it was worth it to see his face. He pulled his gun on the tattoo artist. It was the best day.

"You gonna stare at me all day or get your ass up here and fight?" Junior bounced on his feet and gave me a glare that meant he really needed to get some aggression out.

"Fight." I peeled my tank top off, then grabbed the tape he'd tossed and started wrapping my knuckles and wrists. I was quick, tearing the white tape with my teeth when I was done.

My fingers still had hairline fractures, so I'd have to attempt not to make them worse. "Ready."

He eyed me up and down. "I almost feel guilty that you're fighting me in a pink sports bra, you know blood's a bitch to get out, right?"

I smiled and bowed with my fist pressed into my palm. "I doubt I'll even get a splatter."

He returned my bow. "Let's just say I'm apologizing in advance, and if I knock out a tooth, don't go to Nixon, all right? He'll have my balls even if it's a fair fight."

I smirked and bounced on my toes. "Cute, that you think you still have balls."

He growled low in his throat. God, he was devastating when he looked at me like that. Those aqua eyes might as well hold me in a damn trance the way they locked on me with the precision of a knife.

He moved first.

I ducked and landed my roundhouse near his right ear. He batted my leg out of the way and nearly caught my ankle as I stumbled back. "That all you got, princess?"

I bared my teeth and charged, this time aiming for a kick to his shin while throwing a right hook.

My right hook didn't hit, but my shin kick did. He stumbled a bit and then threw a right punch, then an elbow. His elbow landed right on my chin, splitting it wide open. Well, *that* was gonna need stitches.

"Whoops." He winked.

I went for his feet again in a double leg takedown and managed to get him to stumble. Then I wrapped myself around him, taking him to the ground in an attempt to get a reversal.

He rolled me to my back and was able to get an elbow into my side before jumping to his feet and muttering, *"Zuffa."*

Shit, an Italian term for fighting with no rules. I crooked my fingers at him and whispered, "Bring it."

"Hey, Serena, you got a bit of blood, right here." He motioned to his chin.

I landed a blow to his right cheek only to get back-handed with his hand. I stumbled and ducked as he tried to rush me. I knew that maneuver; he wanted to throw me to my back or side and try to get a rear naked choke, his favorite. We all had them, just like we all had weaknesses.

I moved away and landed another blow to his nose. But it was almost like he let me. I frowned as his massive chest heaved, then his eyes flashed as he ran at me, going low, knocking my legs out from under me and flipping me onto my back with a huge thud.

He straddled me, hooking his legs around me as he braced me against the ground, our faces inches away. "Tap out."

"No." I struggled beneath him.

"Tap the fuck out before you get hurt, princess."

I knocked my head against his, making him lose his tight grip and then used my body weight to get him onto his stomach, I tried to get my arm beneath his chin, but he was already pulling me away like I weighed nothing at all when I knew I trained hard to be able to play with the big boys.

I cursed when he threw me onto my back a second time; the wind knocked out of me as I gasped for air and still refused to tap my fingers.

His fist came down next, but it was a soft hit, I knew it, he knew it, which just pissed me off. "You used to hit harder."

"Son of a bitch, Serena, seriously." Blood oozed from his right eyebrow. Fingers crossed, I broke his nose—again.

Both of us were panting as he pinned my arms above my head. I squirmed beneath him, trying to flip him with my legs, digging my heels in but meeting only muscle.

He let out a strangled groan when I thrust my hips up again in an attempt to gain some separation so I could get my hands between us.

He shuddered. "Stop playing dirty."

"I never promised to play fair." I shot him a flirty smile, and then I thrust my hips up against his already growing erection. He would typically pull away, it was my secret move, almost like he was afraid I was going to break his dick in half, except this time, he pinned me harder against the mat.

Panic seized my chest. He was supposed to pull away, not push me harder, or grow harder for that matter.

His eyes searched mine as blood dripped from his face onto my chest. "I can do this all day, princess."

"Me." I bucked my hips. "Too."

He muffled a series of curses but held steady. He was so clearly not wearing a cup.

I squirmed beneath him. "Someone's feeling brave."

"Someone didn't think you'd take a junk shot."

"And I didn't."

"What the hell do you call this then?" He gritted his teeth. He was rock hard against my stomach, and then he pulled back just enough to press himself exactly where he wanted to go. "Fine, I'll play."

"Shit," I muttered as he started to thrust against my spandex, between my thighs, where I was growing hotter and hotter.

I couldn't tell if it was my sweat, his, or something else as he continued his slow, achingly hard thrusts between my thighs.

Eyes wild, he clenched his teeth. The last time we were like this was before he took my virginity, we'd been going at it like the horny teens we were, using our clothes as a flimsy sort of protection that was more annoying than helpful.

It brought me back.

I arched to meet his next thrust and must have lost my damn mind because this time he met me halfway, a groan of satisfaction erupted from his throat as he hurried his movements. I was stuck beneath him, like his own personal sex toy, I couldn't move my hands, but I could move my body, and the torture was so severe I ended up spreading my legs wider, inviting him more.

"Fuck, Serena." He was hot steel pounding into my core like we had no choice but to get off. I licked my lips as he hurried his hips forward surging so hard against me that the pleasure almost equaled the pain, he moved a leg between mine, and I hooked my right foot around his ass, bringing him closer.

I was losing my mind.

We both were.

We hated each other.

Nothing good would come of this.

Our dads could murder us.

But all I kept thinking about was the savage look in Junior's eyes and the way his hips rocked against me. "I'm close."

"Me too." I squeezed my eyes shut and felt a slight tap to my face as he shook his head.

"Open, always open, on me," he commanded.

I bit down on my lip, and then that same hand moved lower as he rubbed hard between my thighs. It was too intense; between his palm and his dick, I couldn't take it anymore and fell apart against my enemy.

Somehow fully clothed.

He pulled away, then jerked himself out of his pants. I watched his hand move, up and down just once before he spilled on top of my stomach.

I would be insulted if I wasn't so turned on.

And angry.

And confused.

So, I just lay there while he stumbled back and sat on his ass and hung his head in his hands.

We were like addicts, coming back for more, no matter how many times we knew the risk, no matter how many times we broke each other, it was something we always came back to, wasn't it?

I sighed and slowly got up on my elbows. "I won."

His head jerked up. "The hell you did!"

"We're both bleeding, but—" I smirked. "—I did go first..."

He burst out laughing and laid back down against the mat. "You're welcome."

I smacked him in the leg and crawled over to the edge of the ring, grabbing my shirt and wiping my stomach off.

A hollowness spread in my chest when I realized what this meant; it meant we were back to not being friends. The line had been crossed, which meant we would retreat like we always did when we played with fire.

I hung my head.

The music suddenly stopped as my dad walked through

the door in nothing but pajama bottoms and a scowl. "Are you sparring at midnight?"

"Well, it's twelve-thirty now, sir," Junior said from his spot on the mat, he had moved to a sitting position for obvious reasons.

My dad just rolled his eyes. "Don't kill each other."

"No promises!" I laughed, even though my entire body was in shock. Had we been going at it any longer, my dad would have seen it, would have seen what we did, would have known.

I almost puked when dad smiled at me and then went back upstairs.

With wooden legs, I jumped down from the ring and started peeling my tape off.

Junior did the same.

I was waiting for the words.

This can't happen again.

Or *this was a mistake.*

Or *I still hate you for as long as we both shall live.*

Instead, he said, "Tomorrow, midnight."

I turned over my shoulder. "You really think you can handle me two nights in a row?"

His eyes were molten as he rasped, "The question is, can you handle me?"

One eyebrow arched up. "Clearly I already did."

"That wasn't handling, that was cheating. Tomorrow, wear more clothes."

I stuck out my tongue. "You were shirtless; you should talk."

"I can see both of your hard nipples and have been able to for the last half hour, again, cheating."

"You're not a boob guy," I pointed out.

And then squealed when he gripped my ass with his hands in a way that could leave bruises. "Things change."

"Grab my ass again, and I'm knocking you out." I pulled away.

Funny, we both knew it was an empty threat as we cleaned up and went upstairs to our rooms.

And like before, when I went into the shower and heard the familiar *thunk* of his door shutting, I tossed him the body wash and ignored the tension between us.

And when we both went our separate ways, I did something I hadn't done since he broke my heart.

I left my door open.

And waited.

It was maybe five minutes before I saw him standing in the doorway, and then he was walking over to my bed, and I was pulling the covers back, and he was crawling in next to me.

A tear slid down my cheek as he pulled me against his chest, and like he knew I would be crying, a thumb wiped the tear away as he whispered, "For old times' sake, but Serena, this can't happen we can't—"

"I know," I snapped. "Just—sleep."

"I've never been able to sleep when you're in my arms, Serena."

"So, what did you do the whole time?"

He hesitated and then, "Wait for you to fall asleep and wish that I wasn't in love with my best friend…"

CHAPTER
Twenty

Junior

I woke up that next morning with my enemy in my arms. How could something so wrong... so forbidden... feel so right? The voices in my head were quiet, the anxious stir in my soul to fight, to bleed, to do something, was gone. All I had was perfection in my arms. I reached out and twirled a piece of her blond hair between my fingers.

With a moan, she turned to face me.

Both our eyes were open.

My chest heaved like I'd just gone for a two-mile sprint then jumped back into bed with her.

Our gazes collided, locked.

"Serena!" Nixon's voice was loud enough to scare me shitless as he knocked. "You up yet?"

I froze.

Serena gulped. "No, Dad, I'm not dressed, so no barging in."

He chuckled. "No repeats of when you were sixteen and pulled a gun on me?"

I shot her a questioning smirk only to have her smack me in the chest. I grabbed her hand when she did it and held on tight even though I promised her that this was it for us, that this couldn't happen again, already I was going back on that, willing to sell my soul just to touch her.

"What do you need, Daddy?" she asked, her eyes not leaving mine.

"The university called," he said after a few seconds. "And I'm sure you know why they called., Junior wasn't in his room, but I texted him. I'm calling a meeting right now, and I need you ready."

My heart thudded against my chest.

"'Kay," she finally said. "Give me ten minutes."

"Yup." Footsteps sounded as he walked away.

"Shit." I fell back against the mattress and pulled her on top of me in the process. She didn't protest, just straddled me as her hair fell in a soft curtain over her right shoulder. "He's either going to kill me or kill me."

Serena smirked and then dug her nails into my chest and scraped down until she got to my low-slung sweats. "Yup, pretty much."

"Bitch." I laughed. "You're not even going to lie to me, are you?"

"Nope." She hooked her fingers into my sweats and tugged them down.

I flinched. "What are you doing?"

She shrugged. "Just in case he shoots you in the dick, I'll at least have this to focus on whenever I'm alone in my room with nothing but two hands…"

I jerked as she grabbed me with her right hand, torn between telling her to stop or to hurry.

"Serena," I hissed as she bent over my cock. "We shouldn't—"

I lost all train of thought as her tongue slid over me. "You were saying?"

"Nothing." I gripped the sheets with my hands as she sucked me dry, her tongue swirling around my head like I was her favorite flavor. "So good, always so good with you, damn your mouth is hot…"

She pulled away. "Back to enemy number one after this, Junior, so you better enjoy it."

"Doesn't have to be like that." But even as I said it, I knew it was a lie, we had no choice, and we had too many sins between us to have anything like a healthy relationship and what would that even look like? One day we'd be fine, the next day we'd draw blood, the day after that we'd get caught and killed.

My hips jerked as she went back to work. Her lips tightened around my dick while she looked up through a hooded gaze. That look was all mine, just like that mouth. She softly grazed her teeth up my length, then earned a smack in the ass from me before I grabbed her head and forced her deeper. My balls tightened almost painfully as I thrust against her tongue.

I clenched my teeth and tried to shove her head away, but instead, she sucked harder. I saw stars as release hit me, and when she pulled away, she fucking grabbed the sheet and dabbed her swollen lips then said. "Breakfast of champions."

I groaned and moved to a sitting position. "Hate you for as long as we both shall live?"

She grabbed my hand and squeezed it. "Hate you for as long as we both shall live."

"Good." I dropped her hand then shoved her off the bed onto the floor, only to have her trip me when I tried to walk by.

I smiled the entire way to the guest room.

Well, if Nixon killed me, at least I would have one up on him.

Because minutes before my execution, I'd had his daughter's mouth on my cock, and nothing could take that away from me.

Even my own death.

It was a giant F U to one of the most powerful bosses in the known world, and part of me liked that I had something to hold over him, something that would make him see rage because what better way to destroy his sanity than for him to find out, before I took my last breath, that every single time he thought he was keeping his daughter safe during all our family dinners...

I was going down on her for dessert.

I eyed my gun on the nightstand and sighed. I was dressed in minutes, wearing my Eagle Elite uniform of black slacks, white button-down shirt, and black jacket with our insignia on it.

People thought it was weird that a university had uniforms. They didn't realize that it was like wearing a badge that said "property of the mafia." The uniform was how we protected the students.

I sighed; it sure as hell wasn't going to protect me now, was it?

I shoved my gun in the back of my trousers and went into the bathroom to brush my teeth and attempt to do something with my hair.

I stared at myself in the mirror; I looked like I just got off. My eyes looked like I'd just taken a hit of something. Serena's mouth.

I ran my hands through my golden-brown hair and called it good when Serena joined me and shoved me to the side with her hip.

"Could your skirt get any shorter?" I wondered out loud.

She had on thigh-high tights that made me want to bend her over the sink, spank her ass, then say something stupid like, *my office, detention, wait with thighs wide open.*

"Probably." Her mask was back in place, meaning she was wearing makeup, probably to cover up the split in her chin that I'd put there. I wondered if it made me a horrible person that I liked that she was wearing something on her face I had caused.

And not in the way that I got off on hitting her. I got off on the fact that she fucking hit me back.

Already I was having trouble controlling my arousal around her, and it wasn't helping that she was bending close to the mirror as she put on purple lipstick that by all means should look like she was dressing up for Halloween but instead showed me just how luscious those lips were, and how good they felt when they sucked me dry.

"Better stop staring." She finished and then rubbed her lips together and stared at me in the mirror. "The last thing you need is to confront my dad, point down, and go damn it even after I got the best blowjob of my life by your daughter, I still can't keep my shit together."

I sighed. "I hate you."

"I know." She winked.

I grinned and then sighed. "Let me take care of it."

"Your boner?"

Another sigh. "No Serena, I mean today with your dad, let me take care of it, this is on me."

Her gaze softened. "We all let it happen."

"I know, but this is on me, I just, I can't let my blood—" I clamped my lips shut.

She frowned. "Your blood what?"

"You know," I whispered.

She looked over her shoulder like there was a camera or something and then lowered her voice. "Don't."

It was the first time I saw fear in her eyes.

She was afraid of what would happen if I brought it up.

And I knew there was no choice but to bring it up.

"We should go." I ignored the pleading look in her eyes.

And when she shoved me in the back, I welcomed the pain of nearly falling into the closed door.

She wanted to pick a fight. Fighting made her feel better. I knew her too well.

"Junior!" She hissed my name, then grabbed my elbow and turned me around, her eyes pleading. "Promise me."

I sighed and then leaned over and kissed her on the forehead, then whispered, "No."

She cussed me out the entire way down the hall. Hell, I was surprised she didn't try restraining me and cutting off my blood circulation so I couldn't confess.

The bosses, all except the one that would protect me, my father, were all standing in the kitchen.

Intimidating, but in a way that made me so angry I wanted to fight, because how dare they ask us to fix something, how dare they ask and ask and ask and then get mad when we do what's best to protect the Family?

Rage filled my veins.

It pulsed in my ears as my blood roared to life.

And it must have shown because Nixon took a step back and then shared a look with the Capo.

Uncle Tex smirked. "Finally grow a hair on your tiny dick, or are you just gonna throw a tantrum?"

I didn't answer. I lunged and punched, landing one across his jaw.

He went sailing to the ground, probably because he didn't expect me to hit him. Immediately Nixon and Chase restrained me while Tex got back on his feet.

Blood spurted from Tex's lip, and then he threw his head back and laughed. "Ah shit, I wish your dad was here to see you now. Hey, anyone get a video of that?"

Seriously?

My chest heaved.

"No?" Tex asked the room and then approached me. We were both tall, but he still had more muscle than me despite the fact that I punished my body for hours on a daily basis in the gym. "Well that's unfortunate, maybe we should just FaceTime?"

Chase held me tight against him while Nixon's hands dug into my biceps muscle. Great, was he going to just rip the muscle from my body? Was that a thing?

Ash, Breaker, Izzy, and Claire were a few feet away, most likely waiting for me to say something.

And Serena.

She was behind me.

I could feel the shock in her system as nobody said anything.

"Speak." Tex shrugged and leaned against the kitchen

counter. "Because there better be a good reason that we just enrolled twelve suspected De Lange orphans into Eagle Elite."

I shrugged away from Chase and Nixon and stood my ground. "You guys did this, not us."

Tex's eyes widened as he shared a look with all the bosses. Andrei was in the corner watching me with amusement, and the rest of the bosses sat around the table like they were waiting for my execution. Dante Alfero was the only one who seemed tense like he wanted to be anywhere but here. Then again, he was young like Andrei, in his late thirties and was one of the guys that offered to burn down Eagle Elite when he went there.

If anyone understood why I did what I did, it would be Andrei and Dante, but they remained silent.

And my dad wasn't here, so I explained the best way I could by repeating myself. "You guys did this; you guys had the hit on the De Lange Family. I hate to break it to you, but as parents, you're full of shit. You teach us to honor blood, that blood's everything, and yet, you're asking me, a twenty-one-year-old college student to go around and murder innocent people just because you're afraid of what could happen if I don't."

"Can I kill him now?" Chase asked in a calm voice.

I rolled my eyes. "You know I'm right. The fact that they were next door scared everyone shitless, so you wanted them executed, but instead, I invited them into the only place where we can watch them. If they make any bad moves, I'll be the first to pull the trigger, but until then, I'm doing what you guys didn't. I'm doing what you've taught us since we could walk. I'm protecting my blood." A hush went over the room. "De Lange blood."

Tex squeezed his eyes shut, then opened them. "You realize that we cut the De Lange Family from the Cosa Nostra. They ceased to exist."

I smirked. "And yet they fucking do. He's married to one." I jerked my chin toward Chase on my right. "You guys make justifications if it's something you want, but when it comes to kids that grew up with no parents because this guy fucking killed them all?" Again, I pointed to Chase.

He flipped me off.

Whatever, I was used to it. For a senator, he looked anything but calm and reserved. Nope, he looked like he was seconds away from ripping my head from my body.

Fantastic. "We have the chance to start over, that's all I'm saying. Don't ask us to repeat your own shitty history. You asked us to step up as the new Elect at Eagle Elite, so let us fucking do our jobs and stop questioning us when it doesn't go the way you planned it. We're adults now. We're made men." I sighed. "And women. So trust us, and leave us the hell alone."

Tex was silent for a few minutes, and then he smirked. "You get that, Nixon?"

"I think Phoenix shed a tear." Nixon grinned.

I turned and saw that Nixon had his phone pointed at me and that my dad was watching me with so much pride; I wanted to collapse to the floor and puke.

"This—" My dad nodded his head. "—is why we've been so hard on you. And you're right. You're ready. Forgive us for—how did you put it? Making you pay for our shitty sins." He grinned. "And, son…"

"Yeah?" I croaked.

"I've never been more proud of you." He smiled—a

genuine smile, which was rare—and my mom blew me a kiss with tears in her eyes.

"So." Breaker cleared his throat. "Does this mean my dad doesn't get to kill you during breakfast?"

Tex sighed and then gave Breaker a little shove. "No killing in front of the bacon."

"Thank God because I've been sneaking pieces during that entire speech, so hungry." Breaker stole another piece only to get it smacked out of his hand by Tex.

I relaxed a bit, and then I realized that I couldn't relax.

Because this meant that I'd just stood up to the most powerful bosses in history without getting my head chopped off.

And on top of that, my dad said he'd been proud.

Which meant me and Serena would never happen, couldn't because I'd finally been given what I'd wanted my entire life.

Freedom and acceptance to do things my way.

And loving her would take that from me.

Nixon held up his phone to his ear. "You did well raising him, Phoenix, despite all odds…" He looked up at me. "Yeah, he's been great other than sparring with Serena at midnight and catching her chin." He barked out a laugh. "Yeah, well, she should have blocked him better."

Weird. Our life was so weird.

They hung up, and then Nixon put both of his hands on my shoulders and stared me down with his icy blue eyes. "You did good, son. Keep your enemies close, and you did just that while saving lives." I frowned as he reached into his pocket and pulled out a ring. "Each boss has an underboss in the organization, a second in command. Chase is mine, though he's horrible at it now that he golfs with the president—"

"He says hi, by the way." Chase laughed and moved away from us.

Nixon kept talking. "It's yours now." He placed the heavy ring in my hand, it had the Nicolasi crest, and I knew what it meant, why it felt so heavy—because it was.

Nixon Abandonato, dad to the girl I was in love with but had to hate, had just crowned me king.

CHAPTER
Twenty-One

Serena

Nothing crazy happened during classes. In fact, it seemed like the new De Lange kids were shyer than middle schoolers on their first day. When they did see us, they gave us a wide berth.

Tank had texted that he wanted to bring me coffee, and even though I wanted to tell him no because I knew I was leading him on, I said yes.

Which was how Junior found us an hour later, Tank asking me about what I wanted to do with my life and me fighting boredom as I lied about wanting to be a teacher. My life was already determined, and if Tank knew how ruthless I could be, he'd probably shit his pants.

"That's cool." Tank took a sip of his coffee. "I've kind of always wanted to go into law enforcement."

I choked on my next sip. "You're kidding, right?"

"No." His grin was the perfect mix of sexy and cute. Too

bad I liked lethal and off-limits. "It's just an interest; a family friend used to work for the FBI before he retired."

"Good thing we have the FBI on lockdown then," I muttered, semi-joking, but not really because we actually did.

They loved us because our crime was organized and it kept money in the United States so really, they had no complaints.

Tank smiled again and shook his head. "Yeah, good thing."

"Is this the part where you tell me you're actually an undercover agent who's thirty but just looks young?" I wondered out loud, causing him to laugh so hard we had people staring.

Junior made his way over.

And suddenly, Tank stopped laughing and tensed up like he was getting ready for a fight when Junior had been nothing but nice to him, treating him like a friend.

Weird.

"Hey guys," Junior took a seat on the picnic table across from us. "Serena, I'm headed home. I know you rode with Ash, but—"

"Ash had to do something for Chase," Tank piped up. "So, Annie and Claire took the car to go shopping or something. I think they mentioned a dress to match the boots."

I froze. "When did they leave?"

He frowned. "I don't know an hour or so ago?"

Panic hit me square in the chest. I wasn't even sure why something felt wrong; it just did. I mean Claire was with Annie of all people, it wasn't like Annie was going to suddenly pull a knife out of her cardigan.

I shot a look at Junior, who was already on his phone.

There are moments in life that take you by surprise. I'd like to think that I was the type of person that was so weathered down by what my family did that I didn't really shock easy.

But seeing the phone fall from Junior's hand, watching his face visibly pale as he fell to his knees and shouted was enough to traumatize me for life.

"Junior?" I shot to my feet. "Junior, talk to me, what's wrong? What happened?"

I would remember this moment the rest of my life, I knew it, I knew it in my blood, in the way he shook his head like he couldn't believe it.

We were mafia; nothing shocked us.

But I knew this would.

And I prayed it wasn't any of our parents; I prayed that something awful hadn't happened to them.

I grabbed Junior by the shoulders and shook him. "Junior, talk, now!"

He swallowed and looked up at me. "It's Claire."

"Claire?" I hated how relieved I felt. "What happened to Claire?"

"The brakes had been cut." He slowly stood and ran his hand through his hair. "It was a hit meant for Ash, but he let her borrow his car..." His eyes flashed with anger. "She's in the hospital—they don't think she's going to make it."

"No." I shook my head. "No, that's not true. She's strong; she wouldn't, she can't—"

Junior pulled me against his chest while I tried to process what he'd just said. Tank cursed behind us. "Was Annie with her?"

Junior let out a heavy sigh. "Yeah, she was in the passenger seat, Claire spun the car so that the impact hit the driver's side... she saved Annie's life."

We got in Tank's car after realizing that not only had someone tampered with Ash's brakes, but they had tampered with Junior's as well.

Claire getting in her accident, didn't just save Annie's life, but ours.

Tears filled my eyes as Tank drove his truck to Mercy West in downtown Chicago. Already there were reporters outside the ER along with enough men in suits to make the place look like it was ready to host a political campaign for Uncle Chase.

The minute we pulled up, Ax, one of Andrei's men, came over, grabbed Tank's keys, and said, "Get inside."

We didn't need to be told twice.

Breaker was sitting with Izzy and Violet while the bosses were all pacing the floor, most of them on the phone, most of them yelling—and then there was Ash, in the corner, sitting by himself, staring at his hands like they held her blood.

Junior and I made our way over to him at breakneck speed.

He didn't even look up; he just stared at his hands.

"Ash," I reached out to touch his shoulder, he flinched and jerked away.

Shit.

Junior sat down next to him. "How is she?"

Ash sighed and then looked up. His eyes were bloodshot like he'd been crying. Then again, he loved her; he'd loved her faithfully, had done anything he could to protect her. He knew she had Petrov blood in her, knew that she would need the protection of his name, and lucky for us, he fell for her even though it would eventually be revealed that he had been set up.

Not that he needed to know that detail, that Nikolai Blazik

had basically made it so that Ash was obsessed with Claire the minute he saw her at her high school graduation.

It was a secret my dad made me promise to take to my grave, the fact that Ash never really had a chance to choose who he loved.

It was chosen for him.

I never thought it would end up like this, though.

He took another breath and leaned back, pinching the bridge of his nose with his fingertips. "She's in a coma."

I breathed a sigh of hope. "Medically induced?"

He swallowed slowly and rasped out. "No."

I reached for Ash's hand and held on tight. "Is she in surgery?"

"It wouldn't matter." Ash's voice broke. "There's too much damage, even if she did wake up—they did everything they could. We're just waiting for Nikolai to get here."

I was almost afraid to ask. "Why are we waiting for Nikolai?"

His eyes met mine; I'd never seen so much pain in another human being in my life. "So he can say goodbye."

"But—" My eyes filled with tears, I wanted to yell at Ash, to lash out and tell him he had to fight for her! That he loved her, and that's what you did when you loved someone! You fucking fought!

I couldn't find my voice.

I couldn't breathe.

There had to be something someone could do. We were untouchable, right? The great Cosa Nostra?

I pushed my hand against my chest as a sharp pain sliced through me like I was getting chopped in half.

For once, Junior pulled me against him while I tried to

swallow the knot of emotion in my throat. Claire had been part of us.

And I'd put a tracker on her.

I'd doubted her.

And now I was never going to be able to tell her sorry.

Ever.

I clawed at Junior's shirt only to realize that I was trying to get skin, to touch his skin because if he was warm, breathing, I knew he was still there.

I knew we were still holding each other.

Because had Claire not gotten in that car, it could have been any one of us, it could have been Junior in that hospital bed.

It could have been me.

Pain, like I'd never known, slammed into me as I realized I would do anything, anything on this earth to keep Junior safe even if it meant keeping him safe from my love.

Because he was it for me.

I loved him so hard that it turned into hate so lethal I was sick with it. Because if I couldn't have his love, I wanted something equally as strong. His hate would be all I had.

But for the first time since our fight over a year ago.

I wanted to risk everything for more.

He held me tight against his chest.

I opened my eyes and stopped breathing when my dad eyed Junior and then me with curiosity—at least that's what I thought it was until I saw his clenched fists.

Why did he hate him so much when he trusted Phoenix with his life?

It made no sense.

For now, I ignored the questions and held Junior close; I

breathed in his cologne, and I pressed my face against his chest and told myself that I was already close enough to his body when my heart screamed more.

Time went by.

I wasn't sure how much. What I did know was that I felt like I was outside my body when a hush fell over the room, and Nikolai Blazik, made man, one of the most famous doctors in the world, entered the ER with tears in his eyes and walked toward us.

The crowded room shifted.

Every single suited-up man bowed his head while the bosses parted, giving him the respect he deserved, each making the sign of a cross over their chests.

Nikolai didn't stop until he was in front of a stoic Ash.

He went to his knees and grabbed Ash by the hands, then kissed each one and whispered, "Her blood is not on these hands."

Ash shook his head. "I should have been there."

"Had you been there, you'd be dead," Nikolai said in a harsh voice. "And the Abandonatos need more than one heir." He sighed. "Her parents just landed at the airport. They'll want to see her, but to make things easier on them, I came first."

Ash's eyes snapped to his. "What do you mean?"

Nikolai stood and then very strategically pulled a needle from the inside of his jacket and whispered. "A gift for her final moments. Follow me."

They went into the private room.

The door clicked silently behind them.

And we waited.

Ten minutes later, the door opened. And I saw Ash age in

front of my eyes. No longer was he the carefree college student who had an easy joke or an eye roll when things got too serious.

He was changed.

Altered in a way that I couldn't explain.

And then I heard Uncle Chase say something that nearly stopped my heart. "His heart may not survive this."

My dad nodded and said, "Are you saying that because yours never did?"

Chase squeezed his eyes shut and hung his head. "He's more Luc than he is me, and now her death, it will bring out all the bad parts I tried so hard to hide from him. My son... will become the monster."

"Annie," Tank whispered her name, gaining everyone's attention. Her face was bandaged, and she was holding her right arm in a sling. Bruises marred her cheeks as her eyes fell to the busy ER. "I'm so sorry." Tank pulled her into his arms, but she shook her head and moved away from him, her eyes landing on Ash.

Ash clenched his jaw as she approached, tears streaming down her face. "She said..." Her words were muffled by her own sobs. "She said 'tell him I loved him.'"

Tears streamed down my cheeks as Ash closed his eyes like he couldn't bear to look at her, and then they jerked open as he lifted his head and glared, fists clenched at his sides. He walked right up to his dad, grabbed the gun from his hand, and walked out of the ER.

"Where's he going?" I whispered.

Junior sighed and slowly pried me away from his body and sighed. "To kill them all."

"What do we do?" My chest ached as Junior straightened and pulled the gun from his pants, and turned off the safety.

"We do what we were born to do," he said with a hard edge to his voice. "We back him up."

"Okay." I nodded and shot a look to Breaker, who was already joining us, and side by side, we walked by the bosses, our eyes locked straight ahead.

Our blood had been spilled.

Now, we would spill theirs.

I stopped in front of Tank and held the gun to his head. "Was this you?"

He paled. "No."

"Do you know who?"

He was silent and then released a breath. "Yes."

"Give me one good reason not to shoot you." I gnashed my teeth and waited while the men around me kept silent.

He stared me down and then said, "Because I'm an FBI plant."

I almost burst out laughing at the ridiculousness of it. Maybe I was going crazy. I called over my shoulder. "Is it true?"

Chase answered first. "Yes. We knew yesterday."

"Cool." I pulled my gun away from his temple and shoved him toward the door. "You're driving."

He sighed and muttered. "Figured."

CHAPTER
Twenty-Two

Junior

We pulled up to Eagle Elite when it was starting to get dark. I didn't hide the fact that my Glock was out just like Serena didn't hide the fact that she looked minutes away from executing Tank if he blinked wrong in her direction.

He pulled out his own fifty caliber that I'm sure he'd been packing the entire time and walked with us toward the dorm.

"Before you go in, just know—" He put his hand on my shoulder. "—it's not all of them; most of them are innocent."

"Innocent." I snorted. "They're about as innocent as I am."

He swallowed and looked away. "I'm a De Lange too, you know."

I cursed while Serena looked ready to scratch his eyes out.

He kept talking. "Your dad gave us options," he said thickly. "Either for or against, and since I was a fucking twelve-year-old when I lost both parents to a De Lange cleansing, I chose to work for the law and keep the FBI on our side." He shot Serena a look. "I'm good at pretending."

She lunged for him, which only earned a laugh from me. "Holy shit, and why didn't my dad let us know?"

"It was need to know, and then you invited everyone into Eagle Elite, which was brilliant, by the way."

"Thank you."

"And I knew my cover was about to be blown." He sighed. "Last night I got a text from one of the guys, said he was tired of being a charity case and that somebody needed to make an example. I texted Serena to meet for coffee as an excuse to get in and talk him from the ledge, but his roommate said he'd left for the weekend." A spasm of emotion twisted his face for the briefest moment. "I wrongly assumed he'd changed his mind and was a big talker. If you want to blame someone, blame me."

I slid my key card and jerked the glass door open. "No blaming in this life, we're all at fault. Let's just hope that Ash hasn't already killed everyone since we're about four minutes behind him."

We piled into the building then took the elevator to the top floor.

I heard a gunshot and then a scream.

Shit.

The minute the doors opened, I saw Ash, standing with his gun pointed up and dust coming from the ceiling.

"Who?" he shouted.

One of the girls started crying while guys surrounded all the girls, hugging them, protecting them.

Not how I'd seen my Friday going.

We stepped in behind him.

He did a double-take, and then his face softened. "You guys don't have to do this."

"Neither do you," Serena said in a quiet voice. "It was one person, Ash, not all of them."

"It doesn't fucking matter!" he roared.

"It does." I stepped next to him. "Because we aren't our parents, and you, Asher Abandonato, are not your dad."

My words hit him like a blow to the chest as he very slowly lowered his gun. Tears filled his eyes as he stared ahead. "It hurts."

"Then let it hurt," I rasped. "But hurting someone else who didn't do shit, isn't going to make your hurt any less severe. You're bleeding man, sometimes the only way to heal is to let the blood do its job—cleanse."

"You're a De Lange," Ash said bitterly. "You're technically the heir!"

"Then shoot me." I took a step back and held up my hands. "If that's going to make you feel better, fucking shoot me!"

More screams erupted around me as Ash lifted his gun again. "And what if I do?"

"Then you prove to everyone around us that we're broken, that the system's broken, that history can't help but repeat itself over and over again." I shook my head. "We're better than this, Ash. We're better than our parents. We need to fix this. Not make it worse."

"Shit, I hate when he makes sense," Breaker muttered under his breath while Serena shot me a panicked look.

I nodded slowly in her direction and mouthed, "Banana."

It was our code word for her to turn on her psycho flirt mode. It was impressive as hell to watch.

With a shocked smile, she sauntered up to Tank and

pressed the gun against his back, then pressed a kiss to his cheek, using tongue. "Which one?"

Tank let out a little moan that I know he felt all the way past his dick to his toes and back up again. "I was going to tell you regardless."

"But this is more fun." She grinned, kissing the side of his neck, distracting him enough to grab the gun from his hand and point it at him. He had two guns on him; it was going to be either him or the guy that did this.

"Cute," Tank said in an amused voice. "And his name's Benji." As he said it, his eyes darted away from Serena's face and locked onto mine. "And he's standing behind you right now with a gun."

"Well, that's fun," I muttered and slowly turned to face the guy who thought he was tough enough to try to take out Ash, me, and my Family, my blood. Rage like I'd never known coursed through my system as the little shit-looking freshman pointed a gun that I was one hundred percent certain would turn out to be stolen at my face.

I would be shocked if he could grow a mustache. "It's always the quiet ones."

He shoved his glasses up his face. "It's your fault!"

"My fault?" My eyebrows moved up in surprise. "My fault that you decided to cut the brakes on Ash's car? My fault that the love of his life just died while you sit here ready to piss yourself? Do you even know how to fucking shoot that thing? Because the safety's on."

He looked down at the weapon he held. And that was all the time I needed as I kicked him in the stomach and smacked the gun out of his hand. Ash picked it up immediately.

And just like that, little Benji had nothing.

He held up his shaking hands and spat on the ground. "It was worth it. You guys all deserve to die for what you did to our parents!"

"That's where you're wrong," Serena said in a chilling voice. "Because we did nothing, just like you did nothing. We were all born. Some of us in the right place at the right time, some of us in the wrong place. We can either fight or join sides. Benji's chosen his. What about the rest of you?"

She looked around the stunned expressions. Nobody said anything.

And then she looked back to Benji. "Looks like you're the only one stupid enough to try to hurt what's ours." She held up her gun and then whispered, "Ash, I'll let you do the honors since this is your loss." She moved away, and Ash stepped forward. He grabbed Benji by the shirt and slammed him against the wall.

Benji's head made a crunching noise against it as he started to cry.

"No." Ash gritted his teeth. "You don't get to cry. You don't get to beg for mercy. My soul mate is dead because you thought you had something to prove, revenge gets you nowhere, just ask our parents." He shoved him to the floor. "Too bad you won't get the chance to."

I was shocked Ash made it quick.

Two shots directly to the forehead, and it was done.

No torture.

No screams.

Ash pulled out his phone and barked into it. "Cleanup on campus. One dead."

He hung up and held out his hands to the rest of the students on the floor. "Speak up now if you have a problem."

225

They were silent.

"Good." He put his gun away. "Don't forget curfew's at midnight, and mid-terms start in three weeks."

And just like that, he walked away.

And just like that, we followed.

The hush hung heavy in the elevator as we rode down.

The minute we got outside, one of the Escalades pulled up, Dante jumped out and sighed. "Just one body? You sure?"

"He's sure," I said quickly. "Hey, let the parents know we're all crashing at Nixon's, and no shit about all of us getting ridiculously drunk, okay?"

Dante nodded solemnly. "Two twirls, man."

"Two twirls," I repeated and looked at Ash.

After a few seconds, Ash finally repeated, "Two twirls."

Tank got into his truck with us and started the engine. "What does two twirls mean?"

"Everything," Serena said, tears in her eyes. "It's a long story, but it means that you need to capture every moment when you get it, don't waste life doing just one twirl when you can do two." She stared straight ahead but slid her hand toward mine and gripped. "Life's too short to worry about too many twirls, take as many as you want, and be thankful you have the opportunity to twirl in the first place."

I squeezed her hand right back.

Tank pulled out into traffic. "But why twirling?"

"It's a long story," I answered for everyone. "The point is, we lost someone today, so we aren't going to go home and get sad. We had our vengeance; now we get drunk."

Ash was deathly silent as we drove the entire way, his jaw clenching and unclenching every few seconds like he was about to lose it, so when we got to Nixon's, I grabbed a bottle of whiskey and pushed him toward the basement door. "Just don't kill me."

"No fucking promises," he ground out as we made our way down to the gym.

He hurt, so he needed to hurt.

And I was going to be the punching bag.

I took a swig of whiskey and winced.

Fingers crossed, I kept all my fingers.

CHAPTER
Twenty-Three

Serena

Most everyone skipped the wine and went straight to the hard stuff, choosing to crash in our huge theater room while happy movies played in the background.

Breaker made Tank take enough shots that the guy had let go of all of his inhibitions and was trying to adorably hit on me as if he knew what to do with me once he had me.

Most men didn't.

Junior did, a voice reminded me.

My hands shook as I downed the rest of my vodka shot. It could have been him. It could have been any of us.

I wasn't afraid often; today, I was terrified, and no amount of booze or Disney movies was going to take that away.

He could have been taken from me.

He was mine.

Mine, damn it!

The world felt thick around me as I made my way toward the door.

Tank blocked it with his massive body and then gave me a sloppy grin that was too adorable to be sexy. "Going slomwhere?"

I sighed. "Tank, Tank, Tank." I patted him on the shoulder. "I would eat you alive."

"I might like it." He leaned closer, tilting my chin toward him.

"You also might bleed to death." I winked.

He barked out a laugh. "I like your sense of humor."

"Wasn't kidding," I pulled him in for a hug. "We'll find you a nice girl, don't worry. Also, give me your keys."

He dug into the front pocket of his jeans and took at least five attempts before he dangled them between us. "Done."

"Yeah, you need to hydrate. It's hard to hang with Italians who drink wine for breakfast." I pointed his body toward one of the leather couches. "Sleep."

"I'm not shleeepy!" he argued, but his eyes were already closed as he stumbled across the couch face down.

In the corner, Breaker snickered, a bottle of gin in his hand. "Lightweight."

"Did you drink all of that?" I pointed at the bottle.

He made a face and then held up his fingers and then hid it behind his back like I'd somehow forget a fifth was over half gone, and he'd been the only one drinking it.

Something flickered in his gaze, an emotion I knew well.

An emotion I was dealing with right now.

Fear over the future.

Fear for Ash.

And fear that the guys still hadn't returned from downstairs.

With a sigh, I nodded to Breaker. "Stay with everyone; I'm going to go check on them, all right?"

"Yeah," Breaker croaked just as Dom made his way into the room, took one look at all the cousins laying around with alcohol, and smiled to himself.

"Make sure nobody dies," I teased.

My brother grinned. "Babysitting, my favorite."

"How'd it go?" I asked once I was almost past him.

His eyes flickered away while his jaw clenched. "He was nineteen, had the whole world ahead of him, and was in the foster care system since the age of eight. How do you think it went?"

I squeezed my eyes shut and whispered, "The bosses did wrong by them, Dom." His gaze froze over, but I had to say my piece. "They were just kids."

"You have no clue what the fuck you're talking about, or what hell they were put through. They gave them choice after choice Serena, step off that damn pedestal, and take a look around you. You're alive because they did the hard thing. Now it's your turn to do what needs to be done, no matter how bad it hurts." He put his hand on my shoulder. "And trust me, it hurts all the time."

I looked away.

"This is your kingdom now," he murmured. "Yours, Ash's, Junior's—but don't for one second think the bosses won't take back the keys if you guys go soft."

"We would never."

"Then there's no reason for you to be afraid, is there?" He said in a clipped tone before making his way into the theater room.

Breaker started chanting. "Dom, Dom, Dom."

And dread filled my stomach as I made my way down the hall and toward the basement.

I stopped when I heard my dad's hushed voice. He sounded pissed. When I rounded the corner, he barked something else into the phone at his ear. "We'll talk later, Phoenix. Yeah, okay. You too."

"Everything okay?" I asked once my dad slid his phone back into the pocket of his black slacks.

"Depends." My dad relaxed a bit. "How much have you had to drink?"

I rolled my eyes. "I like control; you know this—makes me the worst partier in the world."

My dad cursed under his breath and then, in a totally uncharacteristic show of weakness, pulled me against his chest and kissed my forehead. "I've never been so fucking terrified in my entire life."

I clung to him. "Dad, I'm fine; I'm here."

"I would send you away," he rasped. "If I knew it wouldn't bring down an entire kingdom."

I relaxed against him, then drew back. "Don't take away my only purpose in life, Dad. I'm good at this; you made me good at this. I'm not your princess anymore, I'm your assassin, I'm your right hand, and I was born to be ruthless, just like my dad."

His expression softened. "You're right; you'd be a horrible doctor; you'd probably just let patients bleed out because you'd be annoyed they got shot in the first place."

I burst out laughing. "That's why Violet gets to practice pre-med, and Izzy law, and me, well…" I grinned. "I'm more comfortable with a gun than I am with a scalpel."

"God help us all." He winked. "Promise me you'll come to

me when it gets dark, Serena, and know it will, but know I'm never going to leave your side. I would burn the world, cut out my own heart, and give it to you if I knew it would make you happy. You, Dom, Bella, your mother—you're my world."

I leaned up and kissed his cheek. "Shh, I won't tell Bella I'm your favorite."

"Odd how you inherited both my arrogance and my love of violence."

I shrugged. "I'm just special, I guess."

"You are," he deadpanned. "You're everything."

"Stop." I felt my eyes starting to fill with tears. "You'll make me cry, and mafia princesses don't cry, we fight."

"Yeah, well, by the looks of what's going on downstairs, you may be fresh out of sparring partners for a while."

My stomach sank. "Junior getting his ass kicked?"

He frowned. "Seems sort of even to me at this point, though I saw a tooth go flying, so let's hope it's not the front one."

I winced. "All right, on that note, I'm going to go see if they need a sub."

Dad sighed. "They break you in any way, I break them. Make sure they get the message."

"Dad, you cut off someone's hand and mailed it to their family as a warning. Trust me, they know you mean business."

"Hey, I was proving a point."

"Yeah, pretty sure they got it!" I laughed and made my way down the stairs.

The sound of Rage Against the Machine filled the gym, Killing in The Name was one of Ash's go-to songs. Usually, I ignored his taste in music, but today it held a certain death factor that was hard to ignore.

Both guys had been down there for two hours.

An empty bottle of whiskey was sitting on the bench, and another empty one was completely shattered against one of the walls on the far side of the gym.

My heart pounded as blood flowed over Junior's face, dripped down his chest. His left eye was already bruising, and blood was caked to his upper arms as he ducked, barely missing another blow from Ash.

Both of them were shirtless angry gods among men throwing punches like they hadn't been taking shots every time someone scored a point.

I knew the game well.

It was angry.

It was necessary.

It was also a hell of a lot of alcohol by the way they were both staggering around each other. Then again, they were bleeding profusely so it could have been the numerous flesh wounds.

I felt hands wrap around me from behind, and then Breaker was resting his drunken chin on my shoulder, though he looked stone-cold sober again. He smelled like gin.

He sighed against me. "They're alive, so that's good."

I clung to his muscled arms and jerked when Ash landed a blow to Junior's gut only to have Junior take Ash's legs out from underneath him as he slammed him to the ground and landed a punch across his face.

Breaker whistled under his breath. "That's gonna be a bitch tomorrow morning."

I smiled despite the fact that they were beating the shit out of each other. "Can I ask you something?"

"Depends, do I get to see you naked if I answer right?"

I rolled my eyes even though he couldn't see me. Breaker had always been a flirt, but we'd never crossed that line, and he was very aware that I'd crossed it with Junior when Ash had drunkenly told him.

Cousins.

Basically, he was fishing for information in the only way he knew how—offering up his godlike body in exchange.

But I had another god I worshipped.

And it wasn't the bronze one holding me against his muscled chest.

It was the one with blood dripping from his chin.

The one with vengeance in his eyes.

"You don't want to see me naked," I answered truthfully, finally taking my eyes away from Junior and looking over my shoulder. "It will seriously ruin all women for you."

He barked out a laugh. I'd always loved Breaker's laugh, even though he was part of this dark world, he still laughed like he was able to find a bit of light, where the hell did this guy come from anyway? "This is why you're one of my favorite people, and don't worry, I won't catch feelings..." He was quiet as his lips brushed my ear. "Sometimes, I don't think I have them."

I clung to him tighter as he pulled me back against him. He was too young to be so jaded. Then again, we all were. "You have feelings; you're just forced to ignore them for the greater good."

"And the greater good is what? Survival?" His voice was gritty, full of well-suppressed anger because after all, he was the calm one, right?

"Blood," I said quickly, trying to distract him from snapping. "Are you going to let me talk or what?"

His one hand slid down my side and gripped my hip, trapping me against his heated body as his fingers drummed against my bare skin. "So talk."

"Junior's going to kill you," I said in a sing-song voice.

"Ah, so she finally admits it out loud."

"You already knew," I snapped.

His chest felt warm, strong, as he tightened his grip around me. "Ash was drunk; he could have been full of shit."

"Yeah well." I licked my suddenly dry lips. "Say you did accidentally catch feelings, would you…" I bit down on my lip. "Would you risk your life to keep feeling them, would you give in, knowing you could die?"

Slowly Breaker turned me in his arms. His eyes flashed as he cupped my face. "Serena…" He squeezed his eyes shut then opened them again. He had the most beautiful features, almost too pretty with his almost olive skin and lighter hair. His jaw clenched. "I really want to tell you to stop thinking what I think you're thinking, but after today, I've completely lost my censor, and honestly, I don't think a person should live their life being safe. God knows we only have today. Who knows what's going to happen tomorrow?"

"Thanks." I sighed. "I think."

His grin turned goofy. "Junior looks ready to murder me; it's made my entire shitty night worth it. I so love getting a response out of him."

Before I could ask what the heck he was talking about, he gripped my head and pressed a kiss to my mouth, sliding his tongue past my lips in a dominant way that had me ready to pull my gun on him. He squeezed my ass and then broke off the kiss with a teasing grin in his eyes. "What? I wanted a reward for my honesty!"

"You're such a dick!" I laughed and shoved him away. "And you taste like gin! I hate gin!"

He burst out laughing then bowed. "I know!"

"Go be annoying somewhere else." I shooed him away, still smiling.

"I think you mean go be sexy somewhere else." He winked. "Oh, and tell Junior not to kill me in my sleep. Cool?" He held out his fist.

I tapped it with mine, and then he was zigzag running out of the basement as Junior had already pulled the gun and was trying to aim.

"Doesn't work if nobody's shooting you!" I yelled after him, then felt Junior behind me.

Slowly I turned and then made a face. "Are you okay?"

His eyes blazed with unchecked fury. "No."

"Do you need me to—"

He tossed me over his shoulder and waved off a bleeding Ash, who was wiping his face with his discarded shirt, spreading blood everywhere rather than actually getting clean.

"Put me down!" I pounded against Junior's back.

He slapped me on the ass so hard, my teeth clenched. "No."

"Junior!"

He jogged up the steps with me in his arms like he hadn't just gone a billion rounds with Ash and stomped into the guest room, making sure to lock his door, and then carried me through the bathroom to do the same to my door.

When he was satisfied that all the doors were locked, he went back into the bathroom, me still thrown over his shoulder like he'd completely lost his mind, and then without warning, he shoved me into the shower with my clothes still on.

"The hell, *Junior!*" I roared ready to fight him as my shirt soaked against my skin, my favorite pair of Nike sweats were starting to fall off of me. "What's wrong with you!"

"I'll kill him!" he raged. His aqua eyes were wild as he jerked my shirt over my head and threw it to the ground. "If I leave this room, I'll kill him!"

Blood and water dripped down Junior's face as he jerked my sweats down to my ankles then painfully pulled my thighs apart, his fingers digging into my sensitive flesh as his right hand found my ever-present dagger.

His eyes never left mine as he pushed the tip of the dagger between my breasts and then dug it into my sports bra, tearing it in pieces. He slid the knife down my belly into the front of my underwear and did the same until they slid to the wet floor with my sweats.

"Whose are you!" he screamed inches from my face.

I'd never seen this side of him before, never seen him so unleashed, so wild.

My chest heaved as I tried to catch my breath. "Y-yours."

"Whose!" He roared, slamming his hands on either side of the tile by my face, his mouth pressed against mine as he continued. "Fucking, whose!"

"Yours!" I shoved him and then slapped him across the face for scaring me.

His head whipped to the side as his chest rose up and down. He wasn't calm.

He was ready to commit murder.

"Mine." His teeth nipped at my bottom lip then gave a painful tug as he flipped me around so the cool tile bit into my cheek and stomach, my breasts ached as the cold almost burned my skin. "Mine," he repeated, roaming shaking hands around my body, cupping my breasts before lowering them to my hips.

I let out a gasp when he jerked me back against him. With one harsh thrust, he was inside me. I choked on my next breath as the second surge filled me to the hilt only to pull out again.

"Whose?" he rasped, his voice hoarse as he pumped into me, digging his hands into my hips to pull me back against him only to slam me back against the tile with each jerky movement. "Whose!"

"Yours." Tears streamed down my cheeks from pleasure, from pain, sadness, fear, but most of all, the broken heart that refused to heal between us. "I've only ever been yours."

"I need you." His voice cracked. "I'm sorry, I need you like this, I'm sorry—"

"Junior Nicolasi, you have me; however you need me..." I tasted the salt of my own tears as I looked down at the blood swirling down the drain. "Even like this, Junior, even like this."

With a groan, his movements were wild as he got me closer to release, and when I clenched around him, trying to dig my nails into the tile, trying to grab hold of something, anything, he drove in one more time and stayed there. Out of breath, his head resting on mine, his arms wrapped around my body like he was afraid I was going to disappear.

He'd never been rough with me before.

Not like this. In fact, I'd always found it odd how tender he was during sex since it was the exact opposite of how he was in real life. Now I knew. He'd been holding back. He'd given me the prettiest pieces, keeping the jagged ones to himself.

Part of me wondered if this was a piece of him that he'd hidden on purpose—or if Claire's death didn't just crack Ash—but the rest of us too.

Because it was suddenly real, wasn't it?

Because we'd always been told to embrace the monster—because I knew Junior's number one fear was to lose himself in it.

And now, I wondered if it was too late.

If he was already gone.

And if I was the only thing keeping him sane.

"I'm sorry." Junior kissed down my neck. "I'm sorry I can't—" He pulled away, and then he was gone, leaving me with my clothes tattered on the floor and my heart even more broken than before.

Woodenly, I grabbed a towel and felt more fresh tears when I noticed that his door was closed.

And worse, when I tested the doorknob, it was locked from his side.

What the hell had just happened?

CHAPTER
Twenty-Four

Junior

I was a monster.

I pressed my palms into my eyes until I saw black dots, and even then, nothing made me forget the rage that had swarmed over me when Breaker touched her, kissed her. Breaker was one of my best friends, he was family, but I'd snapped, something in me had snapped.

From the hospital to fighting with Ash, to watching him down his whiskey and then burst into tears before I even had a chance to hit him, I had become acutely aware of the last human parts of me breaking in two. I didn't know how to fix them, how to fix me when all I saw was a red wall of rage.

"I'm fucking lost." He fell to his knees in the middle of the gym, and then he threw the whiskey bottle across the room, smashing it into the wall. His scream pierced my ears so loud that I was surprised the building didn't come down around us.

"Fuck!" He slammed his hands into the floor and then his knuckles, breaking the skin immediately, causing blood to drip from his fingertips.

"Ash!" I pulled him back against me.

He didn't even fight at first; he just let me hold him while he sobbed in my arms.

"I love you." I held him tight. *"I love you, and I have you."*

His entire body shook in my arms.

I don't know how long I held him like that.

He finally relaxed his grip on me and walked over to the ring, peeling his shirt over his body and sitting on the edge of the mat, his head lowered.

"I was going to marry her," he whispered, and then in a horrifying moment, my heart crashed to the floor as he very carefully pulled out a blue Tiffany's box. I hoped to God it was a promise ring, a necklace, a bullet—anything.

He opened it.

Three karats.

Bile rose in my throat as I took the box and looked down. The ring was inscribed, "My heart for yours."

"Take it." His teeth snapped like he was ready to go feral. *"Take it; I can't look at it. I can't—"*

"It's done," I said softly, tucking the box against my discarded shirt on the bench.

"She's gone," he whispered. *"And so am I."*

My body chilled at his admission.

Because I knew a part of him would never be the same, and that her death would unleash something otherworldly into our family.

"I wish it was me," I admitted, taking a swig of the other

bottle of whiskey and handing it to him. "I want you to know; I would have died so you could be together. I still would."

Ash chugged the whiskey and stared me down his expression bitter. "If you knew the truth, you wouldn't say that."

"The truth?" I frowned as he passed me the whiskey back. "What truth?" Chills erupted on my skin at his dark expression.

"It was me." His voice was hollow. "Me and Claire. We were given instructions to break you and Serena apart. My dad knew about you guys, and he knew it was only a matter of time before the rest of the bosses found out and killed you for breaking one of their biggest rules. And selfishly, I didn't want to lose my best friend. I wanted to make my dad proud. That first day at Eagle Elite, when we made our statement to the students and the staff, I goaded you into making out with that girl in front of Serena. I pushed you when you started stripping her in front of the faculty, and then Claire taunted Serena, both of us knowing full well that in order to make a statement, you couldn't choose each other, but also knowing that you pretending not to love Serena would break her heart. Claire was so fucking obedient, going along with it even though I could see it killed her to do it. But you guys broke the rules, so the only way to keep you safe, to keep both of you safe, was to put you in a position where you had no choice but to choose Family over each other." He lifted his chin. "I knew you'd take the bait because you didn't know how to back down, I knew we needed to make a statement, and I knew that Serena wouldn't show weakness."

My mind reeled when I thought about that day, where I'd chosen the Family over Serena, where her eyes begged me to choose her, to leave the girl I'd been seducing in order to make a point.

"You're supposed to be my best friend," I rasped.

"And Claire's not supposed to be dead," he snapped back at me.

With a roar, I threw a punch, hitting Ash square in the face. He smiled through the blood. I hit him again, knocking a tooth out.

Ash just smiled even harder and then said. "You're pissed. Good. Now hit me harder."

He'd done it on purpose.

Told me his secret, so that I'd be all in.

So my anger would match his hurt.

I sat up in my bed and ran my injured hands through my hair. I'd wrapped three of my fingers with tape and knew that I probably looked as shitty as I felt. It wasn't supposed to be like this.

And I'd taken my anger out on Serena. All I kept seeing was her crestfallen face that day we took over Eagle Elite again. The way her eyes begged me to say it was bullshit, that we didn't have to prove this. Instead, I went along with exactly what Ash had wanted me to do. And the sick part of me liked making Serena angry, liked the control I had over her, preened when I touched another woman in front of her. It was the first time I had realized something wasn't quite right with me. It was the first time I'd realized I was just like my bloodline: sick, twisted. And I'd done nothing but unleash that same twisted fuck on Serena today.

I couldn't see past the hurt of all the years we could have been together, and then I couldn't see past the pain of Ash's betrayal, and then I couldn't see past the fear of death if we had stayed on that path.

But now that Claire was gone, all I kept thinking was... I deserve one thing, right? Just one thing that brings me joy in a world so dark and lonely.

And my one thing was Serena.

I'd needed to own her.

Needed her to feel the lack of control I had when I was with her and needed to mark her as mine, so she never forgot.

Instead, I completely lost my mind the minute I touched her smooth skin and almost blacked out during sex because it had been too long.

I left marks on her hips.

I didn't warn her.

I didn't kiss her.

I just wanted. So I took.

Monster.

I'd proven one thing.

I was worthy of the same death sentence that hung over every one of my cousins' heads.

"Shit!" I slammed my fist into my pillow again and again. Not satisfied, I grabbed my knife and ripped into it. Feathers went flying in a puff of white.

"Sex usually calms you down." Serena's voice interrupted my rage-filled tantrum.

I looked up and blinked. She was stunning, always so stunning it hurt to look right at her. "How the hell did you get in?"

"Magic." She sighed. "Oh, and also, I picked the lock."

I swallowed the lump in my throat. "I can't, not right now, Serena. I can't fight, I don't want to talk to you, so unless you're here to suck my dick, leave."

"Ah, there it is." Serena's smile was sad. I needed her to go before I hurt her. Before I destroyed what was left between us with my anger. "The Junior Nicolasi charm. Is this the part where you push me away to make me angry, so you don't get hurt? Or am I supposed to be into it and just get on my hands and knees? Should I be wearing more clothes or less?" She looked down at her tank and shorts.

I fell back against my bed and groaned. "Why don't you ever listen?"

"Because I know you." I could feel her walking toward my bed, and then she was crawling onto it through the mess of white feathers. "And I know that you need me right now, and I don't care how painful, how terrible, how much—I'm here because that's what friends do and no matter what happens between us, you have always been and always will be, my best friend." A tear slid down her cheek and dripped onto my stomach as she waited for me to say something.

A thousand words and sentences filled my head, romantic ones, promises, vows, but all I kept thinking was how damn pretty she was and how I didn't deserve her, would never deserve her. I could imagine only one happy ending to this scenario, to us being together, and it was my own death.

And I knew... it would be worth it.

To have her.

To own her.

To love her.

Even if it meant I had her for a few days, or maybe if we were lucky, I'd get her for a few weeks.

Serena Abandonato was my suicide mission.

And my heart couldn't help but beat... *yes.*

Nothing good would come of this, but maybe in the end, at least the bosses would understand that we had to cling to the good, so the bad didn't destroy us, and she was everything good in my life.

This time. I wasn't letting go.

This time I'd sign my own death contract.

This time, it would be on my terms.

"Love you." I squeezed my eyes shut because it hurt to look at her. "For as long as we both shall live."

And in what felt like a holy moment, Serena Abandonato, my first and only love, bent over and pressed a kiss to my forehead and then moved to her feet. Slowly, she pulled every stitch of clothing off her body until she was naked, and then she whispered, "Take whatever you need because I've always, only ever been. Yours."

CHAPTER
Twenty-Five

Serena

It was either the stupidest thing I'd ever done or the bravest. I held my breath when he said he loved me, and then I froze.

I wasn't sure what he needed.

I wasn't sure if talking would help.

But something in Junior's face darkened as his eyes slowly roamed over me, his expression was anything but calm as his hooded gaze locked on my breasts and then drifted lower.

The covers on his bed were pulled back to his hips, revealing such godlike beauty that my chest ached.

Muscles strained around his midsection as he put his hands behind his head and watched, waited, looking ready to pounce.

"Junior?" I took a step toward him, unsure of what he actually wanted me to do now that I was naked in front of him, now that we were doing this… wait, were we doing this?

Confusion must have marred my expression because he finally spoke. "Do you remember your sixteenth birthday?"

Searing heat flooded my face. "Yeah, I cornered you in the hall and asked for my present early."

His smile was dark, wicked, as he moved to a sitting position and reached out his hand, brushing my right breast with the back of his knuckles, it was so brief and yet I felt an electric current shock me with each touch. "And what did I give you?"

I gulped. My eyes darting to his mouth and then lower as I took in his naked torso and then looked toward his lap.

I squeezed my eyes shut as a shiver wracked my body. "You finally gave me what I'd been begging for."

"What was that?" He said on a growl. "What were you begging for?"

Slowly I lowered myself to the mattress. It sunk under my weight, sending our bodies sliding toward one another. "You gave me you."

"What part of me?" His hand moved to my shoulder as he slowly pulled me down over his body.

I straddled his waist and moved my hips. He was completely naked underneath the sheets. I could feel him pulsing against my ass as he watched me, waited for me to tell him.

"You said I could suck your dick, and then you said happy birthday like a complete asshole as if I should say thank you for your present." I remembered the day well. I'd been so pissed, so embarrassed, that I'd slapped him across the face then punched him in the gut. "I shoved you against the wall, which only seemed to encourage more laughter on your end— and then I kissed you."

"You kissed me." He repeated. "So fucking hard that my teeth hurt for two days."

I smacked him on the chest. He caught my hand and brought my fingertips to his mouth and then slowly took my hand and brought it lower until I was touching between my thighs, dripping wet, ready for him to do something other than travel down memory lane.

I let out a hoarse cry when he made me touch myself, and then he brought my hand back up and licked my fingertips. "I got off so many times on that day, alone in my room, just thinking about that kiss, how aggressive it was, how much more I wanted it to be."

I wiggled against him.

He winced and then slowly flipped me onto my back, hovering over me. "And what happened later that day, Serena?"

I let out a shaky breath. "You caught me."

"Caught you." He pinned my wrists above my head and rocked his naked hips against me. "Doing what?"

So good. He felt so hot it almost hurt.

My cheeks heated. "Thinking about you... wondering how it would be if we could finally..." I bit my lower lip. "I was touching myself."

"Mmm..." He teased my entrance a bit. "Tell me, do you regret it? That day? That night? Those years? Knowing who I was. Who I am. Knowing we would only ever have this?"

"Never," I vowed. "The only thing I regret is that we have to pretend we don't—"

"Don't what?"

I bit the bullet. "We have to pretend that we hate each other because it's the only thing as extreme as our love."

He surged into me. "Right answer."

"Was it a question?" My head fell back against the pillows as he kissed the side of my neck.

"No," he said between kisses. "I just want to make sure there are no regrets, no matter what. Just promise me you'll remember this forever. That Serena Abandonato was the most tempting poison, and that I, Junior Nicolasi..." His lips lingered against mine for a heart-stopping moment as he deepened the kiss, then murmured against the corner of my mouth, "...drank."

"Junior..." I clung to his back as he deepened his thrusts. "You're scaring me."

"Have me now." He pressed a painfully slow kiss to my mouth. "Remember me forever, okay?"

"Okay." Tears filled my eyes as I clung to him. "Love you as long as we both shall live?"

He gulped and then. "As long as we both shall live."

"You didn't say you loved me." I tried teasing, even though my body was already on the brink of exploding as he moved inside me.

"Yeah, I did." He finally smiled. "With every fight, every shove, every insult, I told you I loved you, and with my body right now—I fucking worship you."

I dug my nails into his back as he slammed into me, causing the headboard to hit the wall.

"Don't stop, don't stop!" I scrambled to hang on to his muscled body as he loved me, as he showed me forever.

And when I felt his release inside me, I hooked my ankles around his body, keeping him pinned where I needed him.

Because the thought of him letting go, was the most terrifying thing I could possibly imagine, and part of me wondered why it seemed like he was saying goodbye when we'd finally decided to be together again.

While we were still connected, he looked down at me, his aqua eyes flashing as he whispered, "You will always be worth it, Serena. Always."

He kissed my forehead and muttered a curse as we both stared at one another, panting.

"What happens now?" I asked.

"Well, my princess just said I could have her any way I want. What do you think happens now?"

I grinned. "We might need some red bull."

"Speak for yourself." He slapped my ass on the side. "I have over a year of pent-up sexual aggression to get out."

"It was only one time!" I blurted.

He frowned. "What was?"

"It was one guy, and it was one time, and it was horrible, and I only did it to make you mad and—"

He devoured my next words. "Promise me?"

"It's always been you, always." I kissed him deeper, harder, warred with his tongue as he tried to dominate the kiss, his fingers digging into my hips.

He pulled back, out of breath. "Never thought I'd see the day the ruthless princess surrendered to the dragon."

"Dragon?" I smirked. "Nah, the ruthless princess just surrendered to her King."

CHAPTER
Twenty-Six

Junior

I wanted nothing more than to pull Serena into my arms and sleep in since it was a Saturday, but the last thing we needed was to get caught before this even really got started because believe me, there were things I was going to do to her that would keep her body humming for hours.

My body ached as I moved to a sitting position and then leaned over and pressed a kiss to her forehead. She moaned in her sleep, then blindly reached for me, brushing up against my dick.

"That's not your phone, Serena," I whispered.

"No." She yawned. "My phone's bigger."

I tackled her onto her back while she burst out laughing. "Take it back…" I slid my hands down her sides and tickled her sensitive skin.

"Never!" Her laugh was so damn carefree my heart cracked in its darkness, wishing that I could keep that laugh, this version of her forever, hating that we all had a role to play, masks to wear.

A knock sounded on my door.

Thank God it was locked.

"Junior!" Nixon barked. "If Serena finds out you brought another whore home, she's going to chop off your balls, cook them into your favorite dish, and feed them to you."

"Yeah, Junior." Serena murmured with a smirk. "I'm gonna grab these—" She reached for my dick, but I kept her pinned. "What? Afraid I might have a sharp object?"

"You're nothing but sharp objects," I whispered. "But don't worry, I'm into it."

"Yeah, you are." Her eyes zeroed in on my mouth.

"Junior!" Nixon yelled again. "I'm serious, let the skank out the back and get ready for breakfast. We need to talk anyway."

"Sorry, Nixon, right on it." Actually, I was right on her.

I flipped off the door and pressed a heated kiss to her mouth before peeling myself away from her naked skin, and then walking toward the bathroom.

I heard Serena jogging behind me, felt the slap on my ass, then burst out laughing as I chased her into the shower.

"Mmm..." She rubbed soap up and down her body. "You need some?"

"Nah," I gripped her breasts and squeezed lightly, then massaged up and down her stomach, using the slickness of the body wash to roam all over her nakedness.

Her breath hitched when I pulled us under the water and captured her mouth in a watery kiss that starved us of oxygen.

She clung to me, her arms wrapped around my neck, her hair sticking to my chin as our foreheads touched.

"Are you sore?" I asked softly.

"Even if I was…" She reached for me and stroked. "…do you really think I'd say no to having you any way I can?"

I cursed as she lifted her right leg and then hooked it around my hip, heaving herself up against my body as I pressed her against the wall, thrusting into her beneath the hot water, covering her would-be moans with my mouth. She was slippery everywhere, I dug into her ass harder, angling her down onto me. It always felt like a holy experience, being with her, maybe it was because she was it for me.

My soul mate.

My everything.

The other half of my dark, twisted heart.

She gripped my head with her hands and licked a trail of water down my neck as her thighs tightened around me. She was close; I could feel it in the way she met me thrust for thrust, the way her eyes flashed wild even though she tried to pretend she was calm.

"You with me?" I rasped.

She gave me a jerky nod. "Always with you."

I might have filled her then, but I could have sworn her body was healing me as we both found our release and stared at each other.

"I'm never letting you go. You know that, right?" I slowly pulled back and let her slide down my body.

She turned around and gave me her back as I jerked her against me. Her breasts teased my forearm. "I think I would die if you did."

We were quiet through the rest of the shower, though I did get my ass grabbed at least a dozen more times before I made it back to my room and changed.

I wasn't sure what Nixon wanted, but the last thing I needed was to look like I just fucked his daughter.

The only problem? When I looked in the mirror, I looked way too excited to be headed to breakfast.

My saving grace was that Ash had landed a few good blows causing my cheek and my right eye to bruise.

Add that to the cuts on my knuckles, and I could fake it that I was sore, I could make it look like I was depressed as hell.

All I had to focus on was the fact that one of my best friends was hurting and that my love for my other best friend would one day kill me.

Happiness. Gone.

I jerked open the door to the guest room, and when a shadowy figure pushed off the wall, out of instinct, I reached for my gun in the back of my jeans.

Nixon frowned. "Are you going to shoot me?"

"Depends. Are you going to scare the shit out of me all the time?"

He looked over my shoulder. "Where's the girl?"

I shot him a smug grin and patted him on the shoulder. "We all have our secrets, Nixon, right?"

His eyes narrowed. "I heard her."

"Yeah, I did too." I started walking down the hall. "Allll night long."

"Really?" Nixon scowled. "Where do you find these girls?"

"Eh, you'd be surprised…" I shoved my gun in the back of my pants again. "Some may say they just fall right into my bed, no questions asked."

"Who falls into his bed?" Breaker asked from the kitchen,

holding a glass of orange juice in one hand and bacon in the other.

"Some girl." Nixon sighed. "She snuck out already, though. According to Romeo over here." He jabbed a hand in my direction.

Breaker choked into his orange juice and then rasped, "Yeah, bet she did, because that's so easy to do in this house, sneak in and out, right Junior?"

I flipped him off, knowing exactly where he was going with that, and I was still pissed at him, which meant I owed him one. "Hey, Nixon, did you know Breaker had his tongue down Serena's throat last night for three-point-two seconds?"

"BETRAYER!" Breaker threw his bacon at me. "After all I do for you!"

"WHAT?" Nixon roared.

Breaker ran to the other side of the table and held up his hands.

"You did what!"

"I was teasing her!" Breaker argued. "Plus, Junior's just trying to—"

"Why is everyone yelling?" Serena waltzed into the kitchen, leaned up on her tiptoes, and kissed her dad on the cheek.

His anger disappeared as he pulled her in for a hug. "Nothing, just don't let Breaker's dirty mouth anywhere near yours."

"Ew, he tasted like gin."

"See!" Breaker really needed to stop talking. "If I were actually meaning to kiss her, I'd drink whiskey. You know she likes the taste better, right Junior?"

I glared. "How the hell would I know where Serena puts her mouth?"

Serena started charging toward me.

Here we go, back to the hate. I waited for her to punch me in the face.

Instead, she grabbed a fork and held it dangerously close to my cock. "What was that Junior?"

I grinned. Did she have to be so damn pretty? Her eyes were wild, outlined in black, her lipstick was pale, her blond hair was pulled back into a tight ponytail, and she was wearing the tightest black jeans I'd ever seen, not to mention a tank top that showed a bare midriff. "Nixon, don't you think she should put a sweater on or something?"

Her eyes widened even more as she lowered the fork.

Nixon sighed. "Serena, don't castrate him. We may need him later. And he's right, put on a cardigan or something."

"Fuck!" Ash's voice sounded from somewhere in the room. "Could you guys please keep it down? I'm trying to die in peace!"

I saw a flash of color; he was in the living room lying on the couch with an empty bottle in one hand as he stared up at the ceiling.

Breaker, Serena, and I all shared a look before Nixon sighed and said, "We have to wait for everyone else anyway."

"What for?" Serena asked.

Nixon gulped and then, "Funeral preparations."

Shit.

In an instant, I was up and making my way over to Ash. He looked like complete shit, both eyes were swollen, one almost completely shut, thanks to my right hook, his body had a few bruises near his shoulder, and his knuckles had dried blood on them. He must have crashed on the couch without bothering to take a shower last night.

"Bro…" Breaker sat on the floor next to him. "You smell like shit."

"Go away." Ash covered his face with his hands. "Please."

"Can't do that, cousin." Serena helped Ash to his elbows then scooted underneath him, cradling his head in her lap. "What do you need? What's going to make you feel better right now?"

"Death."

"Other than death," I snapped. The last thing I needed was to lose him too; the last thing he needed was to lose someone else.

When did things get so messed up?

And how the hell were we going to survive, not just Claire's death? But mine if it came to that? How?

The thought haunted me the entire morning as the bosses came over to make arrangements. It was a steady stream of black suits coming in and going out of the house.

And Ash refused to get up.

At one point, Tank finally found his way into the living room. Breaker offered to share some clothes with him and show him where the showers were.

Tank didn't know it yet, but he was in this, part of this now, so him going home and having a normal life now?

Probably not in the cards.

But we'd let him choose, we always did.

"I loved her." Ash's voice was so broken. "It wasn't supposed to end this way."

"It's not the end." Serena kept rubbing his hair back from his forehead in soothing strokes. "You have to live for her. What would she want you to do? Waste away?"

I'd seen Ash angry.

I'd seen him hurt.

But I'd never seen the sort of pain twisting his features like I did now, it was uncomfortably raw like he was broken and could never be fixed.

He opened his mouth, but nothing came out, and then he finally confessed something I didn't see coming.

"She was pregnant." A sob escaped his throat, and then it was like he couldn't stop talking. "We were fighting so much because she was terrified to bring up a baby in this lifestyle. That's why she wanted the normal, that's why she pushed it. She had no clue the thing she fucking pushed was going to end up getting her killed." Eyes wild, he gripped me by the shirt and pleaded. "Please, I can't live like this, I can't. Don't make me—"

His eyes rolled to the back of his head before he could finish, and when I looked up, it was to see Nikolai with a needle protruding from Ash's neck.

"The hell!" I roared, jumping to my feet.

Nikolai sighed. "Let him rest." His eyes were lifeless. "He's been through a lot."

"Did you know?" Serena asked.

Nikolai nodded. "His dad's on his way."

"You think angry Chase Abandonato is going to help the situation? Are you insane?" I would protect Ash even if it meant from his own father.

"He needs his family right now, and the only people in this room who know what it's like to love and lose are Sergio and Chase, and I think it should be his own father who helps him heal… if he can at all."

With that, Nikolai walked away.

Tears streamed down Serena's cheeks as she whispered. "I can't imagine, Junior, we can't—"

I gripped her hand. I knew what she was saying. We couldn't let that be us. We needed to be careful. But more than that. We needed each other.

"Let him sleep," I whispered, helping her out from under his lap.

And without thinking, I wrapped an arm around Serena and pulled her against my chest, because it was as natural as breathing.

Unfortunately, it was the worst timing in the world, because that was about the time Chase came around the corner, his gaze flickering from her to me and back again, calculated, cool.

He walked right up to us and whispered, "I hope like hell you two know what you're doing."

"Says the man who told his son to break us up," I sneered under my breath. "Forgive me for not feeling very grateful right now."

"You should be." Chase's eyes were sad. "I was trying to save your lives."

"Don't fight," Serena whispered. "Ash needs you."

Chase's stance tensed. He was a lethal son of a bitch who was barely restrained by the rage he kept in his soul, the revenge that lurked beneath the surface where his heart should be. "I would take it from him if I could."

"I know," Serena answered. "And do me a favor?"

"Anything." Serena had every single boss wrapped around her little finger, didn't she?

"Don't tell my dad." She touched his arm. "Ash needs you." Her lower lip trembled as she flicked a glance at me. "But, I need him."

"Fuck." Chase bit down on his lip. "This conversation never happened, all right?"

"Right," I agreed.

Chase held out his hand.

I shook it, wondering what the hell he was doing, and then I realized as Serena's eyes filled with more tears.

He was giving the blessing... her father wouldn't.

CHAPTER
Twenty—Seven

Serena

We'd all gravitated toward the gym downstairs, maybe because the upstairs was filled with too much grief. From the minute Claire's mom arrived, she didn't stop crying, which made me suddenly thankful that Ash was out.

We'd grabbed his limp ass body and brought him downstairs, worried that he would wake up in shock and shoot something.

Phoenix and Bee decided to cut their trip short and were already en route so they could attend the funeral in two days.

Being strong for Ash was one thing, being strong for all the younger cousins that we'd all but shoved into the theater room, not to mention my little sister… was harder.

Violet and Izzy came downstairs with us, and Breaker begrudgingly let his younger brother King join us even though King seemed to be really into whoever he was texting. The guy was in his senior year of high school, and let's just say he left nothing but broken hearts in his wake.

"Girlfriend?" I teased, ruffling his golden tipped hair as he smacked my hand out of the way. "Let me see!"

"First off." He very gently patted his mess of curls down. "And second, I don't do girlfriends; they're too clingy."

"Ew." Breaker was sitting next to him, tossing a football in the air. "Please don't list your sexcapades for us, little bro, plus there's only room for one slayer in this family."

"Both of you." I shook my head. "Disgusting."

"But, we're so pretty." Breaker winked and then licked his plump lower lip. I hoped to God he'd get saddled with a girl even more power-hungry than me; it would be insanely gratifying watching someone put him in his place.

Junior was holding vigil next to Ash while Izzy and Violet tended to his bloody hands.

They weren't as close to Claire as I had been, but it didn't matter. In their eyes, they hadn't just lost their future sister-in-law—they had lost their future niece or nephew.

I didn't ask how far along she was because part of me didn't want to know; I was afraid it would break me even more, make it more real. She hadn't looked like she'd been putting on weight, so I assumed she was in her first trimester.

We'd all decided that we needed to make something for Ash to remember the baby by as well, Violet and Izzy said they would be on it once they got all the blood off of him.

"You know what bothers me?" Tank looked completely different in Breaker's skinny jeans and black hoody. He'd been good looking but now was more so. Even more, he looked like he belonged. I wasn't sure if I was relieved or worried.

Undercover FBI didn't often work well with our families, just ask Junior's dad how that ended.

"What bothers you?" I said since nobody answered him.

"It's probably nothing, but all the De Lange kids that we know of are now at Eagle Elite, but that doesn't explain the College. When I dug, I couldn't find anything traceable, and neither could your guy Sergio. Someone made a cash offer on the school, offered scholarships to several of the De Lange kids, but nobody can trace it. I guess I'm just wondering what we do in the meantime."

"We wait." Junior was first to speak. "And we watch our backs like always."

"Sounds safe," Breaker grumbled under his breath.

Tank frowned. "If we wait, someone else could die."

"We wait." Junior moved to his feet. "We have no choice but to be on the defensive, especially since we don't know enough about the offense." Junior's eyes flashed as he pulled his Glock from his jeans and pointed it at Tank's head.

Power radiated from Junior's body as the white Henley wrapped tightly around his muscled body, paired with tight ripped jeans and black combat boots that somehow looked more rocker than anything and I was in heaven, licking my lips, waiting for him to get this over with so I could take him into my mouth.

"Whoa!" Tank held up his hands. "What the hell?"

"We need you to stay undercover." Junior sighed like he was bored. "That much is obvious, but we also need you to swear fealty to the Family."

"Now?" Tank's panicked look did nothing but annoy me.

"No, dipshit." I yawned. "Tomorrow. Can we pencil you in at three?"

Junior smirked. "You scared Tank?"

"No." His hands stopped shaking as he stared Junior down. "Just tell me what I need to do."

Junior scratched his chin with the barrel of the gun. Cockiness and arrogance oozed from him. Breaker and King slowly got up and grabbed their own guns then moved behind Tank, standing watch like guards while Junior spoke. "Denounce the De Lange Family line, and blood must be spilled to prove you'll bleed for the Family, for any one of us. The only way out of this is death; the only way in is sacrifice." He held up his gun again. "So, you get a choice. Leg or shoulder?"

Tank slowly stood and then ground out, "Shoulder."

"Good choice," Breaker said behind him.

"Really?" King shrugged. "I think the leg shot has a better chance of skimming because of Junior's aim."

"Oh, right." Breaker snickered. "His aim is shit, Tank; I'd pray he doesn't accidentally hit your heart."

"Are you shitting me right now?" Tank roared just as Chase, Phoenix, my dad, Sergio, Dante, Andrei, Nikolai, and Tex made their way into the basement.

Most of them were in black trousers with their white shirts rolled up past their forearms like they were ready to get dirty. So many tattoos swirled on arms and hands and necks that I had to just shake my head and look away.

Junior was catching up, so were Ash and Breaker.

But I think Chase took the cake for the amount of ink covering his body.

My dad probably came in second.

I nodded in his direction and earned a wink back as the bosses waited for Junior to finish.

We hadn't planned for them to watch this. It was just necessary, and I knew Junior would get it done before the funeral.

"He's lying," I finally said. "Junior's a crack shot."

Junior's face broke out into a cruel smile. "She only says that because she wants me."

"In your dreams, asshole," I spat.

The bosses just chuckled. They were used to our verbal sparring.

"Leg, I changed my mind, shoot my leg." Tank stuttered over his words while Junior lowered the gun.

"Ah, man." Breaker winced. "That's gonna hurt like a son of a bitch, right, Dad?"

Tex grinned. "Might even get lucky and hit some bone."

"What the hell is wrong with you people?" Tank roared. "Just get it over wi—"

Junior shot him in the leg, and then fired off another shot in the shoulder, then put his gun away while Tank bellowed and writhed in pain on the ground.

Money exchanged hands between the bosses.

I rolled my eyes. "What were you betting on?"

Chase grinned. "If he screamed."

"I had a hundred on him crying." Tex sighed while he handed Andrei his cash.

I noticed Nikolai standing in the background watching with amusement before his eyes flickered to a resting Ash in the corner next to a completely unfazed Izzy and Violet.

I knew that look.

It meant that he was going to wake up soon.

It meant we had to talk about it.

It meant they were going to tell Ash about the funeral.

It meant, as it always did when one of our own has fallen that he had to give Claire's eulogy.

I was pissed for him, hurt, so hurt that I wanted to hurt someone else, so when Tank groaned on the floor, I kicked him in the back and then leaned down. "Relax, you could be dead, plus Sergio and Nikolai can fix your booboos."

The bosses slowly moved around the room; a hush fell over everyone as Chase pulled off his shirt and tossed it on the ground. "Who's first?"

"Me." Andrei's grin was pure evil.

And just like that, money exchanged hands again.

I slowly snuck out of the room and prayed that Junior saw me do it, that Junior would follow—because while my dad was sparring in the ring—I wanted to spar with Junior in bed, or maybe even against the wall, I didn't care.

I just needed him.

CHAPTER
Twenty-Eight

Junior

I watched her slip out the door and go upstairs. I looked over my shoulder to make sure all the bosses were busy watching the fight, and then I slowly made my way to the basement door.

Right when I was almost home free, I felt a tap on my shoulder.

Shit, slowly I turned around; it was Breaker and King.

"What's up, guys?"

They exchanged looks, and then Breaker whispered, "Need us to cover for you?"

I exhaled in relief. "If anyone asks, she had a headache and went to lay down."

"Ohhh, a headache, nice one." King smiled. "And your dick is like her Advil, or what?"

"Look, you either help me or you don't, I'm still going up those stairs." My chest heaved as a frenzy washed over me, the crippling feeling of needing another hit of Serena was almost my undoing.

"We've got you." Breaker said softly. "Please just don't die, no sex is worth that."

"It's not just sex," I snapped, feeling my blood boil beneath my skin. "I fucking love her."

"Well, shit." King paled. "Just don't get caught. I don't want to plan another funeral."

Worth it, my heart pumped while I nodded and then took the stairs two at a time until I was running down the hall in anticipation of her taste.

Her door was shut. I knocked. "Serena?"

"You alone?" She asked through the door.

"Yeah."

"Come in, then lock the door."

I quickly opened the door, shut it and locked it, then turned around and nearly died of a heart attack.

She was completely naked except for the ever-present knife strapped to her thigh, her hair was down covering both of her breasts and hanging almost to her waist.

I'd never wanted to pull someone's hair so desperately in my entire existence. I wanted to wrap it around my fist and tug until her eyes burned with tears, until she screamed my name.

Her lips pressed into a wide smile as she put her hands on her hips, her black fingernails stark against her white skin. "Wanna spar?"

"Hmm…" I sauntered over to her and ran a fingertip down her arm, then looked behind her. Something flickered near her shelf. "Hold that thought."

I went over and grabbed the sparkly silver crown, the same one she'd worn when she'd won prom queen. I'd been so pissed that her dad even let her go that I crashed it even though I'd already graduated.

I'll never forget the look on her face when they set the crown on her head; it wasn't an expression of excitement or even happiness; it was weariness, and I knew why.

That crown was her reality.

And that crown—was fucking heavy.

I lifted it off the bookcase and brought it over to her, then very gently placed it on her head. "Your majesty."

With trembling hands, I gripped her hips and moved to my knees. Then I drew a heavy breath, glanced up at her, and whispered, "With my mouth—I worship."

And without hesitation. I, a mere servant. Feasted.

She held onto my head for balance, but I needed to taste more of her, I needed my tongue to slide deeper, I wanted my mouth coated in everything that was my queen.

Her hips bucked against me as I held her in place, and then, irritated that I wasn't getting the perfect angle to quench my hunger, I stood, picked her up by the ass and tossed her backward onto the bed.

She bounced up, and her crown slipped sideways, but her eyes locked onto me, refusing to let go.

I crawled onto the bed, wordlessly gripping her thighs and pulling them over my shoulders while she went limp and gave in, her eyes hooded with lust.

"Watch me," I hissed. "Watch me claim you with my mouth."

A little whimper escaped from between her parted lips as I lowered my head, bowing to her, loving her, giving her every dark, twisted piece of my soul that I had left.

Her taste was my poison.

My addiction.

My soon to be benediction.

And I would never have enough.

Her fingers twisted in my hair as I sucked, and when her body went completely rigid, I abruptly stopped.

"Junior." She shook her head back and forth. "Why? Why'd you stop?"

"Because." I pinched her sensitive skin and grinned. "I want to watch."

She didn't hold back.

And I didn't stop watching.

It was burned in my brain, the way she responded to my mouth, my hands.

With a shudder, she finally sat up, pulled the crown from her head and placed it on mine, and with a smug grin said. "It's my turn to serve."

CHAPTER
Twenty-Nine

Serena

I told myself I wouldn't fall asleep in his arms.

And I did exactly that after we physically exhausted each other.

Junior's arm was heavy around my body as he held me possessively with his left, while the right was tucked under his head like a pillow. His hair was mussed like a halo around his head, even though it was shaved on the sides, the top was so long it flopped to the side and looked so ridiculously sexy even in his sleep that I wanted to throat punch him.

His full lips parted as he sighed and pulled me closer.

The eagle tattoo on his neck seemed darker this close up; actually all his tattoos seemed darker. I started tracing the Nicolasi crest on his chest when he suddenly gripped my hand, his eyes flashing open. "Shit."

"What?" My heart almost stopped.

"We fell asleep." His eyes searched mine. "I'm sorry," he

groaned and then stretched his arms above his head, making the muscles in his abs clench and damn I wanted to lick my way up while working him into another sex-fueled frenzy.

"Stop looking at me like that." His voice was low, sleepy, so sexy that I couldn't help but spread my hands across his chest and then dig my nails in.

A throat cleared.

Without thinking, I reached for the gun on my nightstand at about the same time Junior did the same, both of us aiming toward the throat clearing by the door.

"Fuck, man." Junior lowered his gun. "How long have you been standing there?"

Ash shrugged, running his hands through his thick whiskey-colored hair before leaning against the dresser. "I was sitting at one point… I think."

"You think?" I said incredulously. "Ash, are you—"

His blue eyes flashed to mine. Hurt. Pain. So much pain that I wanted to look away, I wanted to take it all away. "Do. Not. Ask. If. I'm. Okay."

I held up my hands and gulped while his bright blue eyes locked onto Junior like some sort of understanding was passing between them.

"What's going on?" Junior finally asked, leaning back against the headboard, appearing way more relaxed than I felt since the assassin of the group, aka Chase's son, had just caught us in bed naked.

If this had happened before, I would have had a gunshot to the head. I wasn't stupid back then; immature yes, stupid no. I'd just had no idea Ash would do anything to keep us safe, including listening to Chase when he said to break us up.

Ash's eyes were wild as he shoved away from the dresser

and started pacing back and forth. I didn't realize he had a knife in his hand until he used it to scratch the back of his neck like it was normal to use the point of a dagger to get the job done.

Junior gripped my thigh under the sheets in warning.

And I knew what that warning was.

Ash was either about to go crazy, or he needed us.

Both did not bode well for our current naked situation.

I stared blankly ahead. Trying to mask the fear lurking beneath my skin at the thought that my final moments in this world would be my cousin seeing me naked in my best friend's arms while he slit my throat.

Asher finally stopped pacing and then moved down until he was resting his arms on his haunches. He didn't look up. "I need a favor."

Not what I expected. I almost breathed a sigh of relief.

Junior's grip on my thigh deepened. "Anything you need, brother."

Ash slowly lifted his head. His eyes were wild, and then as if a switch had been flipped, a calmness descended over him. His shoulders relaxed, his lips pressed into a firm line. "I need you to swear fealty to me. Loyalty to me and me alone as the heir to the Abandonato Family."

I stilled. "What?"

Both of us were heirs, but technically Ash's blood was purer than mine because a long time ago... people fell in love, then they fell into hate and cheated, and the result? My dad and Chase almost being closer than cousins.

Ash sighed. "Each of us will be bosses or underbosses one day, one way or another. But I need you to swear fealty to me as your leader. I need you to make a blood oath to sacrifice yourself for me. To keep our secrets." He was quiet and then. "To create a new family line within the families."

It was death.

It wasn't done.

And it wasn't just frowned upon, it was a slap in the face to the bosses, to our fathers who protected us, bled for us.

It was a slap in the face to me since I was the heir, but that wasn't exactly true, because we all knew that the true heir had always been Chase, which meant Asher was next in line if I chose to hand over my crown.

A peace washed over me as I realized it was exactly what needed to be done in order to protect myself—in order to protect our future. A leader was needed, and I'd been leading so long that I was sick of it.

For the first time in my life, I wanted to follow.

And I wanted to choose Junior despite the expectations that were thrown on us.

Even though this wasn't right, I realized I would do it. Because if I kept Ash's secrets.

He kept mine.

Protect the kingdom at all costs, right?

Heavy was the crown that Ash would wear, and even heavier? The keys, the secrets that our new kings would carry.

Junior must have had the same thought because his next words were, "Did you set us up? Hope to find us like this, so we had no choice?"

"Yes." Ash didn't even hesitate as he clenched his jaw and lifted his chin in defiance. "But even if I didn't. You owe me. You fucking owe me. And you owe Claire!"

"You're right," I whispered as guilt slid around my neck

and squeezed until I almost stopped breathing. "What about the others."

"Waiting for my text," he rasped.

"So the kids, the next generation…" Junior bit his lower lip and shook his head like he was trying to put it all together. "We create our own alliance."

"The Elect," Ash whispered. "We are what they made us. And we protect our own. This is our way of making our promises, our bond, just as powerful as that to each of our families. And in the end, if you have to choose, you choose each other."

It was madness.

It was blasphemy.

It was right.

A tear slid down my cheek. "You ask us to swear our lives to you over our own blood promises to our fathers?"

"They can co-exist," Ash said in a harsh voice. "I just need to know that no matter what, you're fucking *with* me."

"No matter what," Junior repeated thickly, "we are with you."

The next few minutes went by in a blur as I quickly got dressed and pulled my hair into a ponytail.

Ash turned toward the door and texted King, Breaker, Maxim, Violet, Kartini, and Izzy.

And one by one, they all came to my room.

A room I'd just made love in.

Ironic, how minutes later, we would start a war.

Ash held a blade over his hand and sliced as drops of blood fell to the hardwood floor in slow motion.

"Our kingdom," he said through clenched teeth. "Our rules."

"Our kingdom. Our rules," we all repeated.

He passed the knife around as each of us made a cut across our palms.

And as we all stood there holding our bloody hands, Ash locked eyes with us and said. "This is our clean slate. May the sins of our fathers—" He shared a look with Junior. "Be forgiven. Amen."

"Amen," I murmured.

Each of us shook hands across our wounds.

And when it was all done.

I turned to my cousin and fucking bowed.

CHAPTER
Thirty

Junior

Nobody asked the older cousins anything when we all asked to crash at Nixon's a second night in a row.

They didn't know that we'd made a blood oath to let Ash lead us into the future, our future.

The bosses didn't know that the very monsters they were trying to keep at bay—had just been set free by the tip of Ash's knife, by the blood of Claire's death.

We needed each other.

But we also needed a plan of action because as much as I knew Ash was losing his shit—he was right. We couldn't go on carrying the sins of our fathers, and we couldn't go on punishing innocent people out of fear.

We'd always been known as the Elect. Some said we were a secret society; others knew we were mafia.

Last night, we had become both.

An almost religious experience had happened between all

of us as we'd realized that we couldn't do this alone, and we couldn't do this with the bosses constantly breathing down our backs.

We had to have our own rules. Our own terms.

Or we wouldn't survive.

We would end up just like Claire.

That morning, the ride to school felt different.

For the first time since going to Eagle Elite, we rode in two SUVs.

For the first time since enrolling, we all packed, no matter what.

And for the first time since stepping foot on campus—I fucking held my girlfriend's hand.

Because the blood bond between all of us trumped the one I'd given her own father.

I had my family.

I was looking at them.

I had my future.

I was holding her hand.

We made our own rules.

Because death made it so you didn't give a fuck anymore.

For the first time since I could remember, I smiled as I walked to class with my princess by my side.

It was turning out to be the perfect day—until lunch happened, and Annie, as she always had with Claire, tried to come up to Ash and talk to him.

"Hey!" I pulled Ash away from her. "Cool off, man, give it some time."

"It's your fault!" Ash roared.

Annie flinched and then ducked behind Tank, who was trying to mediate the out-of-control situation while the rest of us waited for the inevitable, for Ash to snap and for Annie to cry or just run in the opposite direction.

Instead, she shocked the shit out of me, jerked away from Tank, marched right up to Ash, and slapped him across the face shouting. "You have no idea what you're talking about! She was my friend! The only person who offered to help me."

"Help?" Ash roared. "How the hell did she help you!?"

With tears streaming down her face, Annie pulled off her cardigan and tossed it to the ground, stomping all over it like it pissed her off.

I wanted to make a joke about how relieved Ash should be, and then I froze when I saw the bruises on her arms, bruises that were covered by the sleeves of her cardigan in the hospital.

Ash completely paled. "Annie, what the hell?"

"No." Her lower lip trembled. "You don't get to give me that look. She was helping me. Trying to get me s-safe from them! And now…" She sniffed. "Now—"

Ash just stood there while Tank pulled Annie into his arms and hugged her. I couldn't fathom what had given her that many bruises, but I was ready to kill someone.

And by the looks of Ash and the rest of the guys… they were in.

Some of the De Lange kids witnessed the exchange with fear in their eyes, and then I just wondered what the hell we were doing with our lives if we weren't protecting those who couldn't protect themselves.

I slammed my hand down on the park bench before I could stop myself and screamed. "WHO!"

Annie jumped a foot. "Wh-what?"

"Who did this?"

She gulped, her face white. "Leave it alone."

"No." Ash took a tentative step toward her and then, in an eerily possessive voice, whispered, "Tell me who touched you so I can break their hands off. Tell me who marred your skin so I can mar their faces. Tell us so we can fix this; otherwise, I'm going to start randomly beating up people who look like pieces of shit who feed off of innocent women."

She gulped and seemed to pull into herself as she whispered. "My adoptive dad was always nice to my adoptive mom, really nice and then…"

Ash shook his head, grabbed his gun, handed it to a confused Annie, and said, "You get the right to kill him. We'll cover it up."

"What? NO. I could never!" Annie tried to hand the gun back. But Ash wouldn't have it; instead, he pulled her into his arms and whispered something I will never forget.

"To be who you're meant to be—you must. When power's taken—it must be stolen back."

In minutes, both Escalades were pulling up.

Twelve of the De Langes watched us prepare for war. I wondered if they understood what was happening.

And then one by one, each of them walked up to Asher, put a shaky hand on his shoulder, and kissed his right cheek, only to walk past him and into the waiting SUVs. We didn't have room for everyone, which Tank solved by driving his truck.

Did Ash realize how dangerous this new alliance would be if his father found out? How dangerous it would be for all of us when the kids realized there was no out once you were in?

Pride filled my chest as every De Lange kid got in. They weren't even fucking armed, but they had their pride, they wore it like armor.

And without using words.

They swore their alliance, their allegiance.

To the next generation.

To the Elect.

To us.

We had successfully done something that our parents had failed at. We'd given them something to fight for.

We'd given them a reason to fight in the first place.

And we'd given them a leader.

I just hoped like hell that when our dads eventually found out, they didn't see us as a threat—but a savior.

Annie gave us directions to her house and after arguing with a pissed off Ash, stayed in the car shaking while Serena held her in her arms, some of the other De Lange girls handed her Kleenex while Ash walked in to scout the house with Tank.

When they came back, both of them had empty expressions.

They just got into the car and wordlessly drove every single person back to Nixon's house.

I gripped Serena's hand and watched in awe as the gates opened.

And as we let the very "evil" that our parents had tried to destroy.

The very evil that lived in my soul.

Inside the kingdom.

And for one fleeting moment, I had hope. Hope that maybe, just maybe, the King who'd just crowned me—would kneel instead of drawing his sword.

CHAPTER
Thirty-One

Serena

The house was quiet. The suits that always waited around the house watched us with horror on their faces, and yet they did nothing.

Because they couldn't lift a finger to mafia royalty unless the bosses allowed it.

So, in we marched, with the enemy of our fathers shaking next to us.

Wordlessly, Junior and I marched ahead and opened up the door to the basement.

"Downstairs," Junior barked.

I nodded to him as they all filed down, our own private army, our new family.

The Family of the Elect.

One by one, they made their way into the basement near the ring, Asher and King held up the back of the group.

The door to the basement locked with a resounding click.

And there we stood, lined up in front of them like the generals we were. Ash, me, and Junior in the middle. Maksim, Breaker, King, and Tank on the outside, with Izzy, Annie, and Violet in the middle.

"You know why you're here," Ash said in a harsh voice, his face twisted with pain as he looked at each of them, four girls, eight guys.

I pulled out my gun and held it lowered in front of me.

"Yes." One of them stepped forward; he looked like he was my age, his eyes flickered to mine and then to Asher. "We want in."

"The minute you got in that car," Junior said with a smirk. "You already were…" He took a step forward and held out his dagger. "Kneel."

Shit.

The guy's jaw flexed, and then he very slowly lowered to his knees as Junior held the knife over his head. With a grimace, Junior dug the knife into his palm and sprinkled the blood over the guy's bent head.

"Who do you answer to?" Junior barked.

"You," the guy yelled.

"WHO!" Junior screamed, this time getting in his face. It was a moment I won't ever forget a moment where a switch was flipped, maybe a moment where blood recognized blood.

The guy looked up into Junior's face and whispered, "The true heir and our true boss."

Junior sucked in a sharp breath, and in an instant, I saw a family line go from being cut out—to being reborn.

And the ultimate betrayal to our fathers…

Began.

Every single person swore their loyalty to the De Lange-

Nicolasi line, and then to Ash as our leader.

I was emotionally exhausted by the time everything was done. I mean, how did someone explain the rules of the mafia to kids who had only grown up knowing they had to hide from the very thing that created them? The very blood that called to them? Screamed for vengeance from the ground.

"We have a slight problem," Breaker said once we'd made the formal introductions and basically told them we owned the very blood that ran through their veins.

"Slight?" I almost laughed.

"Oh, this?" He waved his hand around. "This is a big problem, not talking about this. I'm talking about the fact that none of them know how to fight."

I gaped. "Wait, none of them?"

"Watch." He whistled one of the guys over. "Matt, throw a punch."

Matt had his hair buzzed short to his head, baby skin with no tattoos, and green eyes that looked so innocent I wondered if he was going to burst into tears.

"Uhh…" He rocked back on his feet and then sloppily threw a right hook.

Breaker moved out of the way and shoved him to the floor then sighed. "See? What good is an army if they've never learned how to throw a punch?"

"Maybe if they'd had parents who taught them…" Tank said, all passive-aggressively next to us.

I glared. "Point made."

He held up his hands. "Just saying…"

"We'll train them," I said like it was just that simple, earning irritated looks from all the guys. "What? We can't train here, I mean obviously, but we can train at The Spot, turn it from party central to, mafia base."

"Ash?" Junior looked to him. "What do you think?"

"I think once the parents find out we did this, we may need to hide out for a few days anyway." He sighed. "Until then, let's get everyone out of here before Nixon calls all of the bosses, and we have a blood bath. Best to tell them to their faces than to tell them to—"

The sound of the basement door opening was our only clue.

And then footsteps.

Several.

They were hard.

Purposeful.

Angry.

And slow.

Junior shoved me behind him while Ash did the same to the girls. The De Langes looked ready to shit themselves— as they should, and they stood in the very back. I mean it wasn't like we were going to be able to hide much, plus you could smell the fear, it had this metallic shimmer in the air that seemed to somehow make it harder to breathe the closer the footsteps got.

My dad was first. His sleeves rolled up to his elbows, his black pants almost casual looking, as his eyes flashed in my direction.

Part of me almost laughed, because if he thought this was pissed, then well, just ask me who I had in my mouth last night.

Or was that morning?

Junior cleared his throat ahead of me.

Phoenix was next. I knew he had flown back. He ran a hand through his hair as he looked at us with such disappointment and rage, I could feel Junior flinch beside me.

Tex and Sergio filed in behind them.

And then Dante and Chase flanked each of their sides. It was a little alarming that Andrei had also shown up with Vic, one of Chase's number one men, and what was even more alarming?

My grandpa Frank stood with them, and next to him, my uncle Luca Nicolasi, who we hadn't seen in at least a decade. He'd gone into hiding years ago along with my grandpa Frank, but at least I knew Grandpa was still around; he sent me cards on my birthday even though he'd disappeared.

"So, this is a fun family reunion," Breaker said under his breath.

I shot him a look. "Could you not be *you* right now?"

He winked. "What can they do? Shoot us?"

"Yes," Junior and Asher said in unison, not making me feel at all better about the anger directed at us.

The funeral for Claire was to take place in one more day.

And I had to wonder—would our caskets be joining hers?

"Serena!" My dad barked my name so loudly that I jumped in place.

But I didn't move.

I lifted my chin in defiance. "Yes?"

"Come here now."

I gave him a sad smile. "I can't do that."

"You'd make me shoot through you, then?" he asked innocently.

"If that's what it takes," I said in a strong voice. "But I'm not standing here to play human shield; I just have to defer to someone else right now."

"Defer. To. Someone. Else," he repeated slowly. "And who is this someone else?"

"Me." Asher took a step forward, and the ripple of shock that went through the group of men would have been hilarious had they not all been armed.

Chase's eyes were wild. "What the hell have you done?"

"What you didn't," he snapped. "I offered them a choice."

Chase roared, "You have no idea—" and then stopped himself. "No idea what sort of betrayal this is. Bringing that filth into Nixon's home! Into the safety of these walls, you had no *right* to even ask them to join the ranks! That right goes to the boss! And that line is officially dead!"

"You can't kill blood that still flows," Junior spoke up. "Trust me; I've tried."

A shadow crossed Phoenix's face, but Junior kept talking. "Right, Dad? You can't forget who you are, *whose* you are, no matter how many times you fucking change your name."

"Enough!" Chase snapped.

"You want us to be our own people, but only if we follow your rules. Well..." Ash shrugged. "Your rules suck. So, we created our own. We'll stay loyal to the Family, to our bloodlines, to *all* of our bloodlines."

"All of them," Junior echoed and then in a move I did not see coming, he grabbed the tip of his tagger and dug into his forearm, red blood slid in streams down his arm as he made slash after slash, and then the knife clattered to the floor.

I gasped as he pulled his shirt off and wiped the blood away.

He'd marred his perfect skin.

He'd created a bloody scar of the Phoenix.

The De Lange crest.

Phoenix took a step closer and then another, until he stood in front of Junior, gripped his forearm, and jerked him forward.

I'd never been so terrified in my entire life as Phoenix touched his forehead to his son, and then kissed each of his cheeks and whispered, "You're right."

We exhaled as he eyed each of our faces and then shook his head. "I'm gone for two weeks…" He turned around. "All this under your roof, Nixon?"

"He was too busy getting his wife naked," Dante said under his breath.

"I just have one question." Phoenix dropped Junior's arm. "Whose idea was this?"

Oh, shit was about to very much hit the fan as Ash took a step forward and said in a commanding voice. "They all swore their fealty. Every last one…" He eyed his father and narrowed his gaze. "To me."

Chase charged forward but was stopped by Nixon and Dante.

"How dare you!" Chase roared. "YOU KNOW what they did to us! YOU KNOW!"

"Chase—" Tex shoved him back. "Get ahold of yourself."

But the damage was done, wasn't it?

The trust between father and son… broken.

All because Ash's heart wasn't his own anymore—he was burying it into the cold hard ground. He had nothing left to lose.

So, he chose to get revenge the only way he knew how.

Embracing the enemy and rising to power in a way that would make it impossible for the bosses to challenge.

Because they wouldn't kill their only heirs.

Not when they needed us so desperately.

Not when we were one and not divided.

"The sins of our fathers," Ash spoke evenly. "Are no longer on our shoulders. We rebuke them. We won't make your mistakes, so don't ask us to, because it just forces us to say no to your faces. You want us to fight for blood." He pointed at Junior. "Well, congratulations, we just fought for it."

Slowly, Junior and Ash started walking forward; the bosses parted, most of them with smirks on their faces or looks of pride.

In fact, they all looked quite pleased with themselves, which was confusing, everyone except Chase.

No, he had murder in his eyes, and for a split second I wondered if there would be a blood bath since his only job for a while had been to hunt De Langes and kill them, since he'd been singlehandedly responsible for cleansing their family line after his deceased wife's betrayal.

But Tex held him firm, whispering something under his breath that made Chase still.

And then he whispered something else. "Leader."

Chase squeezed his eyes shut as a grimace crossed his face, and then with a firm nod in Ash's direction, he let them pass.

Along with the entire mass of De Lange kids, who were trembling from the encounter.

We took them up to the theater room and closed the door. My hands were shaking as I quickly went over to Junior and wrapped my arms around him.

Asher cleared his throat, and I immediately jumped back. "What?"

"Not in public." His eyes searched mine. "We're already

on thin ice. If they find out about you guys, it may just tip the scale."

I wanted to tell him to go to hell, but I couldn't. Not anymore. So I whispered, "I understand." And tried to keep the tears at bay.

Tears of pride that Junior had stood up for his family, for his blood, no matter how evil.

And tears of stress that he could have so easily been taken from me, in a heartbeat, in a few seconds, gone.

"You should get something for that," I said, pointing at his forearm, it hadn't stopped bleeding and was scary accurate when it came to the family crest. "Come on."

There was a bathroom that led to the hall but also had a door to the theater room, I grabbed his hand and pulled him into that bathroom, then made sure to close and lock both doors.

Before I could turn around, Junior had me in his arms, lifting me onto the sink, getting blood all over my black skirt and the top of my thighs.

He kissed me while he bled.

His mouth claimed me over and over again as his anger and desperation violently clashed.

With a grunt, he tugged my thighs open. "I need you."

"You have me. You always have me. Whenever you need me," I pulled back, lips swollen. "After all, I live to serve my king." Slowly, very slowly, I opened my thighs wide as he walked between them, pulling me against his hard length. He was so hot and ready; I reached for his trousers only to have him shove me back against the mirror, looking like an angry god as his wild eyes locked on mine.

King and Queen.

Pleasure and pain.

Had there ever been a love like ours, I wondered? Saint and sinner, Heaven and Hell.

We were every extreme and everything in between.

And I wouldn't want it any other way.

His fingers slid up my thigh and gripped my underwear. When he gave an aggressive tug, they became nothing but scrap in his bloody hands. Really, I needed to just stop wearing them if he'd keep finding so much pleasure in destroying them.

I leaned back and directed a lazy gaze in his direction. "All yours."

"Yes." His eyes flashed as he gripped me by the knees and pulled me forward. "All mine."

"Greedy." I let out a breathless moan as his lips found my neck, between bites and kisses, I was squirming for more of him, and then with one swift movement, he freed himself and impaled me on his cock.

He swallowed my cry with his mouth and thrust deep. I gripped his head with my hands while we watched each other, no words were said, only actions, only the jerky movements of my body as he claimed me.

That and the murmur from the other side of the door that sounded like my dad, as he said, "Let them do what they want, Chase."

Junior clapped a hand over my mouth while I squeezed my eyes shut and tried to stay quiet, and I probably would have been able to, but Junior refused to stop moving if anything his thrusts grew wilder. In one movement, he was out of me, pressing me face forward on the door, my palms flush against it while my dad talked with Chase.

"They're strong," Chase said, almost annoyed. "Stronger than we were."

"We made them that way." Phoenix joined in.

A muffled cry escaped from between my lips as Junior pounded into me while I was mere feet from the bosses, mere feet from my dad, while the heir to the Nicolasi throne claimed me as his.

"You hear them?" Junior whispered, pulling me lightly back by my hair as his lips found my neck. "Remember whose you are... remember who you serve."

"You, you," I whimpered in a soft whisper.

"You stopped being Nixon Abandonato's daughter the minute you let me into your soul, the minute I tasted you—now, you're mine. And one day." He thrust into me harder as pleasure squeezed me so tight, I couldn't breathe. "One day, he'll know just how dirty his princess got. Because while you're letting the Nicolasi King give you release—you're simultaneously letting the De Lange Fallen give you pleasure. You get both. Good and bad. Monster and man and one day, he'll know. It's me who holds your allegiance, your body, your heart," My release was crashing all over me as he finally whispered. "Your soul."

"Yes." Out of breath, I rested my forehead against the door and sighed. "Yes."

The voices disappeared.

Junior held me close, still pulsing inside me. Still making me want to move my hips.

And as I looked down, I realized his bloodied forearm was pressed against my chest, against my heart.

And in a hushed voice, I said, "The Phoenix has risen."

CHAPTER
Thirty-Two

Junior

Nixon's place had officially become the place to crash. I think some of the cousins were petrified that if they went home, their moms would lay into them over what had happened with the De Langes, my mom included.

Because if you think a mob boss is scary, then you really don't want to piss off one of the moms.

I shuddered.

I remember my ma telling me that if I got a girl pregnant out of wedlock, she'd actually stab a fork into one of my balls, make it look like an accident, then serve it to me like a meatball.

I was fourteen.

To this day, spaghetti and meatballs make me want to hurl, which she so lovingly used to serve every single time I had a so-called date in junior high or high school.

Joke was on her since all those girls were just a way to get Serena to wake the hell up, and when that did happen, we used the girls as a way to cover up the fact that we were the ones sleeping together.

It worked until my ma asked why I never touched any of them at dinner. I used the meatball as explanation enough.

It was nearing midnight, and we'd sent the De Langes back to the campus along with one of the SUVs and enough suits to keep them safe, so they didn't shit themselves during the twenty-minute ride.

It was a very real possibility with how many of them were shaking during our amateur movie night, another way to try to calm them the hell down.

And when that didn't work, we gave them wine.

I was waiting to sneak into Serena's room and knew Nixon was a night owl, so while I waited for the guy to finally give it a rest in his office, I jogged down the stairs and decided to work out for a bit.

Nixon wasn't in his office, though; he was in the ring, and Asher was on the ground bleeding under him.

"The hell?" I roared. "Did you kill him?"

Nixon frowned over at me, sweat dripping down his muscled stomach. "Why would I kill him?"

"Because of today? Look if you're that pissed to just single us out then—"

Asher raised a taped hand into the air. "Asked him. Wrote… eulogy."

"Shit." I grabbed one of the water bottles and tossed it to Nixon and watched as Asher groaned and moved to a sitting position. Blood dripped from his chin and somehow from his right ear. "You look like hell."

"That's what happens when you ask someone scarier than

you to fight," Ash grumbled. "I said 'make me forget,' not 'kill me please.'"

"Yeah, I get those phrases confused often." Nixon flashed a smile. "I think my work here is done. Don't stay up too late. We have the funeral tomorrow, and don't either of you show up drunk."

"We would never," I lied and then smirked.

Nixon just stared me down and then reached out and grabbed my forearm; I'd let the scar scab as it should.

"Your dad rose from the ashes," Nixon sighed. "Then burned his entire family back into the cold dead ground only to have his son, his heir, resurrect the very evil we tried to keep out. I hope for your sake, you two know what you're doing."

I pulled my arm away and shrugged. "We're doing the right thing, and we're doing the only thing we know how. Putting more De Langes into the ground doesn't keep you any more safe Nixon—it just steals more pieces of your soul, pieces that none of us really have extra of. If someone crosses us, we know what to do, but until then, the sins of the father..." I didn't finish, but something flashed in his eyes, something that made me want to throw a punch.

"The sins of the father," he repeated, giving me another strange non-Nixon like stare. "And do you admittedly take after him more or your mother?"

"What do you think?" I snapped.

"He's all Phoenix," Asher grumbled from the floor. "Down to the way he fucks."

I knew it slipped before Ash could stop it.

And I knew in that moment that I flinched like I couldn't stop it, which just proved what Ash said as truth—which meant I now looked guilty in front of my girlfriend's father.

The air stilled, took on a tangible chill.

"Something you need to tell me, Junior?" Nixon leaned in until I could smell the blood and sweat from his skin.

I lifted my chin and ground out a, "No, sir."

His blue eyes narrowed into tiny slits as he pressed a hand to my shoulder. "You sure about that?"

"Yes," I lied. "I'm sure."

"Okay, then." His eyes flickered to my other arm. "Funny how you have a De Lange crest on one forearm and my trust on your other." His teeth gritted together in a sneer. "Don't break it."

"Don't tempt me," I snapped.

"Whoa, whoa." Ash stood on wobbly feet. "It's been a long day. Nixon just beat my ass, so his testosterone can probably be smelled from upstairs." He gave a gentle shove toward his uncle then joked. "Want me to kick his ass for you, Nixon?"

I snorted. "Like you could."

Nixon finally smiled and then stepped out of the ring and grabbed his shirt. "Remember what I said, guys."

"Yeah, yeah," I called after him, trying to sound like I wasn't ready to bang my head against the closest sharp object.

"Really, Ash?" I hissed once Nixon was gone. "You just had to say that?"

"My girlfriend's dead, and I have internal bleeding. Sorry if I'm missing my filter—hell, any filter. I hurt."

"Yeah, you look like you hurt." I eyed his bruised body.

"Not here." Tears filled his eyes. "Here." He tapped his chest and jerked his head toward the bench where his bag was waiting. "I wrote out her eulogy about a hundred different times, but nothing did her justice, nothing made what I felt for her sound like anything except infatuation, lust, and *maybe* a bit of love sprinkled in. How do you tell the ignorant that your soul is missing from your body? That you may never get that part of yourself back? That half the time, you just wish the pain would end."

I pulled him into a tight hug, blood, sweat, and all. "You have nothing to prove to anyone at that funeral tomorrow. All you have to do is honor the life she lived by your side, do that, and you'll be fine."

He hugged me tighter. "Will you stand with me?"

My chest and throat grew tight. "I'll stand with you in life and in death. I'll stand by your side forever, Ash."

"No matter what?" he repeated.

I pounded my fist onto his back. "No matter what. Even if the world burns around us. You've got me."

"Same, brother. Same."

CHAPTER
Thirty-Three

Junior

I hated funerals.

They reminded me that life was fleeting.

They also reminded me that I probably wouldn't live to see my next birthday, especially with how the conversation had gone with Nixon last night, he suspected something.

I would need to be more careful.

My black suit felt tight around me as I waited for Ash to stop puking in the bathroom.

The guy was a mess.

He'd taken one look at the casket and lost it.

Every single one of us had been to the open casket, but he couldn't do it, he said he wanted to remember what she looked like with real life in her cheeks, with the life of their baby in her body.

None of us had told the rest of the bosses, and I assumed

Nikolai kept that silent. It wasn't his secret to tell, but it also wasn't Ash's secret to keep, at least not from her parents.

They, too, would need to mourn, not just Claire, but the baby she and Ash had created.

He'd confessed she was only eight weeks along, but that didn't matter, did it? That baby had been alive, growing, and now was in heaven with its mom.

Because of someone's hatred.

That baby never got the chance to see the light of day.

I swallowed the thickness in my throat as I pulled out my flask of whiskey, brought it to my lips, and took one swig when I noticed Violet stumbling out of the girls' bathroom of the church.

She tugged down her form-fitting black dress and then fixed her hair. She took after Luc, classic beauty that you felt in your soul whenever you looked at her and so damn sweet, I was thankful she was studying medicine and that the bosses gave her a free pass since she'd be the Family doctor one day.

Her full red lips pressed into a secret smile.

I almost waved her over, instead choosing to hide back in my spot around the corner.

A few seconds passed, she looked over her shoulder, and then Breaker was grabbing her ass.

My jaw dropped as she smiled and then told him to be quiet.

His hair was in complete disarray, his shirt unbuttoned by at least three buttons as he tucked it back into his pants.

No. They couldn't.

I mean, they could.

Was it the funeral?

Emotions were high, people were sad, sex happened probably just as much at funerals as it did at weddings.

Thankfully, we were in a private part of the church that had been sectioned off for security reasons for the Family.

And everyone was already sitting down.

"Hey." Ash walked out of the bathroom and took my flask, downing two gulps, and getting ready to turn in the very wrong direction.

I wrapped an arm around him and then patted him on the chest, directing him away from Violet and Breaker.

Because the last thing he needed was to murder one of his cousins on the day he had to give his girlfriend's eulogy.

"You're tenser than I am." Clearly, the alcohol was affecting Ash. His eyes were glassy, but he wasn't swaying yet. He'd get through it, and then I'd knock him out, so it didn't hurt anymore. Because that's what brothers did, right? I just wish I could take the pain from him, all of it.

"Yeah well, you know funerals, they make everyone a bit… tense."

"Yeah," he croaked.

"You can do this," I said softly. "I'll be right by your side."

"Doing this means goodbye forever." He barely got the words out. "It means it happened. It means it's not a bad dream. It means I'm burying them."

Them.

I squeezed my eyes shut. "Do you truly think that with the world we live in, a soul suddenly goes silent because of death?"

"I don't know anymore." His voice caught. "But I know it hurts. And my only solace is knowing that at least I get the pain—while they get to rest."

My heart burned in my chest as I slowly nodded my head

in agreement and then walked side by side to the back of the church where Nikolai continued to speak.

Two minutes later, he introduced Ash.

And we walked side by side down the aisle to give her eulogy. To say a final prayer of peace.

And to mourn—his best friend.

My eyes flickered to movement in the back row. All of the De Lange kids were here, some with their adoptive parents.

Slowly but surely, the De Langes, the cut off line, the line that was hated the most, rose to their feet in solidarity as Ash and I walked.

I'd only ever heard of it happening once before.

And it was at Mil De Lange, Chase's first wife's funeral. They stood with Chase despite what his wife had done—they stood with Ash now, despite what their blood had done.

And as we walked, all the people in the church rose to their feet, while honoring the ones who fell, honoring the ones left behind, honoring the ones left to pick up the pieces.

And when Ash looked out at the congregation that day, I swear it felt like his crown was finally and firmly pressed onto his head, just like mine.

I'd been baptized in bad blood.

While he'd been baptized in death.

Both moments had created us, formed us, and both moments would define us.

"You can sit," Ash said boldly into the microphone. "I asked my best friend to stand up here with me because I wasn't completely sure I could make it through. But more than that, sometimes you just need people you love by your side to remind you that in a world full of hate, love still exists." The room was so quiet I could hear my own slow breathing as I locked gazes with Serena and refused to look away all the while thinking, let them see who owns my heart, let them see because even in death, I would only ever be... hers.

Ash continued. "All it takes is one second, and life can get ripped from you. I actually had a fight with Claire that morning. She wanted to go shopping, and I wanted to send security with her. She finally won because she was part Russian and absolutely terrifying when she needed to be."

The room fell into chuckles.

"But I would take that fight over and over again; I would take blood and war and beatings just to hold her one last time. To tell her that I'm sorry I couldn't protect her. To tell her I'm sorry I couldn't keep them safe—" His voice cracked. "It's heavy, that moment when you realize your life isn't ever going to be the same, when you realize your love created a life you'll never get the chance to see."

Serena's eyes filled with tears. As one spilled over, I still didn't look away. I couldn't.

Ash took a minute. "She was pregnant." The room stilled with tension. "And we were trying to figure out how to navigate this world, we were shaken with the brutal truth that bringing up kids in this atmosphere is anything but easy, anything but innocent, and we were broken with the absolutely horrifying idea that we would fail, but she reminded me, in a time when I desperately needed it, that our parents succeeded. That they raised up a generation of warriors, of mafia royalty that would forever protect their blood until their last breath. She reminded me who I was, whose blood ran through my veins. She reminded me that fear only steals, makes you powerless, that walking through that fear is what makes you a man."

"I love you," Serena mouthed to me.

"You too," I mouthed back.

Let them see our love.

Let them hate us for it.

I was done. So done.

"I will miss my best friend until my last breath, but I refuse to walk in fear. I refuse to cower. If anything, Claire's death hasn't woken the beast. It's risen within me the sleeping giant that was always there, that just needed a little push from a very wise woman to understand what life meant. I will be forever grateful to the love of my life. And I'll mourn her until I join her, whenever that may be. Thank you for honoring her today, and thank you for honoring the Families by your presence." He looked out to the crowd and took a deep breath then finished with. "Blood in. No Out… except death."

"Blood in." The congregation responded. "No out."

"Amen," Ash whispered.

I released the breath I'd been holding and looked to my right as we made our way back down the stairs to our seats, and what I saw chilled me to the bone.

Nixon looked from me to Serena silently crying in her seat, and then back at me. It was a moment when I should have ducked my head, or rolled my eyes, done anything except what I did.

Fucking stare him down and challenge him for the treasure in his kingdom.

Her.

I was supposed to sit with my family, but in that moment, I made a choice, one I should have made all those years ago when Ash broke us apart.

Today.

Today. I would choose Serena Abandonato.

And I would do it knowing my moments were counted, my seconds numbered, knowing I was choosing her, the way I was choosing my own death.

Trace gaped at me in shock as I stared Nixon down and sidestepped him, then sat next to his daughter and held her hand.

Chase turned over his shoulder and shot me a nod of approval, but my dad, my dad looked at me like he was going to lose me. I didn't realize my mom was crying into her hands until he put his arm around her to keep her from making any noise.

They'd seen everything.

They knew.

And I would pay the ultimate price.

Down into the darkness, I walked with my princess by my side, toward blood, beatings, uncertainty in utter blindness. And never had I felt so happy.

"Why?" Serena whispered as more tears slid down her cheeks.

"Because… I choose you." I held her hand tightly. "Because you own my heart." She started sobbing quietly. "Because as Ash said, we're only given moments, and I'm choosing to live mine with the truth."

The funeral ended with a prayer.

And I confidently wrapped an arm around Serena and walked her away from everyone.

She could ride with me back to her parents' house for food.

She could hold my hand if she needed comfort.

And she would be kissing my mouth for sustenance.

I was hers.

She was mine.

"As long as we both shall live," I swore.
"As long as we both shall live," she repeated.
Amen.

CHAPTER
Thirty-Four

Serena

We held hands the entire drive back to my house. Junior's eyes were locked on the road, but his hand gripped mine so tight I could swear I felt the imprint of his ring on his finger.

The Nicolasi ring.

The crest.

The heaviness of the Nicolasi Kingdom resting on his shoulders as well as a fallen kingdom that he'd helped resurrect.

Who knew a few weeks ago, we would be in this position?

"His speech was beautiful." I tried to keep the terror out of my voice, but it was nearly impossible. All I kept thinking was what happened if that was Junior, and how I wouldn't live if it was.

I would never forgive the person who took him away from me.

Never.

"You're beautiful." Junior brought my hand to his lips and

then turned down a dirt road outside the city. We were still miles from my house.

"We could go out like Romeo and Juliet," I suggested.

Junior cursed and turned off the car; then his hands were in my hair as his mouth devoured mine, his tongue tasted like whiskey as it flicked and teased me, making promises we both knew he couldn't keep.

Like forever.

We broke apart, panting.

"I love you." Tears formed in my eyes as I crawled over the console and straddled him, I'd never been more thankful he had a stupid Maserati.

Junior's mouth parted as he pressed hungry kisses to my chin and down my neck, his hands already lifting my form-fitting thankfully, stretchy, bodycon dress up to my hips.

He let out a curse when his hands hit bare ass.

I grinned down at him. "Well, you keep ripping them—"

"Fuck, I love you." Our mouths crashed together as I worked the front of his black dress pants, pulling him free. He was always so ready for me, so hard, every huge inch of him... hard and throbbing for me.

We broke apart as he helped lift me onto him, and then I was taking him as slowly as I could, until I felt him in my soul, so deep I had to suck in a sharp breath to keep from tensing up.

"In another life..." He pressed a tender kiss to the corner of my mouth. "We had ten kids."

"Ten?" I laughed through my tears. Through my pleasure. Through my heartache. "Why ten?"

"Because you can't keep your hands off of me," he growled against my mouth then nipped my lips before sucking them so hard that I cried out against him, the feeling of his mouth sucking, his body moving beneath me was almost too much to take.

"That's true," I panted.

"And in another life, your father wouldn't kill me for loving you. I would have seen you pregnant with my children; I would have my ring on your finger. I would have your blood etched on my fucking soul, and I would give you my name."

Tears dripped off my chin as I nodded my head. "Serena Nicolasi." I gasped and then changed my mind. "No. Serena De Lange-Nicolasi. Because if I get to marry the king, I want him all. The bad parts, the good. I want the forbidden. I want the Phoenix."

"I don't want to let go," Junior confessed. "I'm so close, always with you, so close to the edge."

"I'll jump with you," I swore. "And Junior…" My body shook as he filled me harder as I took him deeper. "You aren't alone."

We both came apart, Junior whispering my name with reverence, me screaming his name like a claiming.

When I looked down, he had pulled the Nicolasi crest ring from his finger and slid it onto my left hand. "Just in case."

"Don't say that, please don't—"

He kissed away my protests.

My fears.

I realized in that moment, I might have been kissing a Nicolasi heir, but it was the De Lange blood that had claimed me, over and over again, and it was that crest that I wanted pressed against my skin, that name I would shout over and over again until the world heard my outrage.

He was mine.

And if he went down.

I was going down right by his side.

"They'll be waiting for us." Junior sighed.

"Let them wait, just a little bit longer..." I kissed him softly. "Let them wait until we're ready."

"Until we're ready," he said against my lips.

But even then, time was steadily ticking by.

And we were nearly out of it.

CHAPTER
Thirty-Five

Junior

All the cars were at Nixon's. And waiting outside was the man himself, standing next to my dad.

The moms were probably inside crying or at least pleading with Tex to change the rules, to say something—anything to make this better.

But what could they do?

We knowingly defied the bosses' rules.

What was worse—in Nixon's eyes, I knowingly defiled his daughter's pure blood with mine.

Serena and I both got out of the car and slammed the doors. We walked toward each other.

She grabbed my hand and then pulled me against her in a hug, our mouths met in an achingly slow kiss that felt like goodbye, and then we broke apart.

"Whatever your dad says about mine, about—" I sighed. "It's true. All of it. I just want you to know. I was sworn not to tell anyone the full story since it would tarnish everyone's view of my dad. Just know, I've never once in my life lied to you, but this... was not my secret to tell."

Her eyes filled with tears. "It's worse than I think it is, isn't it?"

"It's why your dad wants me dead..."

"If it were anyone else..." Serena repeated as if remembering Ash's words all those years ago, and then we were out of time.

"Inside," Nixon said in a cold voice, his eyes flashed *murder* each time he blinked.

My dad's jaw clenched as he held his old Colt King Cobra gun in his right hand, resting against his thigh.

I gripped Serena's hand as we slowly walked through the doors and sighed in frustration when every single boss present—and all of them were present because of the funeral—held their guns in their right hands.

And not just any guns.

No, each of them had a special gun that represented death.

My dad had his, which meant the rest of them had theirs.

The world was full of murderers who just grabbed a gun and pointed—but my world? It was full of a certain way of doing things, a respect for the hardware that took the life, and escorted the soul to the afterlife.

I wanted to protect her so desperately. I wanted to stand in front of her and tell her to fucking run.

But she just gripped me tighter as a storm built inside my chest.

All of the cousins were on the outside of the bosses, some were eating and or drinking quietly, but not Ash, he had a gun in his hand, as did Breaker, and slowly but surely, I saw that my cousins, the Elect, were not going to go down without a fight.

"I wonder..." Uncle Tex took a step toward me. "...did you ever think that your love would start a war?" His face was livid, contorted into rage as he got right in my face. "You think with your dick, and you divide this entire family! You divide kid from parent; your fucking selfishness is going to bring down an entire dynasty." He sneered in disgust. "I hope it was worth it."

I lunged even though Serena had my other hand, and managed to hit him across the face with my fist. "Take it back!"

I'd just hit our godfather.

Again.

If I wasn't already dead.

That did it, sealed my fate.

He spat out some blood. "Sex is never worth breaking up a family. I don't care how good it is."

"Say something like that about Serena one more time, and I'm going to fucking rip your lungs out through your throat!" I roared.

Someone let out a low whistle, but I didn't care. All I saw was rage, rage that he'd disrespect her like that.

"Serena," Nixon said in a soft and gentle tone. "Give me your hand."

"No!" she said sharply.

I'm positive it was the first time she'd ever yelled at her dad in front of anyone by the look of pure shock on his face.

"Let go of his hand," Nixon growled. "Now."

"No!" she screamed. "I LOVE HIM!"

Her announcement was worse than me hitting the Capo by the curses that exploded around us.

"You're too young to know what—"

"So help me God, Nixon, if you tell your own daughter she's too young to know what love is, you'll be the one peeing through a straw!" Serena's mom Trace piped up, and then one by one, the wives stood with the kids.

Oh, this was not going well.

At all.

"Trace, you know the rules we gave them," Nixon said in an irritated voice. "They knowingly broke them because they're horny college students! You get punished when you break the rules, and we were clear from the beginning what they were! Look at us!" He spread his arms wide. "Of course you didn't think this would happen, did you? If it was any other person—"

"Stop." My dad lifted his hand. "Stop draping my shame on my son's shoulders."

"Wh-what shame?" Serena's clear voice filled the tense room.

Trace slowly walked over to her daughter but didn't try to take her from me. Instead, she shared a look with me and whispered, "Honey, it was a long time ago, but some things are harder to forgive."

"I tried to rape Trace." My dad just out and said it.

Serena sucked in a sharp breath and clung to me tighter. "What?"

My dad's eyes held so much pain that for a second, I wanted to drop her hand and give him a hug.

"It was a dark time." Dad swallowed while my mom came up and grabbed his arm like he needed her strength. "Junior knows, I told him when he was young, just in case, just in case—" He squeezed his eyes shut. "My dad at a young age told me I was just like him, just like his father before him. He said men like us needed to dominate, needed to hurt, needed to break girls in, make them bleed, use them as a currency. At a very young age, my only job within the De Lange Family was to break them, some were virgins, but we were held at gunpoint. Doesn't justify it. The first girl I tried to save shot herself in front of me when we were finished. I was fourteen." His eyes filled with tears. "I was filled with so much hatred over Trace that I couldn't see straight. She showed up on our campus, my campus, and stole Nixon's friendship, stole my only friends, the only solace I had in my godforsaken life, and I snapped. I set her up, and because of that, my dad was no longer boss, and I was cut from being his heir. Our family suffered, so I wanted her to suffer, seeing her as the reason. I never—" He took a deep breath. "It never got that far because Chase ran in and saved the day with Nixon and Tex, but it's something that I will never forgive myself for. It's why Junior wears the mark of your family, Serena. Because no matter what, the Nicolasis will always honor the Abandonatos, no matter what choice is made. My firstborn was always supposed to be a penance, at the beck and call of the Abandonatos as a way to show forgiveness and fealty."

I stared down at my arm and tried not to let the rage hit me again, but it was impossible to stop the shaking as Nixon walked up to me, with my dad's silent permission and my mom's tearful sobs, took his dagger and fucking cut into the Abandonato symbol on my skin, ripping the scar to shredded pieces.

I let out a little groan while Serena still clung to me. The burn was deep. And I knew, in that moment, I had relived the sins of my father.

Because Nixon Abandonato was cutting me from the Families.

All because I fell in love with his daughter.

"Serena," Nixon said in a low tone. "Come here. Now."

"My place is by his side," she answered, her voice clear and bold.

"Serena—" My voice cracked.

"No!" She bellowed. "You don't get to give up right now."

My smile was weak. "When have I ever given up?"

"Then what are you doing?"

I gulped and then. "I don't want you to see me break."

"Too bad." She turned around and held out her left hand. "Where he goes, I go— even if that means you bury me too. And I answer to Asher." She glared at her dad. "Not you."

A gasp resounded through the group.

And the ever-silent Chase finally spoke up. "Let Asher deal with it. It's what he does best."

He left out the "kills people" part, but it was there regardless, in the heavy pregnant hush that settled over the room.

Ash stepped forward and sighed. "Please don't make me force you two."

"You won't have to," Serena answered for me.

We walked in steady cadence down the hall, and then down to the basement, bypassing the gym we so often sparred in.

Down another set of stairs we went until Ash stopped us in front of one of the soundproof rooms.

Two metal chairs were already in there, not facing each other, another curse, dying without seeing the last breath of the loved one. Or maybe it was a blessing. I couldn't decide.

I just calmly walked to one of the chairs and sat.

Serena did the same.

"I won't kill you quickly." Ash's voice caught in his throat. He looked like he was going to puke.

"I know." I locked eyes with him. "Ash, for what it's worth, I'm glad it's you."

"Don't say that to me, man." He shook his head. "I don't know how much more I can take right now. It's fucking hard to breathe, and I wish they knew. I wish they knew how long, because maybe then they'd know this isn't screwing, this is... this is so much more."

"Would they even listen?" Serena asked quietly. "Or would they just assume we're high on sex?"

"You could at least try." Ash looked away from us and walked over to the table. I knew what was there, several guns, torture devices, rope.

He grabbed the rope.

Great choice.

With a pale face, he wrapped the rope around our joined bodies as our backs were pushed hard against the cold metal of the chairs. The knots were tight, digging into my skin like an ever-present bruise.

When I looked up, he had the chains.

Again, solid choice, at least I couldn't fault him for sucking at his job.

"Good choice," Serena muttered.

And for some reason, I laughed.

Because it was so fucked up that we were proud of him for torturing us then killing us later.

"Are you guys seriously laughing right now?" Ash gave us both incredulous looks as the door opened. The rest of the cousins piled in. Maybe to say their goodbyes.

"This is wrong," Maksim said through clenched teeth. "You know it, we know it! So stop it!"

Ash stared pretty boy Maksim down. "Does it matter? Because I guarantee you'll be tied to something if you try to fight for them."

Violet gave a panicked look to Breaker, who grabbed her hand and slowly pushed her behind him.

I knew it.

"Don't worry." I gave them a sad smile. "If it were anyone else, they'd probably just get a warning shot in the leg, nothing fatal." I stared at Breaker.

His eyes narrowed.

I continued. "Chase knew anyway…"

"What?" Ash stopped grabbing the chain. "You mean the first time?"

"Yeah, but the second time too," Serena said. "He told us not to get caught."

"That's…" Ash didn't finish his sentence. He did, however, grab the stupid chain again and start wrapping the heavy thing around us. It pressed into our bodies tight while at the same time pulling us toward the floor with its heaviness. Sooner or later, something would break under the pressure, or crush beneath bone; it was too heavy for either of us to last that long, especially Serena.

And if we moved during the torture, it would slowly slip getting tighter and tighter around our bodies until we suffocated.

So it forced you to sit there and take it and try not to pass out.

Ash went over to the table and braced himself against it, then grabbed his phone. "I need you guys to do me a favor."

"Really?" Serena said with heavy sarcasm. "You want us, the ones about to get tortured to do you a favor?"

God, her strength was incredible.

The rest of the cousins slowly trickled out of the room as the door gave a resounding click behind them.

I smiled despite the pain in my biceps muscles, slowly squeezing me to death.

"I know, right?" Ash suddenly looked way too happy to be inflicting pain on us. "I jus— I want the cousins to hear your story. From beginning to end. They don't know, and I think, when you guys die, they'll understand how important it is to fight for what you loved even if it means dying by their side."

"Was that your pep talk?" I wondered out loud. "Do you seriously do this shit to everyone you torture? That's messed up, even for you, Ash."

"I think—" Ash's eyes flashed. "That this might be a good way to save lives, so maybe stop talking out of your damn ass and tell the story."

Serena's annoyed sigh jumped me out of my stupor. "She sighed like that the first time I fell in love with her."

Ash held out his phone and then walked to the corner of the room. "Yeah, Maksim? It's Ash... Yup, you got the text? ... Good. ...Yes. I'm sorry too. ...Yeah." And then Ash held out his phone and slid it until it was by my feet. "Talk."

"I sighed in annoyance?" Serena asked with what sounded like a small smile.

I needed to keep her awake, keep her alive; the only way to do that was to keep her mind off the pain that was slowly choking the air out of her body.

"Yeah." I snorted out a painful laugh. "You were so easily annoyed by everything, and then I was annoyed you didn't give me any attention even after that time I climbed the tree and threatened to shove you out of it."

"Because boys aren't supposed to go, 'By the way you're pretty, whoops don't fall, don't fall!'"

I choked on my laugh. "Oh, shit, you were so pissed at me you ran to your dad crying that boys were mean. I'm sure that didn't help my stellar reputation with him."

"It's because I liked you, stupid. And you threatened to kill me!"

"Oh, hell, Serena, it was like maybe five feet."

"I was still short!"

"And you aren't now?"

"Take it back, you bastard!"

"Stop moving!" I laughed despite our predicament. "And I would take it back like I stole all those kisses."

"Hah, you think you're sly enough to steal them, I gave those freely, willingly the day I told you I loved you."

"Fifteen is too young." What I said.

"I argued with you until you finally gave in." She sighed. "You looked over your shoulder for a good year every time we had family dinner. But it didn't matter; you made me yours."

"Yeah." My body heated, "Maybe we leave all that part out, so your dad doesn't come back and kill me a second time."

"Let them know," she whispered. "You were so... gentle."

I squeezed my eyes shut as she spoke.

"You took your time, you kissed my mouth like you worshipped me—you still kiss me that way."

"Because I do," I told her softly. "Because I fucking worship the ground you walk on. Would sacrifice my body just to honor yours."

She sniffled. "And then the great disappointment."

"You mean when Chase found us having sex…"

"Awkward."

"It's not like he watched. I mean, it could be worse. Remember Claire and Ash? He was literally inside her, ass naked while his dad came charging in like a bomb going off."

Serena laughed. "Okay yeah, that's worse."

"So much worse. I mean, have you seen Ash's ass?"

"Um… something you wanna share with the class?" Serena asked.

I rolled my eyes. Shit, my lungs felt heavy. Focus on her voice. Focus on my soul mate. "I think you know one hundred percent that I'm all man, and I've only ever been yours."

"Despite your attempts to make everyone believe you're a manwhore."

I swallowed the emotion in my throat. "You know I've only ever given myself to you, only you, forever you."

"I shouldn't have—"

"You wanted to make me jealous. That was understandable after the incident."

"Ash turned our love to hate," Serena admitted. "But the thing about love and hate… the pendulum often swings all the way back."

"I couldn't stop my heart from falling, Serena, even now, know that it beats for you, until the very last faint thump against my chest."

She started silently sobbing. "I love you so much it hurts."

A tear slid down my cheek, hitting the cold metal keeping us tied to each other. "For as long as we both shall live."

"For as long—" She hiccupped. "—as we both shall live."

She let out a sharp gasp.

"Serena? What's wrong? Talk to me, princess. Serena!"

"I'm—" She was shaking. "I'm okay. I think."

"Where does it hurt?"

Suddenly the chains felt loser; I tried looking over my shoulder. Then realized that they were getting pulled from us by my dad and Nixon and that behind them, we had several wives bawling into their husbands' chests, and looks of pure annoyance were being directed at Ash like he was the reason for no bloodshed.

We had all five bosses with their wives packed into that small room, and then the oldest kids with Ash giving each other high fives like they'd just won the lottery.

I stood on shaky legs and barely had time to turn around before Serena launched herself in my arms. "Is this real?"

"I have no idea." She said against my mouth. "But I'll take it."

"Junior," Nixon growled. "The ring. Now."

This time I did listen, because getting the shit beat out of me sounded a hell of a lot better than death.

"Try not to die," my dad said under his breath like that had me thinking happy thoughts.

"I don't understand," I whispered as we all piled out of the room, me with my dad by my side and Serena on the other.

My dad just smiled. "I think this would have been a lot better had you not been idiots, hellbent on keeping it from us."

"Right, because telling you would have what? Saved us?"

"Maybe," Dad said. "Maybe if you would have come to us first, asked permission…"

"But you said by penalty of death…" I reminded him.

"Well, yeah." He shrugged.

"We've killed people for wanting to walk away."

"The rules are there to keep you from being idiots." Dad slapped me on the back of the head. "From thinking with your cock and just taking something because it looks pretty and is forbidden. But love, the kind of love we just heard on the phone. Well, that's different."

Serena shrieked out, "What?"

"Thanks for that replay, by the way," Ash said from his place ahead of us. "Really wanted to relive the moment I fell in love and got caught."

I could tell he meant it.

I could also tell a lot of blood was about to get spilled as Nixon stripped off his shirt and jumped in the ring.

His fingers weren't wrapped.

And I knew firsthand that he was an excellent street fighter.

The only bonus was that my own dad had taught me Jiu-Jitsu to the point that I could hopefully escape without dying.

"Six rounds," Tex called out. "For every year you loved Serena and kept it from her father, from her protector, from your father, from your boss, and from me, your Capo."

Ash let out a low whistle. "That's gonna be really hard after being tied up and—"

I shot him a look. "How about you stand by my side the way I stood by yours?"

"I did." He sobered. "I'm the one who saved your lives."

With that, he patted me on the back and then shoved me into the ring with the very pissed off father of the woman I loved.

He was a big man, six-two, enough muscle on his muscle that his sweat probably had muscle.

He had maybe fifteen more pounds of muscle on him, but I was taller, and my reach would be better—hopefully.

"Nixon, go ahead."

Nixon stepped forward, and then with a cruel smile on his lips, said, "How many times did you sneak into my house?"

"Oh, fuck." Maksim looked ready to puke in the corner.

We really needed to talk about the guy's ability to encourage and lie!

"I didn't really keep track, sir—"

The fist came flying at me so fast and hard that I stumbled to the side. My vision blurred as I moved out of the way and finally answered. "I'm guessing here, but probably..." I gulped. "...a little over two hundred times before—"

His next fist came from the other direction. I saw it. His knee, however, seemed to be operating independently, as it got me right in the chin; had my tongue been in the wrong place, I would have bitten it off.

There was something that felt very wrong about fighting him back when I was the one who went behind his back without his permission.

So, with every question, I took the hit, blocking what I could, making sure that whoever walked out of here the bloodiest, won the girl.

And that would be me.

"How many times did you lie to us!" Nixon roared.

"All the damn time," I muttered, turning my right side toward him as my left eye started swelling shut. "We didn't want to get caught!"

The air left my lungs as a kick got me right in the gut.

I fell to my knees. "Shit, that hurt." I spat blood and wiped what I could from my mouth.

"Who was in your bedroom three nights ago when I knocked on the door?"

Shit, damn, shit. I'm going to die after all. I wasn't innocent, and innocence wasn't getting me out of the pain, so I answered truthfully. "She was, sir, still naked, in my bed, while I lied through my teeth."

A roar of rage fell from Nixon's mouth. I didn't duck that time; I let him hit me, twice in the stomach before I doubled over in pain, and then another time across the face. I spat out more blood and muttered, "Worth it."

"He's not fighting back," a voice said. "He needs to fight back!"

"He won't." My dad piped up. "This is about honor, and Nixon needs to get his. This is about respect, and Junior needs to learn how to give and receive it."

I was starting to see double as I blinked up at a pacing Nixon. His eyes were sharp, focused, clearly intent on ending my life. "Will you die for her? Kill for her? Protect her?" With each question, a hit came until I was nearly blacked out on the mat.

All I remembered doing was whispering "yes" before my eyes caught his fist flying down into my face, I barely held my hands up, but the blow was hard enough to break some of the bones in my hand as I blocked.

I roared in agony and rolled to my side then slowly got up. "Any more questions?"

"You want me to kill you, is that it?" Nixon seemed amused.

"I want you to feel justified enough in your anger so that I can feel justified enough in loving her when I don't deserve her." His fist came and then stopped as he backed away.

"That—" Releasing a frustrated sigh, Nixon grabbed a towel and tossed it at me. "—was a good answer."

"Great." I stumbled to my knees again and briefly saw a

flash of blond hair as it registered that Serena was at my side in the ring. Why'd she look so freaked out? We hadn't even gone six rounds, or had we? I suddenly couldn't think straight... couldn't...

A solitary tear rolled down her cheek and dripped onto my chest, the last thing I noticed before passing out.

CHAPTER
Thirty-Six

Serena

My dad wouldn't let me into Junior's room.

I expected to lay with him, comfort him, wash away his pain, and then cry until he woke up.

Instead, the first thing Junior Nicolasi, my boyfriend and soul mate saw when he opened his eyes was the guy who made him hurt beyond all reason.

My dad said he just wanted to talk.

Well, Junior had been out cold for at least four hours, talking had gone out the window the minute all of us had gotten into it.

Just another day in the life, right?

"Hey." Ash came into the kitchen with a bottle, not a glass, but a bottle of wine in hand. "You hanging in there?"

I frowned. "Isn't that my line? Because I'm pretty sure we were just at a funeral, and you gave the eulogy."

He sighed, shaking his head. "Life is so…" He grimaced. "…strange."

"Tell me about it." I grabbed the bottle and tipped it back. It was full of tequila. I shoved it back against him. "You savage! That's not even wine!"

He gave me a dopy grin. "Yeah, I pretty much ran out of that, two hours ago, and now I see three of you, but I don't give a shit because at least you're alive."

His body swayed toward me; I took the moment to pull him into my arms and give him the hug he deserved. "I love you, Ash."

"Not as much as I love you." His fingers dug into me as he held me tight. "I'm so pissed you almost got yourself killed."

"Says the guy who tied me up." My voice was muffled against his chest.

"I expected you to fight more," he said when he pulled back. "To confess your love in such a huge way, they'd have to listen."

I frowned and took the bottle again. "It never occurred to me they would care. We broke the rule; we suffer the consequences. Isn't that how it's always been? How many times have you had to go down to the basement in your dad's house? How many times have you taken a life because a cousin, a made man, or a businessman broke the rules?"

Ash leaned his massive body against the counter. "The thing about family, Serena. They're always willing to listen… eventually. You did the hard thing, you did the right thing by staying by Junior's side, but you also have to know that your dad would kill himself before letting harm come to you. I've never in my life seen Nixon Abandonato, badass boss, so upset as when he was up here staring at the wall like he'd just lost everything that matters because what you still don't understand is the rules apply to them too. If they give you a free pass, it's the entire Family in jeopardy; it's the boss, his wife, the rest of the kids. It's everyone, so if you don't fight and prove your fealty, they have to let justice and blood run through, get it?"

I gulped. "How drunk are you?"

"Very." He took a heavy step toward me. "Remember this for the future, hell remind me when I'm sober, rules apply to everyone, so if you're gonna fucking break them, make sure you know how to survive it, mmmkay?" He patted me on the face at least six times before finally stumbling down into the living room and collapsing onto the couch.

"He's going to be okay, right?" Violet suddenly appeared, her lipstick was a bit smudged, and her dress was wrinkled.

I eyed her suspiciously. "Did you take a nap in your clothes?"

"No." Her eyes widened. "Why?"

"Uh, no reason." I shook away the haze. It was my imagination, just like it was my imagination that Breaker was stomping into the room looking like he wanted to break something. "Geez, what's his deal."

Violet was quiet. "He's young."

"Yeah, we can't use that excuse with anyone who grew up in these families, plus he turns twenty in like two weeks."

"Yeah," she whispered and swiped her tongue across her top lip. "I know." And then, "It's probably horrible timing but, I just wanted you to be the first to know since everything's gotten a bit crazy. Sergio gave me the green light to finish med school outside of Chicago."

I froze, my mind filled with a million questions. "Why

would you do that? Why would you leave? Why would they let you?"

Her eyes filled with tears before she looked away and shrugged. "Things change, you know? Someone close to us just died, and I think—I think it might be good for me to get away, to learn and come back and help as much as I can, maybe I could have saved someone, maybe, I don't know, just maybe."

"Is that why you look like someone just broke your heart, then?" I reached for her hand. "What's going on?"

"You can't help u—m-me," she stuttered. "Nobody really can, can they?"

"Violet, talk to me, what's wrong?" My stomach filled with dread as she bit down on her lower lip, it trembled so much I was afraid she was going to start sobbing, and I wasn't sure I could handle any more emotional trauma.

"Do you think—" she started when she finally got herself under control, composed and cool like she always was. "Do you think some of us are cursed?"

"What?" I reared back. "No, not even a little bit, and especially not you!"

She was the goody-goody of the entire group. I mean, I would bet a million dollars she'd never seen a penis and had taken one drink in her entire life. If there was ever a perfect daughter, it was her.

And ohhhh, how Chase knew it.

Perfect for his political career, I mean.

"Yeah, well…" She sniffed. "That, at least, makes me feel better."

She went to pull away, and that's when I noticed the mark on her finger, her left finger? It had been smudged away by her tears. What? Makeup? Why would she have cover up on her finger?

It looked like a sickle tattoo, which would be madness because she didn't have tattoos; she didn't have anything.

"Hey, I gotta go make sure Breaker isn't too drunk." She jerked away from me and then walked off, giving me a horrible feeling in the pit of my stomach because I could have sworn I'd seen that tattoo before.

And on someone I knew.

"Serena." My dad barked out my name. I ran down the hall to the guest room, where both he and Phoenix were standing outside its door.

"Can I go in? Is he okay?" Tears streamed down my face. "Daddy, tell me he's okay, and he's going to live because I love him, I really love him, and Phoenix I don't care, I don't care! Everyone gets a second chance; I'm not justifying what you did, I'm just saying that—"

"Shhhh." My dad pulled me into his arms and rocked me like I was a little girl. I instantly relaxed. "We didn't know. And as much as it pains me to admit, we're still fucking up every day as parents. The rules apply to us all, and we thought you were just being you, and Junior was just testing us, testing the Family, breaking rules because he could, sleeping around because it got you attention, and stop giving me that look. We can't let people break those sorts of rules just because they feel like it. When one rule's broken, the house of cards falls."

A heaviness settled on my chest. "I know, I know, I should have told you I just, I didn't even know how to say anything, and then we stopped for a while because we hated each other so much—"

"—Because your love matched your hate," Phoenix said

behind me in a soft voice. "Trust me when I say, I know exactly what that feels like."

He sighed and then held out his hand to my dad. "We're good?"

"We're good." My dad took his hand and then leaned in and kissed Phoenix on each cheek and said. "He's released from his promise. And so are you."

Phoenix instantly relaxed. "I chose well."

"Well?" my dad repeated.

Phoenix just smiled. "For a best friend. All those years back. I chose well."

My dad gulped and then murmured, "Despite our past, I did too, Phoenix, I did too."

Phoenix gave me a small squeeze, and then he was gone, and my dad was opening the door, giving me a slight push and nudging me in.

It closed behind me.

And there was Junior in all his bandaged-up glory looking extremely black and blue and high on whatever they'd given him so he'd stop moaning and jerking out stitches in his sleep.

"So…" I walked over to him and sat on the bed.

He muttered a curse and slowly turned his head toward me. One eye was completely swollen shut the other was getting there, his beautiful skin was turning purple and blue, and I'd never seen him more handsome in all my life.

Because he was alive.

And he was mine.

"So." He blindly reached for my hand.

"Want me to get naked so you can touch me with what fingers aren't broken?"

He laughed and then moaned.

"Sorry." I chuckled and then scooted myself on the bed. "I'll hold you, and you dream, how's that?"

"Living my dream," he said softly. "But you can hold me while I do that, princess."

"I love you." I tried not to let the hot tears fall, but it was impossible.

He turned and looked up at me. "Those for me?"

"No."

"Liar."

"Hate you for as long as we both shall live."

He barked out a laugh. "Yeah, hate you for as long as we both shall live."

Neither of us missed the way he kept trying to grab my ass, just like I couldn't keep myself from running my hands up and down his abs.

Junior De Lange-Nicolasi was my curse and my reward. My treasure, my love. He was my perfect match in every way.

And I would never, never let him go.

He was my King—mine.

CHAPTER
Thirty-Seven

Junior

One week later

The fact that I was alive was still a new concept to me as I grabbed my gun, pulled it apart, and started cleaning it. Nervous habit.

Serena was coming over for dinner, and it was the first time she'd be in my house where we wouldn't have to sneak around—as much, at least.

"So." Dad slapped me on the back, scaring the ever-loving shit out of me, and looked ahead. "You wanna talk about it?"

"If this is the sex talk, you're a bit late, Dad." I kept cleaning and then realized he was way too quiet next to me, which meant he was thinking, which meant something was wrong. Normally I'd get a laugh out of him. Today he just stood next to me, completely void of emotion, like he had gone somewhere he couldn't come back from.

I knew that feeling well.

"Dad?" I placed everything on the counter and turned.

We looked so much alike, it was almost scary, but where his eyes had this icy almost cruelty to them, mine were a warmer aqua, my hair was longer on top, and I had the eagle tattoo permanently etched into my neck. His lips pressed into a line as he crossed his arms and then finally looked at me. "Do you want to talk about it?"

"So not sex," I whispered under my breath. "Are we talking about nearly dying?"

"We are." His eyes drilled into me. "I could have lost you."

A heaviness pressed down against my heart. "But, you didn't."

"But, I could have." He swallowed slowly and then pressed his hands out against the countertop, his biceps flexing like he was ready to rip apart the entire kitchen. "I could have."

I reached for him then, pulled him against my chest, and hugged him tight. "I'm here, I'm right here, and you'll have to kill me to get me away from you."

He clung to me so tight it stole the air from my lungs. "All I ever wanted was for you to know how much you're loved—to find a love like I did, a love that rescues you from this sick pit of despair, and you just had to fucking fall for the one person that was off-limits."

I grinned and pulled back. "My heart couldn't help it."

"Neither could your dick." He rolled his eyes and then finally smiled. "Maybe I was the one that needed the talk."

"Dad," I put my hand on his shoulder. "It goes a little bit like this. When a boy likes a girl—"

"Little shit." He kicked his foot out from under both my feet, sending me to the floor and then had a knife pointed at my still-bruised right eye before I could even finish teaching my sex ed class!

I grinned when I spotted him notice that I had a small dagger trained right next to his temple at what would be a very painful and deadly wound.

One side of his mouth quirked upward in a half-smile. "You're learning."

"It should be weird that you're proud," I grumbled, still not moving.

"And yet, I would have been disappointed had you not been quick enough."

"Boys!" Mom came strolling into the kitchen and stopped; I could see the shadow of her hands on her hips and could almost imagine her look of irritation. "Did you get blood on the food?"

"Great, Ma, not even concerned about your only son!" I roared from the floor.

"Did you get blood on the food?" she asked again with a bit more force. Another shadow fell, a small gun.

"Why the hell did you arm her again?" I gave Dad a shove. "You know she has shit aim!"

"Watch it!" Mom said.

I sighed and let my head fall back against the kitchen floor at about the same time I saw a flash of black spiky stiletto heel. "Aw, you guys having family game night?"

I moaned into my hands.

She laughed. "Just give me a minute, and I'll grab my knife too. Dibs on Junior. I like to see him bleed."

Dad shook his head again at me. "Just had to be Serena…"

"Hey, I heard that!"

He got up to his feet. "Yeah, you were meant to." He

walked over and kissed her gently on the cheek and then. "No weapons at the table."

Serena grumbled.

I grumbled.

Mom shoved her gun in her apron pocket. I mean really, the fact that she was even wearing an apron was hilarious, she could cook around ten things well, everything else was… shall we say, not very Italian, but dad never complained, so I never complained.

I just went to Chase's.

Now *that* was food.

They were like professional chefs over there!

Dad sat at the head of the table and reached for my hand. And slowly, as we all joined hands, I looked up at Serena and winked.

Family dinner.

With my soul mate.

Alive.

I kept my eyes open during the prayer; something about closing them seemed wrong when I wanted to spend every waking moment drinking her beauty in. Some of Serena's dark roots were starting to show, and I realized I liked it, I liked that around me she didn't care.

She was wearing lip gloss I'd lick off later.

And mascara she didn't really need.

But other than that, the armor had been lifted, maybe because the dragon had been defeated.

The dragon being our lie.

Dinner went by in a blur, and then Serena and I were outside because going to my room just meant I'd get her naked, and then my mom really would use that gun. I mean, she knew, everyone knew we'd started having sex early, but that didn't mean that they were handing us condoms and making signs that said, "get there faster."

I wrapped an arm around her and let the silence descend between us. It was almost strange how weird it felt to be out in the open, to touch her without wondering if I was going to get my fingers cut off.

"You ready for this?" Serena asked.

I looked out at the field and then back at her. "Am I waiting for something to happen right now?"

"Don't be a dick."

"That's literally all I know how to be," I teased, pulling her against my chest and stealing a kiss, and then another, and then one more.

She laughed against my mouth and turned just as the sun started to set, and then very slowly, she twirled in my arms, once, twice, and exhaled. "I wondered how many more of these moments I would get with you."

"No more wondering." I tilted her chin. "You get all of them."

"I asked my dad, you know." Her full lips were so plump I wanted to take a bite. "Were they really going to let us die down there."

My body tensed up because I'd asked my dad the same thing, and he'd refused to say yes or no. "And?" I didn't want to remember that sick feeling in my chest, the hollowness that cut itself into my soul at the feeling of losing her. "What did he say?"

"He pulled me into his arms..." Her arms tightened around my body. "...and said, 'what do you think?'"

I burst out laughing. "That's the worst answer ever!"

"Exactly what I said, and his only response was to shrug!"

"Bastard."

"Hey, that's my dad."

"And that's a bastard move," I pointed out. "If it makes you feel any better, mine didn't answer me either."

"Hey, I'm not finished with my story."

My eyebrows shot up. "Oh, so it's a story now?" I started toying with the straps of her tank top, then licked my lips when I realized she wasn't wearing a bra underneath. "I think I'm going to go on a treasure hunt when this story's done."

She crooked her finger as we rounded the corner where the outdoor gym was located. It was an RV garage converted into enough weights and flat screens to make anyone happy, though dad denied it was a man cave.

I found great joy in making signs every year that he had to take down. I'd used two hundred nails last Christmas.

Nixon had helped.

"You're distracting me," she whispered as we walked into the gym.

The lights were off as I led her farther into the room until we were on the other side of the sitting area toward the wet bar my dad rarely drank from but always kept stocked.

I let her hand go and then went about getting each of us a shot of vodka, something we did every year on the day we remembered those who'd died.

"I live to distract you," I said, handing her the shot glass.

We both tilted the alcohol back, and I poured two more. "Now, finish your story so I can see how fast I can finish you."

"So charming, it's amazing you landed me."

"Ah, is that what you were thinking about this morning when I did that thing with my tongue? How fucking charming

I am? Hey, are you blushing right now? I can't tell it's too dark," I grabbed boob and got slapped.

"Girls don't blush there."

I snorted out a laugh. "But, you know where you do blush…"

"Sto-op!" Her laugh was like oxygen. "Okay, keep your hands and cock to yourself. So anyway I went and asked Uncle Chase, but that's like asking the president for his secrets, same answer, right? So then I went and—"

One of the lights flickered on.

Serena dove behind the bar where I was. "I thought your dad went to bed early!"

"He does, he's like a grandpa!" I hissed.

"Huh, hot grandpa—"

"Could you not right now?" I pinched her ass.

We both peered around the bar and heard footsteps, a lot of footsteps, and one by one, all the bosses casually walked into the place. Someone turned on the TV. Nixon grabbed two ping pong paddles and handed one to my dad.

My jaw nearly came unhinged when both our dads started a game of ping pong. Fucking ping pong!

"What sort of warped universe is this?" I whispered. "No guns? No violence? Nobody's even bleeding!" I said.

Serena's shocked expression mirrored my own as laughter ensued around the couch, where Chase was currently watching himself on TV with Uncle Tex, who immediately started throwing Doritos.

I think I nearly shit my pants when Andrei of all people joined in and then asked if they had any fucking chocolate chip cookies. What?

"What are they saying?"

We scooted away from the bar and hid behind another giant couch.

Nixon hit the ball. "We did good, didn't we?"

"Better than I thought, honestly," Dad answered as he slapped the ball back, his expression free. "I'm glad Ash isn't such an emotional screw up like Chase. I imagined we would have had to intervene or something."

"I was ready." Tex popped something in his mouth. "I knew you guys were going to look for an out. They're your kids, after all. But I was ready."

Nixon and Dad said nothing.

And then Phoenix piped up. "Sad about Violet."

Nikolai's voice came next. The hell, he was still here? A week later? He scratched the back of his neck, giving full view to the sickle tattoo on his finger, the one thing that proved he was still with the Russians even though he was Italian. Andrei had the same one.

"What about Violet?" Tex asked.

"She's leaving," Chase muttered as he shared a dark look with Andrei only to have Nikolai change the subject.

I knew my dad did it on purpose; I just couldn't figure out why.

I released a breath. "At least now we know they weren't going to let us die."

"Probably." Serena sighed. "I mean, at least our dads weren't. Tex, on the other hand…"

"Is he tossing a gun in the air and catching it by the tip?" I asked, risking another peek.

"Junior, Serena," Phoenix barked. "Talk any louder, and your friends are going to hear you back at the house."

I flipped him off.

"Saw that." He grinned without taking his eyes off the ping pong ball.

Slowly we both stood.

Nixon gave me a sharp look.

I held up my hands. "Her clothes are on!"

"Dad…" Serena rolled her eyes.

"How'd you know we were even here?" I asked as we walked by my dad and stared at all the scary as shit bosses.

"You breathe loud." This from Chase.

"Well, this has been fun." I grabbed Serena's hand, and we left before the Twilight Zone of the bosses playing ping pong messed me up for life.

Breaker was the first person I saw when we walked back in the house, and then I saw King and assumed they were probably all here.

"Movie night." Maksim jutted his chin out at me. "PS, you still look like shit."

I grabbed my knife.

He grinned and walked in the direction of our rec room. Ash was already there, sitting in the corner, his expression brooding as hell, and everyone else was laughing. Maybe we did need time to focus on things other than death.

Maybe that's what the bosses were doing out there with their weird ping pong tradition.

I sat down and pulled Serena onto my lap. She wiggled a bit too much and then lifted her skirt.

My cock strained through my jeans as I felt nothing but warm heat, naked skin.

I let out a pained groan as I immediately pressed up against her, hard, ready to just unzip my pants and go to town.

Serena grabbed a nearby blanket and tossed it over us

while Maksim turned off the lights, and my wicked princess reached behind her, and slowly unzipped my jeans, freeing me as though she did it all the time while watching movies.

This was a first.

My fingernails dug into the leather theater chair as she slowly appeared to move positions and fucking sank down onto me.

The amount of restraint it took not to grab her and just fuck her in front of everyone and tell them we'd be a minute was unreal.

My dick pulsed while she moved again. I gripped her by the arms and hissed out. "Hate you."

She just laughed and said. "Hate you too."

"Can you guys stop fighting for five minutes?" Breaker snapped back at me.

"I'd say... give it more like three," I muttered.

"Two," Serena countered.

I pinched her ass and whispered back. "I highly doubt I'll even last that long. Just feeling you clench around me makes me want to—"

"Shhh!" Violet threw popcorn at us.

A jump scene happened in the movie.

And then... then Serena was off and back on—and somehow, I managed to get her off me, tuck myself back into my jeans like the calm adult I was, and grab her by the hand.

"Gotta make more popcorn," I muttered.

Before I could even finish that sentence, we dashed to my room. Her shirt over her head, my jeans kicked off, and it was us again.

The love so strong that the hate spurned it on.

"Make it rough." She winked.

I groaned. "I don't deserve you."

"Nope." Her eyes twinkled as she grinned. "What now?"

"Now," I growled as I crawled up to where she was lying sprawled across my bed like a present I couldn't wait to unwrap, her breasts high and begging to be sucked, her thighs trembling just waiting for my touch. "I'm going to make you scream."

"Good thing they're watching a horror movie."

"Doesn't matter. They'll still hear you." I reared up and pressed a hand to her naked ass and then smacked. "Now beg."

Serena's blue eyes locked onto me and refused to let go as she bit down on her lip and squirmed beneath my touch.

I'd always loved looking down at her, drinking my fill, eating even more—because she was made for me, always.

I knew it the minute I set eyes on her.

I just never knew how dangerous loving her would be to my mental and physical health.

Until I was told to stay the hell away.

"Junior..." She reached for me, pushing my hair away from my forehead. "You're mine too, you know. I own you the way you own me."

"I thought you were begging," I teased, lowering my mouth to hers. "And yet I don't hear it..."

"You don't need to hear it to feel the way my body begs you with every single tremor," she rasped, grabbing my hands and lowering them to her hips. "I'm ready for you—I need you."

"Have me," I said, the way she had the first time all those days ago when we finally let go of the hate.

Her eyes filled with tears as I sank into her, pinned her hands over her head, and kissed her hungrily across the mouth.

She moaned with each slow pump of my hips, I was

sinking so deep that I couldn't think straight, and my princess just took every single slam of my body like it was a gift.

I'd always been afraid to be too rough with her. Now I knew; we were born out of murder, made for madness. Of course, she would take me however she could.

A tear slid down her cheek, and then she was holding me in place with her legs wrapped around me like we were getting ready to spar, making it so it was almost impossible to move.

She grinned. "Now, you're trapped."

"You call this trapped. I call this Heaven." I moaned as my dick pulsed inside her, needing more of her heat, needing to move. Release was so close for both of us; I could always tell the way she tried to keep us from chasing it as if she was terrified of the fulness we experienced, that we'd never get it again.

"Serena." I brushed a kiss across her mouth. "Princess, you can finally let go." I hesitated. "We can finally let go."

She nodded as more tears slid down. "You promise? This is it? Just us? Forever? No more—"

I devoured her mouth with mine, tasting the salt of her tears on my tongue as my lips slid along hers, and then I casually flipped us until she was on top.

"Us." We broke apart. I was still inside her, but something told me she needed to have control, to know that this was it between us.

Finally.

Thank God. Finally.

"Look at us," I encouraged. "Nothing but death will separate us, princess. And even then, I'll fight it till the bitter end, to make sure I have as much time with you as humanly possible."

She started moving slowly above me. "And even then, Junior, once death comes calling, promise you'll follow."

"Where else would I rather be than dying with you by my side?" My voice cracked, and then I gripped her ass and started moving while she went wild above me.

I couldn't stop staring at the way her throat moved as she cried out my name, her swollen lips parted like a prayer.

She panted over me, and I felt her body finally understand, as she gave in fully to me—I was hers—she was mine.

She collapsed over me, her hair covering half my face as tiny tremors wracked her body, and then she shoved away from me and said, "Does this mean you're going to marry me?"

"You already have my ring," I pointed out. "But do you really think your dad would let me have sex with you, and not expect me to marry you? I mean, he's old school. He'd probably grab his gun at the altar to make sure I didn't bolt."

She swatted my chest. "I'd shoot you myself if you did."

"I know." I laughed. "But sometimes a guy likes it when a girl chases him."

"You'd be a wounded guy, so maybe rethink that scenario."

I burst out laughing. "I love you."

"I love you too."

We both fell into more fits of laughter as I pulled the blanket over us and tucked her beneath my chin.

EPILOGUE

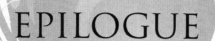

Breaker

Two days later

I knew they were in there having sex again in Serena's room, I mean, who the hell didn't? They were loud, and this was Junior we were talking about, I was surprised he hadn't just peed all over her in front of us the first day of classes this year. The guy was getting more and more possessive. If I even looked Serena's way, he growled at me.

And I was her fucking cousin!

Adopted, but still!

It was madness.

Then again, it was Junior, so... we kind of let it pass. We were each a little mad in our own way.

I sighed and walked past their room, making my way into the rec room. Violet was sitting in the corner like she always was. Confident and calculating.

I wondered if anyone saw what she was about the way I did.

She had this outer persona of class and control.

But I knew the truth.

She was dying inside.

She was a woman trapped with expectations on her shoulders that nobody should have to deal with on their own.

Hell, even her smile was fake, I remembered her going on all those press tours with Chase when he got re-elected for a second term, she was slowly dying inside.

And I hated it.

Because I'd always liked her, but also because I'd always had a massive crush on her, I'd stayed far, far away. You know, death and all that.

I gulped.

My first mistake was kissing her when I was fourteen.

My second mistake was telling her I was in love with her.

And my third? Betraying her the minute I had a chance.

I took what wasn't mine, I took the prettiest thing on the shelf, destroyed it, then tried to put it back.

And now she was broken.

Because that's what I did.

I broke things.

Not just hearts.

I fucking broke her soul.

And now she was leaving.

And it was all my fault.

"Breaker!" Izzy ran over to me. "It's a party; you're supposed to look happy!"

"I'm happy." I had exactly zero smile on my face; my eyes kept flickering toward Violet.

I shoved away from Izzy and pulled out my phone, sending Violet a text.

> Me: Can we talk?
>
> Violet: Go. To. Hell.
>
> Me: I live there. Try again.
>
> Violet: Eat shit.

I smiled, well at least she was still angry? Was that a good thing?

And then I looked up.

Tears streamed down her face.

I had done that.

I was stuck between needing to confess my sins or let the one person I loved walk away forever.

And I hated that right then and there as she slowly walked past me, I chose the latter.

And damned love in the process.]

WANT MORE *Mafia Royals*?
CHECK OUT *Scandalous Prince*,
BREAKER AND VIOLET'S STORY!

ACKNOWLEDGMENTS

Sometimes I think this is the hardest part of a book because there truly are so many moving parts! I'm so thankful to God for giving me inspiration every day and allowing me to wake up and do what I love, to work with readers, bloggers, teams that are so incredible in this book world!

My husband has been so instrumental in helping me get these books done, always giving me those extra hours I need to write and taking Thor on the trampoline, so he doesn't interrupt mom when she's in the zone. He's the best partner a girl could ask for, and I always sprinkle a bit of him in every book I write! He's my hero and my best friend.

To my incredible editing team and beta readers who helped me make sure this book wasn't going to be a complete failure!

Thank you, Jill, for all of your hard work with this entire process! I could not do this without you, and I'm sorry for the constant stress I give you when I'm like hey I had another book idea, and you're like sigh let me look at your schedule!

Thank you to Tracey, Krista, Georgia, Yana, and Candace for all of your feedback along with Jill's haha! It helped so much!

And Nina with Valentine PR, man, this is our FIRST major release since you started your own management company, and I'm so proud of you for taking a leap of faith! This has been such a crazy ride last year, and this year, I'm so thankful God brought us together! You're not allowed to leave me! Haha.

Judi, my strategist, who always has the best ideas on how we can gain a bigger following—thank you for listening to my crazy and going yup, let's do it.

To my agent Erica who again, doesn't call me crazy when I email her and go okay so I'm going to write a book about aliens… she just goes send it to me!

I truly have the most incredible people surrounding me, and I'm so proud of all they do for the book community.

Becca, thank you for an amazing trailer! I so appreciate it and the support you give!

Thank you to all the authors who read early, you know who you are, to all the text messages, DM's, thank you for promoting me and believing in me and thank you for not laughing at me when I asked you to read an early copy! And Amo, your review will forever be imprinted on my soul, girl!

To the readers, aghhhhhhh, I want to cry. This book truly is for you. It's blood, sweat, tears, it's me finally letting go, I've always wanted to write a mafia book like this, and I'm so proud to say I finally did it. I wrote a book where I didn't censor my characters in any way, I didn't edit out any language, anything that I felt might be too much, I just let them live and breathe, and your response has been amazing! Thank you for understanding, thank you for standing by my side, ride or die, you are the best readers in the world!

To the bloggers who read early copies and shared, I adore you guys, your love for books makes doing what I do so much fun. You all work so hard and have such thankless jobs, it's the love of books that keeps you going, and I respect that so much. Thank you for taking a chance on Ruthless Princess!

And to any new readers, I hope you enjoyed this new book! I have a super fun fan group on Facebook: Rachel's New Rockin' Readers, I'm in there daily, and it's a safe fun place to discuss books, you are all welcome to join and hang with us!

Thanks again, blood in, no out.
RVD

ABOUT THE *Author*

Rachel Van Dyken is the #1 New York Times, Wall Street Journal, and USA Today bestselling author of over 90 books ranging from contemporary romance to paranormal. With over four million copies sold, she's been featured in Forbes, US Weekly, and USA Today. Her books have been translated in more than 15 countries. She was one of the first romance authors to have a Kindle in Motion book through Amazon publishing and continues to strive to be on the cutting edge of the reader experience. She keeps her home in the Pacific Northwest with her husband, adorable son, naked cat, and two dogs. For more information about her books and upcoming events, visit www.RachelVanDykenauthor.com.

ALSO BY
Rachel Van Dyken

Kathy Ireland & Rachel Van Dyken
Fashion Jungle

Eagle Elite
Elite (Nixon & Trace's story)
Elect (Nixon & Trace's story)
Entice (Chase & Mil's story)
Elicit (Tex & Mo's story)
Bang Bang (Axel & Amy's story)
Enforce (Elite + from the boys POV)
Ember (Phoenix & Bee's story)
Elude (Sergio & Andi's story)
Empire (Sergio & Val's story)
Enrage (Dante & El's story)
Eulogy (Chase & Luciana's story)
Exposed (Dom & Tanit's story)
Envy (Vic & Renee's story)

Elite Bratva Brotherhood
RIP (Nikolai & Maya's story)
Debase (Andrei & Alice's story)

Mafia Royals Romances
Royal Bully (Asher & Claire's story)
Ruthless Princess (Junior & Serena's story
Scandalous Prince (Breaker & Violet's story)
Destructive King (TBA)
Mafia King (TBA)
Fallen Dynasty (TBA)

Cruel Summer Trilogy
Summer Heat (Marlon & Ray's story)
Summer Seduction (Marlon & Ray's story)
Summer Nights (Marlon & Ray's story)

Covet
Stealing Her (Bridge & Isobel's story)
Finding Him (Julian & Keaton's story)

Wingmen Inc.
The Matchmaker's Playbook (Ian & Blake's story)
The Matchmaker's Replacement (Lex & Gabi's story)

Bro Code
Co-Ed (Knox & Shawn's story)
Seducing Mrs. Robinson (Leo & Kora's story)
Avoiding Temptation (Slater & Tatum's story)
The Setup (Finn & Jillian's story)

The Dark Ones Series
The Dark Ones (Ethan & Genesis's story)
Untouchable Darkness (Cassius & Stephanie's story)
Dark Surrender (Alex & Hope's story)
Darkest Temptation (Mason & Serenity's story)
Darkest Sinner (Timber & Kyra's story)

Ruin Series
Ruin (Wes Michels & Kiersten's story)
Toxic (Gabe Hyde & Saylor's story)
Fearless (Wes Michels & Kiersten's story)
Shame (Tristan & Lisa's story)

Seaside Series
Tear (Alec, Demetri & Natalee's story)
Pull (Demetri & Alyssa's story)
Shatter (Alec & Natalee's story)
Forever (Alex & Natalee's story)
Fall (Jamie Jaymeson & Pricilla's story)
Strung (Tear + from the boys POV)
Eternal (Demetri & Alyssa's story)

Seaside Pictures
Capture (Lincoln & Dani's story)
Keep (Zane & Fallon's story)
Steal (Will & Angelica's story)
All Stars Fall (Trevor & Penelope's story)
Abandon (Ty & Abigail's story)
Provoke (Braden & Piper's story)
Surrender (Andrew & Bronte's story)

The Consequence Series
The Consequence of Loving Colton (Colton & Milo's story)
The Consequence of Revenge (Max & Becca's story)
The Consequence of Seduction (Reid & Jordan's story)
The Consequence of Rejection (Jason & Maddy's story)

Curious Liaisons
Cheater (Lucas & Avery's story)
Cheater's Regret (Thatch & Austin's story)

Players Game
Fraternize (Miller, Grant and Emerson's story)
Infraction (Miller & Kinsey's story)
M.V.P. (Jax & Harley's story)

Red Card
Risky Play (Slade & Mackenzie's story)
Kickin' It (Matt & Parker's story)

Liars, Inc
Dirty Exes (Colin, Jessie & Blaire's story)
Dangerous Exes (Jessie & Isla's story)

The Bet Series
The Bet (Travis & Kacey's story)
The Wager (Jake & Char Lynn's story)
The Dare (Jace & Beth Lynn's story)

The Bachelors of Arizona
The Bachelor Auction (Brock & Jane's story)
The Playboy Bachelor (Bentley & Margot's story)
The Bachelor Contract (Brant & Nikki's story)

Waltzing With The Wallflower — written with Leah Sanders
Waltzing with the Wallflower (Ambrose & Cordelia)
Beguiling Bridget (Anthony & Bridget's story)
Taming Wilde (Colin & Gemma's story)

London Fairy Tales
Upon a Midnight Dream (Stefan & Rosalind's story)
Whispered Music (Dominique & Isabelle's story)
The Wolf's Pursuit (Hunter & Gwendolyn's story)
When Ash Falls (Ashton & Sofia's story)

Renwick House
The Ugly Duckling Debutante (Nicholas & Sara's story)
The Seduction of Sebastian St. James (Sebastian & Emma's story)
The Redemption of Lord Rawlings (Phillip & Abigail's story)
An Unlikely Alliance (Royce & Evelyn's story)
The Devil Duke Takes a Bride (Benedict & Katherine's story)

Other Titles
A Crown for Christmas (Fitz & Phillipa's story)
Every Girl Does It (Preston & Amanda's story)
Compromising Kessen (Christian & Kessen's story)
Divine Uprising (Athena & Adonis's story)
The Parting Gift — written with Leah Sanders (Blaine and Mara's story)

RACHEL VAN DYKEN
www.rachelvandykenauthor.com